PUBLISHERS' FOREWORD

The Pearl was one of the first 'underground' magazines of modern times and, though much imitated, has retained a reputation for originality, unrestrained eroticism, and sheer bawdy fun that has little dimmed over the many years since the last of its eighteen volumes appeared. The first issue was published in London in the summer of 1879 and through a highly efficient 'subterranean' marketing system it was soon being read and enjoyed by people of all stations.

To the modern reader and the sociologist alike, *The Pearl* shows the Victorians as vastly different to their public image; indeed, beneath the facade of respectability and sexual repression there obviously existed the strongest urge for sexual experimentation and enjoyment. In the pages which follow, the publishers have selected further items from the eighteen volumes which appeared between July 1879 and December 1880.

Bawdy, provocative, irresistibly entertaining, *The Pearl* is a vital part of the Victorians' great literary legacy to today's more tolerant society. The publishers are pleased to have played a part in restoring it to general availability

Also available from New English Library

THE PEARL volume 1

THE PEARL

A Journal of Facetiae and Voluptuous Reading

Further Selections from Volumes 1-18
July 1879-December 1880

NEW ENGLISH LIBRARY

First NEL Paperback Edition May 1981
Reprinted July 1982
Reprinted September 1983

NEL Books are published by
New English Library,
Mill Road, Dunton Green,
Sevenoaks, Kent.
Editorial office: 47 Bedford Square, London WC1B 3DP

Printed and bound in Great Britain by
Cox & Wyman Ltd, Reading

0 450 04637 0

CONTENTS

AN APOLOGY FOR OUR TITLE

HAVING decided to bring out a Journal, the Editor racks his brains for a suitable name with which to christen his periodical. Friends are generally useless in an emergency of this kind; they suggest all kinds of impossible names; the following were some of the titles proposed in this instance; "Facts and Fancies," "The Cremorne," "The All Round," "The Monthly Courses," "The Devil's Own" and "Dugdale's Ghost"; the two first had certainly great attractions to our mind, but at last our own ideas have hit upon the modest little "Pearl," as more suitable, especially in the hope that when it comes under the snouts of the moral and hypocritical swine of the world, they may not trample it underfoot, and feel disposed to rend the publisher, but that a few will become subscribers on the quiet. To such better disposed piggywiggys, I would say, for encouragement, that they have only to keep up appearances by regularly attending church, giving to charities, and always appearing deeply interested in moral philanthropy, to ensure a respectable and highly moral character, and that if they only are clever enough *never to be found out,* they may, *sub rosa,* study and enjoy the *philosophy of life* till the end of their days, and earn a glorious and saintly epitaph on their tombstone, when at last the Devil pegs them out.

EDITOR OF THE "PEARL."

LADY POKINGHAM; OR THEY ALL DO IT:

Giving an Account of her Luxurious Adventures, both before and after her Marriage with Lord Crim-Con.

INTRODUCTION.

To the Reader,

Very little apology will be needed for putting in print the following highly erotic and racy narrative of a young patrician lady, whose adventures I feel assured every genuine lover of voluptuous reading will derive as much or more pleasure afforded your humble servant.

The subject of these memoirs was one of the brightest and most charming of her sex, endued with such exquisite nervous sensitiveness, in addition to an unusual warmth of constitution that she was quite unable to resist the seductive influences of God's finest creation; for God made man in his own image, male and female, created he them; and this was the first commandment, "Be faithful and multiply, and replenish the earth"—see Genesis, chap. 1.

The natural instinct of the ancients instilled in their minds the idea that copulation was the direct and most acceptable form of worship they could offer to their deities, and I know that those of my readers who are not bigoted Christians will agree with me, that there cannot be any great sin in giving way to natural desires, and enjoying, to the utmost, all those delicious sensations for which a beneficent Creator has so amply fitted us.

Poor girl, she did not live long, and in thoroughly enjoying her few briefs years of butterfly life, who can think her wicked!

9

The scraps from which my narrative is compiled were found in a packet she had entrusted to a devoted servitor, who, after her sudden and premature death at the early age of twenty-three, entered my service.

As author, I feel the crudeness of my style may be a little offensive to some, but hope my desire to afford general pleasure will excuse my defects.

THE AUTHOR.

PART I.

My dear Walter,

How I love you! but alas! you will never know it till I am gone; little do you think, as you wheel me about in my invalid chair, how your delicate attentions have won the heart of a poor consumptive on the verge of the grave. How I long to suck the sweets of love from your lips; to fondle and caress your lordly priapus, and feel its thrilling motions within me; but such joys cannot be, the least excitement would be my death, and I can but sigh as I look at your kind loving face, and admire the fine proportions of my darling, as evidenced by the large bunch of keys you always seem to have in your pocket; indeed you look to have a key of keys, whose burning thrusts would unlock any virgin cabinet.

This is a strange fancy of mine (the writing for your perusal a short account of some of my adventures); but one of the only pleasures left me is to indulge in reveries of the past, and seem to feel over again the thrilling emotions of voluptuous enjoyments, which are now denied to me; and I hope the recital of my escapades and follies may afford you some slight pleasure, and add to the lasting regard with which I hope you will remember me in years to come. One thing I ask of you, dear Walter, is to fancy you are enjoying Beatrice Pokingham when you are in the embraces of some future inamorata. It is a pleasure I have often indulged in myself when in the action of coition, and heightened my bliss by letting my fancy run riot, and imagined I was in the arms of someone I particularly wished for, but could not come at. My income dies with me, so I have no cause to make a will, but you will find notes for a few hundred pounds enclosed with this outline of my adventures, which is all I have been able to save. You will

10

also find a fine lock of dark brown hair, which I have cut from the abundant chevelure of my Mons Veneris; other friends and relatives may have the admired curls from my head, your memento is cut from the sacred spot of love.

I never remember my father, the Marquis of Pokingham, but have my doubts as to whether I am really entitled to the honour of claiming him as a parent, as he was a used-up old man, and from papers and letters, which passed privately between him and my mother, I know that he more than suspected he was indebted to his good-looking footman for the pretty baby girl my mother presented to him; as he says in one note, "that he could have forgiven everything if the fruits of her intercourse with James had been a son and heir, so as to keep his hated nephew out of the estates and title, and wished her to let him cultivate her parsley bed for another crop, which might perhaps turn out more in accordance with his wishes." The poor old fellow died soon after writing that note, and my mother, from whom this dreadful consumption is transmitted to me, also left me an orphan at an early age, leaving me her jointure of £20,000, and an aristocratic title which that amount was quite inadequate to properly support.

My guardians were very saving and careful, as they sent me to school at eight years of age, and only spent about £150 a year for schooling and necessaries, till they thought it was time for me to be brought out in the world, so that I benefitted considerably by the accumulated interest of my money.

The first four years of my school passed away uneventfully, and during that time I was only in one serious scrape, which I will relate, as it led to my first taste of a good birch rod.

Miss Birch was rather an indulgent schoolmistress, and only had to resort to personal punishment for very serious offenses, which she considered might materially affect the future character of her pupils, unless thoroughly cut out of them from the first. I was nearly seven years old when I had a sudden fancy for making sketches on my slate in school. One of our governesses, Miss Pennington, was a rather crabbed and severe old girl of five-and-thirty, and particularly evoked my abilities as a caricaturist, and the sketches would be slyly passed from one to the other of us, causing considerable giggling and gross inattention to our lessons. I was infatuated and conceited with what I considered my clever drawings and several admonitions

11

and extra tasks as punishment had no effect in checking my mischievous interruptions, until one afternoon Miss Birch had fallen asleep at her desk, and old Penn was busy with a class, when the sudden inspiration seized me to make a couple of very rude sketches; one of the old girl sitting on a chamber utensil; but the other was a rural idea of her stooping down, with her clothes up to ease herself, in a field. The first girl I showed them to almost burst with laughter, and two others were so anxious to see the cause of her mirth, that they were actually stooping over her shoulder to look at my slate, when, before I could possibly get to it to rub them off, old Penn pounced upon it like an eagle, and carried it in triumph to Miss Birch, who was awakened chagrined by the amused smile which our principal could not repress at first sight of the indecent caricatures.

"My young lady must smart for this, Miss Pennington," said Miss Birch, with suddenly assumed gravity; "she has been very troublesome lately with these impudent drawings, but this is positively obscene; if she draws one thing she will go to another. Send for Susan to bring my birch rod! I must punish her whilst my blood is warm, as I am too forgiving, and may let her off."

I threw myself on my knees, and implored for mercy, promising "Never, never to do anything of the kind again."

Miss Birch.—"You should have thought of the consequences before you drew such filthy pictures; the very idea of one of my young ladies being capable of such productions is horrible to me; these prurient ideas cannot be allowed to settle in your mind for an instant, if I can whip them out."

Miss Pennnington, with a grim look of satisfaction, now took me by the wrist, just as Susan, a stout, strong, fair servant girl of about twenty, appeared with what looked to me a fearful big bunch of birch twigs, neatly tied up with red velvet ribbon.

"Now, Lady Beatrice Pokingham," said Miss Birch, "kneel down, confess your fault, and kiss the rod," taking the bunch from Susan's hands, and extending it to me as a queen might her sceptre to a supplicant subject.

Anxious to get over the inevitable, and make my punishment as light as possible, I knelt down, and with real tears of penitence begged her to be as lenient as her sense of justice would admit, as I knew I well deserved what she was going to inflict, and would take care not to insult Miss Pennington again, whom I was very sorry to have so caricatured; then I kissed the rod and resigned myself to my fate.

Miss Pennington, maliciously.—"Ah! Miss Birch, how quickly the sight of the rod makes hypocritical repentance."

Miss Birch.—"I quite understand all that, Miss Pennington, but must temper justice with mercy at the proper time; now, you impudent artist, lift your clothes behind, and expose your own bottom to the justly merited punishment."

With trembling hands I lifted my skirts, and was then ordered to open my drawers also; which done, they pinned up my dress and petticoats as high as my shoulders; then I was laid across a desk, and Susan stood in front of me, holding both hands, whilst old Penn and the French governess (who had just entered the schoolroom) each held one of my legs, so that I was what you might call helplessly spread-eagled.

Miss Birch, looking seriously round as she flourished the rod.—"Now, all you young ladies, let this whipping be a caution to you; my Lady Beatrice richly deserves this degrading shame, for her indecent (I ought to call them obscene) sketches. Will you! will you, you troublesome, impudent little thing, ever do so again? There, there, there, I hope it will soon do you good. Ah! you may scream; there's a few more to come yet."

The bunch of birch seemed to crash on my bare bottom with awful force; the tender skin smarted, and seemed ready to burst at every fresh cut. "Ah! ah! oh!!! Oh, heavens! have mercy, madame. Oh! I will never do anything like it again. Ah—r—re! I can't bear it!" I screamed, kicking and struggling under every blow, so that at first they could scarcely hold me, but I was soon exhausted by my own efforts.

Miss Birch.—"You can feel it a little, may it do you good, you bad little girl; if I don't check you now, the whole establishment would soon be demoralized. Ah! ha! your bottom is getting finely wealed, but I haven't done yet," cutting away with increasing fury.

Just then I caught a glimpse of her face, which was usually pale, but now flushed with excitement, and her eyes sparkled with unwonted animation. "Ah!" she continued, "young ladies beware of my rod, when I do have to use it. How do you like it, Lady Beatrice? Let us all know how nice it is," cutting my bottom and thighs deliberately at each ejaculation.

LADY BEATRICE.—"Ah! oh! ah—r—r—re! It's awful! Oh I shall die if you don't have mercy, Miss Birch. Oh! my God, I'm fearfully punished; I'm cut to pieces; the birch feels as if it was red hot, the blows burn so!"

Then I felt as if it was all over, and I must die soon; my cries were succeeded by low sobs, moans, and then hysterical crying, which gradually got lower and lower, till at last I must have fainted, as I remembered nothing more till I found myself in bed, and awoke with my poor posteriors tremendously bruised and sore, and it was nearly a fortnight before I got rid of all the marks of that severe whipping.

After I was twelve years of age they reckoned me amongst the big girls, and I got a jolly bedfellow, whom I will call Alice Marchmont, a beautiful, fair girl, with a plump figure, large sensuous eyes, and flesh as firm and smooth as ivory. She seemed to take a great fancy to me, and the second night I slept with her (we had a small room to ourselves) she kissed and hugged me so lovingly that I felt slightly confused at first, as she took such liberties with me, my heart was all in a flutter, and although the light was out, I felt my face covered with burning blushes as her hot kisses on my lips, and the searching gropings of her hands in the most private parts of my person, made me all a tremble.

"How you shake, dear Beatrice," she answered. "What are you afraid of? you may feel me all over too; it is so nice. Put your tongue in my mouth, it is a great inducement to love and I do want to love you so, dear. Where's your hand? here, put it there; can't you feel the hair just beginning to grow on my pussey? Yours will come soon. Rub your finger on my crack, just there," so she initiated me into the art of frigging in the most tender loving manner.

As you may guess, I was an apt pupil, although so young. Her touches fired my blood, and the way she sucked my tongue seemed most delicious. "Ah! Oh! Rub harder, harder —quicker," she gasped, as she stiffened her limbs out with a kind of spasmodic shudder, and I felt my finger all wet with something warm and creamy. She covered me with kisses for a moment, and then lay quite still.

"What is it, Alice? How funny you are, and you have wetted my finger, you nasty girl," I whispered, laughing. "Go on tickling me with your fingers, I begin rather to like it."

"So you will, dear, soon, and love me for teaching you such

14

a nice game," she replied, renewing her frigging operations, which gave me great pleasure so that I hardly knew what I was doing, and a most luscious longing sensation came over me. I begged her to shove her fingers right up. "Oh! Oh! How nice! Further! Harder!" and almost fainted with delight as she at last brought down my first maiden spend.

Next night we repeated our lascivious amusements, and she produced a thing like a sausage, made of soft kid leather, and stuffed out as hard as possible, which she asked me to push into her, and work up and down, whilst she frigged me as before, making me lay on the top of her, with my tongue in her mouth. It was delightful. I can't express her raptures, my movements with the instrument seemed to drive her into ecstasies of pleasure, she almost screamed as she clasped my body to hers, exclaiming, "Ah! Oh! You dear boy; you kill me with pleasure!" as she spent with extraordinary profusion all over my busy hand.

As soon as we had recovered our serenity a little, I asked her what she meant by calling me her dear boy.

"Ah! Beatrice," she replied, "I'm so sleepy now, but tomorrow night, I will tell you my story, and explain how it is that my pussey is able to take in that thing, whilst yours cannot at present; it will enlighten you a little more into the Philosophy of Life, my dear; now give me a kiss, and let us go to sleep to-night."

ALICE MARCHMONT'S STORY.

You may imagine I was anxious for the next morning to arrive. We were no sooner in our little sanctum, than I exclaimed, "Now, Alice, make haste into bed, I'm all impatient to hear your tale."

"You shall have it dear and my fingers, too, if you will but let me undress comfortably. I can't jump into bed anyhow; I must make the inspection of my little private curls first. What do you think of them, Beatrice? Off with your chemise; I want to compare our pusseys," said she, throwing off everything, and surveying her beautiful naked figure in the large cheval glass. I was soon beside her, equally denuded of covering. "What a delightfully pouting little slit you have, Beatrice," she exclaimed, patting my Mons Veneris. "We shall make a beautiful contrast, mine is a light blonde, and yours will be brunette. See my little curly parsley bed is already half-an-inch long." She indulged in no end of exciting tricks, till at last my patience was exhausted, so slipping on my *chemise de nuit*, I bounced into bed, saying I believed it was all fudge about her having a tale to tell and that I would not let her love me again, till she had satisfied my curiosity.

"What bad manners to doubt my word," she cried, following me into bed, taking me by surprise, uncovered my bottom, and inflicted a smart little slapping, as she laughingly continued, "There, let that be a lesson to you not to doubt a young lady's word in future. Now you shall have my tale, although it would really serve you right to make you wait till to-morrow."

After a short pause, having settled ourselves lovingly in bed, she began:

Once upon a time there was a little girl about ten years old, of the name of Alice, her parents were rich, and lived in a beautiful house, surrounded by lovely gardens and a fine park, she had a brother about two years older than herself, but her mama was so fond of her (being an only daughter), that she never would allow her little girl out of her sight, unless William, the butler, had charge of her in her rambles about the grounds and park.

William was a handsome, good-looking man about thirty, and had been in the family ever since he was a boy. Now Alice, who was very fond of William, often sat on his knee as he was seated under a tree, or on a garden seat, when he would read to her fairy tales from her books. Their intimacy was so great that when they were alone, she would call him "dear old Willie," and treat him quite as an equal. Alice was quite an inquisitive girl, and would often put Mr. William to the blush by her curious enquiries about natural history affairs, and how animals had little ones, why the cock was so savage to the poor hens, jumping on their backs, and biting their heads with his sharp beak, &c. "My dear," he would say, "I'm not a hen or a cow; how should I know? don't ask such silly questions"; but Miss Alice was not so easily put off, she would reply, "Ah! Willie, you do know, and won't tell me, I insist upon knowing, &c.," but her efforts to obtain knowledge were quite fruitless.

This went on for some time till the little girl was within three or four months of her twelfth birthday, when a circumstance she had never taken any notice of before aroused her curiosity. It was that Mr. William, under pretense of seeing to his duties, was in the habit of secluding himself in his pantry, or closet, from seven to eight o'clock in the morning for about an hour before breakfast. If Alice ventured to tap at the door it was fastened inside, and admittance refused; the keyhole was so closed it was useless to try and look through that way, but it occurred to my little girl that perhaps she might be able to get a peep into that place of mystery if she could only get into a passage which passed behind Mr. William's pantry, and into which she knew it used to open by a half-glass door, now never used, as the passage was closed by a locked door at each end. This passage was lighted from the outside by a small window about four feet from the ground, fastened on the inside simply by a hook, which Alice, who mounted on a high stool, soon found she could open if she broke one of the small diamond panes of glass, which she did, and then waiting till the next morning felt sure she would be able to find out what Willie was always so busy about, and also that she could get in and out of the window unobserved by anyone, as it was quite screened from view by a thick shrubbery seldom entered by anyone.

Up betimes next day she told her lady's-maid she was going to enjoy the fresh air in the garden before breakfast, and then hurried off to her place of observation, and scrambled through the window regardless of dirt and dust, took off her boots as soon as she alighted in the disused passage, and silently crept up to the glass door, but to her chagrin found the panes so dirty as to be impervious to sight; however, she was so far lucky as to find a fine large keyhole quite clear, and two or three cracks in the woodwork, so that she could see nearly every part of the place, which was full of light from a skylight overhead. Mr. William was not there, but soon made his appearance, bringing a great basket of plate, which had been used the previous day, and for a few minutes was really busy looking in his pantry book, and counting spoons, forks, &c., but was soon finished, and began to look at a little book, which he took from a drawer. Just then, Lucy, one of the prettiest housemaids, a dark beauty of about eighteen, entered the room without ceremony, saying, "Here's some of your plate off the sideboard. Where's your eyes, Mr. William, not to gather up all as you ought to do?" William's eyes seemed to beam with delight as he caught her round the waist, and gave her a luscious kiss on her cheek, saying: "Why, I keep them for you, dear, I knew you would bring the plate"; then showing the book, "What do you think of that position, dear? How would you like it so?" Although pleased, the girl blushed up to the roots of her hair as she looked at the picture. The book dropped to the floor, and William pulled her on to his knee, and tried to put his hand up her clothes. "Ah! No! No!" she cried, in a low voice; "you know I can't to-day, but perhaps I can to-morrow; you must be good to-day, sir. Don't stick up your impudent head like that. There—there—there's a squeeze for you; now I must be off," she said, putting her hand down into his lap, where it could not be seen what she was after. In a second or two she jumped up, and in spite of his efforts to detain her, escaped from the pantry. William, evidently in a great state of excitement, subsided on to a sofa, muttering, "The little witch, what a devil she is; I can't help myself, but she will be all right to-morrow." Alice, who was intently observing everything, was shocked and surprised to see his trousers all unbuttoned in front, and a great long fleshy-looking thing sticking out, seemingly hard and stiff, with a ruby-coloured head. Mr. William took hold of it with one hand, apparently for the purpose of placing it in his breeches, but he seemed to hesitate, and closing his right hand upon the shaft, rubbed it up and down. "Ah! What a fool I am to let her excite me so. Oh! Oh! I can't help it; I must." He seemed to sigh as his hand increased its rapid motion. His face flushed, and his eyes seemed ready to start from his head, and in a few moments something spurted from his instrument, the drops falling over his hands and legs, some even a yard or two over the floor. This seemed to finish his ecstasy. He sank back quite listless for a few minutes, and then rousing himself, wiped his hands on a towel, cleared up every drop of the mess, and left the pantry.

Alice was all over in a burning heat from what she had seen but instinctively felt that the mystery was only half unravelled, and promised herself to be there and see what William and Lucy would do next day. Mr. William took her for a walk as usual, and read to her, whilst she sat on his knee, and Alice wondered what could have become of that great stiff thing which she had seen in the morning. With the utmost apparent innocence, her hands touched him casually, where she hoped to feel the monster, but only resulted in feeling a rather soft kind of bunch in his pocket.

Another morning arrived to find Alice at her post behind the disused glass door, and she soon saw Mr. William bring in his plate, but he put it aside, and seemed all impatient for Lucy's arrival. "Ah!" he murmurs. "I'm as stiff as a rolling pin at the very thought of the saucy darling," but his ideas were cut short by the appearance of Lucy herself, who carefully bolted the door inside. Then rushing into his arms, she covered him with kisses, exclaiming, in a low voice, "Ah! How I have longed for him these three or four days. What a shame women should be stopped in that way from enjoying themselves once a month. How is he this morning?" as her hands nervously unbuttoned Mr. William's trousers, and grasped his ready truncheon.

"What a hurry you are in, Lucy!" gasped her lover, as she almost stifled him with her kisses. "Don't spoil it all by your impatience; I must have my kiss first."

With a gentle effort he reclined her backwards on a sofa, and raised her clothes till Alice had a full view of a splendid pair of plump, white legs; but what rivetted her gaze most was the luscious looking, pouting lips of Lucy's cunny, quite vermilion in colour, and slightly gaping open, in a most inviting manner, as her legs were wide apart; her Mons Veneris being covered with a profusion of beautiful curly black hair.

The butler was down on his knees in a moment, and glued his lips to her crack, sucking and kissing furiously, to the infinite delight of the girl, who sighed and wriggled with pleasure; till at last Mr. William could no longer restrain himself, but getting up upon his knees between Lucy's legs, he brought his shaft to the charge, and to Alice's astonishment, fairly ran it right into the gaping crack, till it was all lost in her belly; they laid still for a few moments, enjoying the conjunction of their persons till Lucy heaved up her bottom, and the butler responded to it by a shove, then they commenced a most exciting struggle. Alice could see the manly shaft as it worked in and out of her sheath, glistening with lubricity, whilst the lips of her cunny seemed to cling to it each time of withdrawal, as if afraid of losing such a delightful sugar stick; but this did not last long, their movements got more and more furious, till at last both seemed to meet in a spasmodic embrace, as they almost fainted in each other's arms, and Alice could see a profusion of creamy moisture oozing from the crack of Lucy, as they both lay in a kind of lethargy of enjoyment after their battle of love.

Mr. William was the first to break the silence: "Lucy, will you look in to-morrow, dear; you know that old spy, Mary, will be back from her holiday in a day or two, and then we shan't often have a chance."

LUCY.—"Ah; you rogue, I mean to have a little more now, I don't care if we're caught; I must have it," she said, squeezing him with her arms and gluing her lips to his, as she threw her beautiful legs right over his buttocks, and commenced the engagement once more by rapidly heaving her bottom; in fact, although he was a fine man, the weight of his body seemed as nothing in her amorous excitement.

The butler's excuses and pleading of fear, in case he was missed, &c., were all of no avail; she fairly drove him on, and he was soon as furiously excited as herself, and with a profusion of sighs, expressions of pleasure, endearment, &c., they soon died away again into a state of short voluptuous oblivion. However, Mr. William was too nervous and afraid to let her lay long; he withdrew his instrument from her foaming cunny, just as it was all slimy and glistening with the mingled juices of their love; but what a contrast to its former state, as Alice now beheld it much reduced in size, and already drooping its fiery head.

Lucy jumped up and let down her clothes, but kneeling on the floor before her lover, she took hold of his limp affair, and gave it a most luscious sucking, to the great delight of Mr. William, whose face flushed again with pleasure, and as soon as Lucy had done with her sucking kiss, Alice saw that his instrument was again stiff and ready for a renewal of their joys.

LUCY, laughing in a low tone.—"There, my boy, I'll leave you like that; think of me till to-morrow; I couldn't help giving the darling a good suck after the exquisite pleasure he had afforded me, it's like being in heaven for a little while."

With a last kiss on the lips as they parted, and Mr. William again locked his door, whilst Alice made good her retreat to prepare herself for breakfast.

It was a fine warm morning in May, and soon after breakfast Alice, with William for her guardian, set off for a ramble in the park, her blood was in a boil, and she longed to experience the joys she was sure Lucy had been surfeited with; they sauntered down to the lake, and she asked William to give her a row in the boat; he unlocked the boat-house, and handed her into a nice, broad, comfortable skiff, well furnished with soft seats and cushions.

"How nice to be here, in the shade," said Alice; "come into the boat, Willie, we will sit in it a little while, and you shall read to me before we have a row."

"Just as you please, Miss Alice," he replied, with unwonted deference, stepping into the boat, and sitting down in the stern sheets.

"Ah my head aches a little, let me recline it in your lap," said Alice, throwing off her hat, and stretching herself along on a cushion. "Why are you so precise this morning, Willie? You know I don't like to be called Miss, you can keep that for Lucy." Then noticing his confusion, "You may blush, sir, I could make you sink into your shoes if you only knew all I have seen between you and Miss Lucy."

Alice reclined her head in a languid manner on his lap, looking up and enjoying the confusion she had thrown him into; then designedly resting one hand on the lump which he seemed to have in his pocket, as if to support herself a little, she continued: "Do you think, Willie, I shall ever have as fine legs as Lucy? Don't you think I ought soon to have long dresses, sir! I'm getting quite bashful about showing my calves so much." The butler had hard work to recover his composure, the vivid recollection of the luscious episode with Lucy before breakfast was so fresh in his mind that Alice's allusions to her, and the soft girlish hand resting on his privates (even although he thought her as innocent as a lamb) raised an utter of desire in his feverish blood, which he tried to allay as much as possible, but little by little the unruly member began to swell, till he was sure she must feel it throb under her hand. With an effort he slightly shifted himself, so as to remove her hand lower down on to the thigh, as he answered as gravely as possible (feeling assured Alice could know nothing): "You're making game of me this morning. Don't you wish me to read, Alice?"

ALICE, excitedly, with an unusual flush on her face.—"You naughty man, you shall tell me what I want to know this time: How do babies come? What is the parsley bed, the nurses and doctors say they come out of? Is it not a curly lot of hair at the bottom of the woman's belly? I know that's what Lucy's got, and I've seen you kiss it, sir!"

William felt ready to drop; the perspiration stood on his brow in great drops, but his lips refused to speak, and Alice continued in a soft whisper: "I saw it all this morning, Willie dear, and what joy that great red-head thing of yours seemed to give her. You must let me into the secret, and I will never tell. This is the monster you shoved into her so furiously. I must look at it and feel it; how hard it has got under my touch. La! What a funny thing! I can get it out as Lucy did," pulling open his trousers and letting out the rampant engine of love. She kissed its red velvety head, saying: "What a sweet, soft thing to touch. Oh! I must caress it a little." Her touches were like fire to his senses; speechless with rapture and surprise, he silently submitted to the freak of the wilful girl, but his novel position was so exciting, he could not restrain himself, but the sperm boiled up from his penis all over her hands and face.

"Ah!" she exclaimed. "That's just what I saw it do yesterday morning. Does it do that inside of Lucy?"

Here William recovered himself a little, and wiping her face and hands with his handkerchief, put away the rude plaything, saying, "Oh! My God! I'm lost! What have you done, Alice? It's awful! Never mention it again. I mustn't walk out with you any more."

Alice burst into sobs.

"Oh! Oh! Willie! How unkind! Do you think I will tell? Only I must share the pleasure with Lucy. Oh! Kiss me as you did her, and we won't say any more about it to-day."

William loved the little girl too well to refuse such a delightful task, but he contented himself with a very short suck at her virgin cunny, lest his erotic passion should urge him to outrage her at once.

"How nice to feel your lovely tongue there. How beautifully it tickled and warmed me all over; but you were so quick, and left off just as it seemed nicer than ever, dear Willie," said Alice, embracing and kissing him with ardour.

"Gently, darling; you mustn't be so impulsive; it's a very dangerous game for one so young. You must be careful how you look at me, or notice me, before others," said Mr. William, returning her kisses, and feeling himself already

22

quite unable to withstand the temptation of such a delicious liaison.

"Ah!" said Alice, with extraordinary perception for one so young. "You fear Lucy. Our best plan is to take her into our confidence. I will get rid of my lady's-maid, I never did like her, and will ask mama to give Lucy the place. Won't that be fine, dear? We, shall be quite safe in all our little games then."

The butler, now more collected in his ideas, and with a cooler brain, could not but admire the wisdom of this arrangement, so he assented to the plan, and he took the boat out for a row to cool their heated blood, and quiet the impulsive throbbings of a pair of fluttering hearts.

The next two or three days were wet and unfavourable for outdoor excursions, and Alice took advantage of this interval to induce her mother to change her lady's-maid, and install Lucy in the situation.

Alice's attendant slept in a little chamber, which had two doors, one opening into the corridor, whilst the other allowed free and direct access to her little mistress's apartment, which it adjoined.

The very first night Lucy retired to rest in her new room, she had scarcely been half-an-hour in bed (where she lay, reflecting on the change, and wondering how she would now be able to enjoy the butler's company occasionally), before Alice called out for her. In a moment she was at the young lady's bedside, saying: "What can I do, Miss Alice, are you not warm enough? These damp nights are so chilly."

"Yes, Lucy," said Alice, "that must be what it is. I feel cold and restless. Would you mind getting in bed with me? You will soon make me warm."

Lucy jumped in, and Alice nestled close up to her bosom, as if for warmth, but in reality to feel the outlines of her beautiful figure.

"Kiss me, Lucy," she said; "I know I shall like you so much better than Mary. I couldn't bear her." This was lovingly responded to, and Alice continued, as she pressed her hand on the bosom of her bedfellow, "What large titties you have, Lucy. Let me feel them. Open your nightdress, so I can lay my face against them."

The new femme de chambre was naturally of a warm and

23

loving disposition; she admitted all the familiarities of her young mistress, whose hands began to wander in a most searching manner about her person, feeling the soft, firm skin of her bosom, belly, and bottom; the touches of Alice seemed to fire the blood, and rouse every voluptuous emotion within her; she sighed and kissed her little mistress again and again.

ALICE.—"What a fine rump! How hard and plump your flesh is, Lucy! Oh, my! what's all this hair at the bottom of your belly? My dear, when did it come?"

LUCY.—"Oh! pray don't, Miss, it's so rude; you will be the same in two or three years' time; it frightened me when it first began to grow, it seemed so unnatural."

ALICE.—"We're only girls, there is no harm in touching each other, is there; just feel how different I am."

LUCY.—"Oh! Miss Alice," pressing the young girl's naked belly to her own, "you don't know how you make me feel when you touch me there."

ALICE (with a slight laugh).—"Does it make you feel better when Mr. William, the butler, touches you, dear?" tickling the hairy crack with her finger.

LUCY.—"For shame, Miss! I hope you don't think I would let him touch me"; evidently in some confusion.

ALICE.—"Don't be frightened, Lucy, I won't tell, but I have seen it all through the old glass door in his pantry. Ah! you see I know the secret, and must be let in to share the fun."

LUCY.—"Oh! My God! Miss Alice, what have you seen? I shall have to leave the house at once."

ALICE.—"Come, come, don't be frightened, you know I'm fond of Mr. William, and would never do him any harm, but you can't have him all to yourself; I got you for my maid to prevent your jealous suspicions and keep our secret between us."

Lucy was in a frightful state of agitation. "What! has he been such a brute as to ruin you, Miss Alice! I'll murder him if he has," she cried.

ALICE.—"Softly, Lucy, not so loud, someone will hear you; he's done nothing yet, but I saw your pleasure when he put that thing into your crack, and am determined to share your joys, so don't be jealous, and we can all three be happy together."

LUCY.—"It would kill you dear; that big thing of his would

24

split you right up."

ALICE.—"Never mind," kissing her lovingly, "you keep the secret and I'm not afraid of being seriously hurt."

Lucy sealed the compact with a kiss, and they spent a most loving night together, indulging in every variety of kissing and tickling, and Alice had learnt from her bedfellow nearly all the mysterious particulars in connection with the battles of Venus before they fell asleep in each other's arms.

Fine weather soon returned, and Alice, escorted by the butler, went for one of her usual rambles, and they soon penetrated into a thick copse at the further end of the park, and sat down in a little grassy spot, where they were secure from observation.

William had thoughtfully brought with him an umbrella, as well as a great coat and cloak, which he spread upon the grass for fear Miss Alice might take cold.

"Ah! you dear old fellow," said Alice, seating herself, and, taking his hand, pulled him down beside her. "I understand everything now, and you are to make me happy by making a woman of me, as you did Lucy; you must do it, Willie, dear, I shall soon make you so you can't help yourself." Uubuttoning his trousers and handling his already stiff pego, "What a lovely dear it is; how I long to feel its juice spouting into my bowels; I know it's painful, but it won't kill me, and then, ah! the heavenly bliss I know you will make me feel, as you do Lucy when you have her; how will you do it? will you lay over me?"

William, unable to resist her caresses and already almost at spending point, makes her kneel over his face, as he lay on his back, so that he may first lubricate her maiden cunny with his tongue. This operation titillates and excites the little girl, so that she amorously presses herself on his mouth as she faces towards his cock, which she never leaves hold of all the while; he spends in ecstasy, whilst she also feels the pleasure of a first virgin emission.

"Now's the time, Alice, dear, my affair is so well greased, and your pussey is also ready; if I get over you I might be too violent and injure you; the best way is for you to try and do it yourself by straddling over me, and directing its head to your cunny, and then keep pressing down upon it, as well as the first painful sensations will allow; it will all depend on your own courage for the success of the experiment," said

William.

ALICE.—"Ah! you shall see my determination," as she began to act upon his suggestion, and fitting the head of his pego into her slit, soon pressed down so as to take in and quite cover the first inch of it.

Here the pain of stretching and distension seemed almost too much for her, but she gave a sudden downward plunge of her body, which, although she almost fainted with the dreadful pain, got in at least three inches.

"What a plucky girl you are, my dear Alice," said William, in delight. "As soon as you can bear it, raise yourself up a little, and come down with all your force. It is so well planted, the next good thrust will complete my possession of your lovely charms."

"I don't care if I die in the effort," she whispered, softly. "Never mind how it hurts me, help all you can, Willie dear, this time," as she raised herself off him again, and he took hold of her buttocks, to lend his assistance to the grave girl.

Clenching her teeth firmly, and shutting her eyes, she gave another desperate plunge upon William's spear of love, the hymen was broken, and she was fairly impaled to the roots of his affair. But it cost her dear, she fell forward in a dead faint, whilst the trickling blood proved the sanguinary nature of Love's victory.

The butler withdrew himself, all smeared with her virgin blood, but he had come prepared for such an emergency, and at once set about using restoratives to bring her round, and presently succeeded in his efforts; her eyes opened with a smile, and whispering softly, Alice said:—

"Ah! that last thrust was awful, but it's over now. Why did you take him away? Oh! put it back at once, dear, and let me have the soothing injection Lucy said would soon heal all my bruised parts."

He glued his lips to hers, and gently applied the head of his pego to her blood-stained crack, gradually inserted it till it was three-fourths in; then, without pressing further, he commenced to move slowly and carefully. The lubricity soon increased, and he could feel the tight loving contractions of her vagina, which speedily brought him to a crisis once more, and with a sudden thrust, he plunged up to the hilt, and shot his very essence into her bowels, as he almost fainted with the excess of his emotions.

They laid motionless, enjoying each other's mutual pressures, till Mr. William withdrew, and taking a fine cambric handkerchief, wiped the virgin blood first from the lips of her cunny, then off his own weapon, declaring, as he put the red-stained mouchoir in his pocket, that he would keep it for ever, in remembrance of the charms she had so lovingly surrendered to him.

The butler prudently refrained from the further indulgence in voluptuous pleasure for the day, and, after a good rest, Alice returned to the house, feeling very little the worse for her sacrifice, and very happy in having secured part of the love of dear and faithful William.

How suddenly unforeseen accidents prevent the realization of the best plans for happiness. The very same day, her father was ordered by his medical adviser to the South of Europe, and started next morning for town, to make the necessary arrangements, taking the butler with him, leaving Alice's mama to follow as soon as the two children were suitably located at school.

Lucy and her young mistress consoled each other as well as possible under the circumstances. But in a few days, an aunt took charge of the house, and Alice was sent to this school, and is now in your arms, dear Beatrice; whilst my brother is now at college, and we only meet during the holidays. Will you, dear, ask your guardians to allow you to spend the next vacation with me, and I will introduce you to Frederick, who, if I make no mistake, is quite as voluptuously inclined as his sister.

Part II.

I will pass over the exciting practices myself and bedfellow used to indulge in almost every night, and merely remark that two more finished young tribades it would have been impossible to have found anywhere.

I had to wait till the Christmas vacation before I could be introduced to Frederick, who, between ourselves, we had already devoted to the task of taking my virginity, which we did not think would prove a very difficult operation, as with so much finger frigging, and also the use of Alice's leather sausage, which, as I learnt, she had improvised for her own gratification, my mount and cunny were wonderfully devel-

27

oped, and already slight signs of the future growth of curly brown hair could be detected. I was nearly thirteen, as one fine crisp morning in December we drove up to the Hall on our return from school. There stood the aunt to welcome us, but my eyes were fixed upon the youthful, yet manly figure of Frederick, who stood by her side, almost a counterpart of his sister, in features and complexion, but really a very fine young fellow, between seventeen and eighteen.

Since hearing the story of Alice's intrigue with William, I always looked at every man and boy to see what sort of a bunch they had got in their pockets, and was delighted to perceive Mr. Frederick was apparently well furnished.

Alice introduced me to her relatives, but Frederick evidently looked upon me as a little girl, and not at all yet up to the serious business of love and flirtation, so our first private consultation, between Alice and myself, was how best to open his eyes, and draw him to take a little more notice of his sister's friend.

Lucy, who I now saw for the first time, slept in the little room adjoining Alice's chamber, which I shared with her young mistress. Frederick had a room on the other side of ours, so that we were nextdoor neighbours, and could rap and give signals to each other on the wall, as well as to try to look through the keyhole of a disused door, which opened direct from one room to the other, but had long since been locked and bolted to prevent any communication between the occupants.

A little observation soon convinced us that Lucy was upon most intimate terms with her young master, which Alice determined to turn to account in our favour.

She quickly convinced her *femme de chambre* that she could not enjoy and monopolize the whole of her brother. and finding that Lucy expected he would visit her room that very night, she insisted upon ringing the changes, by taking Lucy to sleep with herself, and putting me in the place of Monsieur Frederick's ladylove.

I was only too willing to be a party of this arrangement, and at ten P.M., when we all retired to rest, I took the place of the *femme de chambre*, and pretended to be fast asleep in her snug little bed. The lock of the door had been oiled by Lucy, so as to open quite noiselessly, but the room was purposely left in utter darkness, and secured even from the intrusion of a dim starlight by well-closed window curtains.

About eleven o'clock, as nearly as I could guess, the door silently opened, and by the light of the corridor lamp, I saw a figure, in nothing but a shirt, cautiously glide in, and approach the bed. The door closed, and all was dark, putting my heart in a dreadful flutter, at the approach of the long wished for, but dreaded ravisher of my virginity.

"Lucy! Lucy!! Lucy!!!" he whispered, in a low voice, almost in my ear. No response, only the apparent deep breathing of a person in sound sleep.

"She hasn't thought much about me, but, I guess, something between her legs will soon wake her up," I heard him mutter; then the bedclothes were pulled open, and he slid into bed by my side. My hair was all loose, the same as Lucy's generally was at night, and I felt a warm kiss on my cheek, also an arm stealing round my waist and clutching my nightdress as if to pull it up. Of course I was the fox asleep, but could not help being all atremble at the approach of my fate.

"How you shake, Lucy; what's the matter? Hullo! who's this; it can't be you?" he said rapidly, as with a sigh and a murmur, "Oh! oh! Alice." I turned round just as he pulled up my chemise, clasping my arm firmly round him, but still apparently lost in sleep. "My God!" I heard him say, "It's that little devil of a Beatrice in Lucy's bed; I won't go, I'll have a lark, she can't know me in the dark."

His hands seemed to explore every part of my body; I could feel his rampant cock pressed between our naked bellies, but although in a burning heat of excitement, I determined to let him do just as he liked, and pretend still to be asleep; his fingers explored my crack, and rubbed the little clitoris; first his leg got between mine, and then presently I could feel him gently placing the head of his instrument in the crack, and I was so excited that a sudden emission wetted it and his fingers all over with a creamy spend. "The little devil's spending in her sleep; these girls must be in the habit of frigging each other, I believe," he said to himself again. Then his lips met mine for the first time, and he was quite free from fear on that account as his face was as beardless as a girl's.

"Ah! Alice!" I murmured, "give me your sausage thing, that's it, dear, shove it in," as I pushed myself forward on his

29

slowly progressing cock; he met me with a sudden thrust, making me almost scream with pain, yet my arms nervously clung round his body, and kept him close to the mark.

"Gently," he whispered, "Beatrice, dear, I'm Frederick, I won't hurt you much; how in heaven's name did you come in Lucy's bed?"

Pretending now to awaken for the first time with a little scream, and trying to push his body away from me, I exclaimed, "Oh! Oh! How you hurt! Oh! for shame, don't. Oh! let me go, Mr. Frederick, how can you?" And then my efforts seemed exhausted, and I lay almost at his mercy as he ruthlessly pushed his advantage, and tried to stop my mouth with kisses. I was lost. Although very painful, thanks to our frequent fingerings, &c., the way had been so cleared that he was soon in complete possession, although as I afterwards found by the stains on my chemise it was not quite a bloodless victory.

Taking every possible advantage, he continued his motions with thrilling energy, till I could not help responding to his delicious thrusts, moving my bottom a little to meet each returning insertion of his exciting weapon (we were lying on our sides), and in a few moments we both swam in a mutual flood of bliss, and after a spasmodic storm of sighs, kisses, and tender hugging pressure of each other's body, we lay in a listless state of enjoyment, when suddenly the bedclothes were thrown, or pulled off, then slap—slap—slap, came smarting smacks on our bottoms, and Alice's light, merry laugh sounded through the darkness, "Ha! Ha! Ha! Ha! Mr. Frederick, is this what you learnt at college, sir? Here, Lucy, help; we must secure and punish the wretch; bring a light."

Lucy appeared with a candle and locked the door inside at once, before he could have a chance of escaping, and I could see she was quite delighted at the spectacle presented by our bodies in conjunction, for as I had been previously instructed, I clung to him in apparent fright, and tried to hide my blushing face in his bosom.

Frederick was in the utmost confusion, and at first was afraid his sister would expose him, but he was a little reassured as she went on, "What shall I do? I can't tell an old maid like aunt; only to think that my dear little Beatrice should be outraged under my very eyes, the second night of her visit. If papa and mama were at home, they would know what to do; now I must decide for myself. Now, Frederick, will you submit to a good whipping for this, or shall I write to your father, and send Beatrice home disgraced in the morning, and you will have to promise to marry her, sir? Now you've spoilt her for anyone else; who do you think would take a cruche cassée if they knew it, or not repudiate her when it was found out, as it must be the first night of her marriage. No, you bad boy, I'm determined both to punish you and make you offer her all the reparation in your power."

I began to cry, and begged her not to be too hard, as he had not hurt me much, and in fact had, at the finish, quite delighted my ravished senses.

"Upon my word," said Alice, assuming the airs of a woman, "the girl is as bad as the boy; this could not have happened, Beatrice, if you had not been too complaisant, and given way to his rudeness."

Frederick, disengaging himself from my embrace, and quite unmindful of his condition, started up, and clasping his sister round her neck, kissed her most lovingly, and the impudent fellow even raised her nightdress and stroked her belly, exclaiming, as he passed his hand over her mossy mount, "What a pity, Alice, you are my sister or I would give you the same pleasure as I have Beatrice, but I will submit to your chastisement, however hard it may be, and promise also that my little love here shall be my future wife."

ALICE.—"You scandalous fellow, to insult my modesty so, and expose your blood-stained manhood to my sight, but I will punish you, and avenge both myself and Beatrice; you are my prisoner, so just march into the other room, I've got a tickler there that I brought home from school, as a curiosity, little thinking I should so soon have a use for it."

Arrived in Alice's own room, she and Lucy first tied his hands to the bedpost, then they secured his ankles to the handle of a heavy box, which stood handy, so as to have him tolerably well stretched out.

ALICE, getting her rod out of a drawer.—"Now, pin up his shirt to his shoulders, and I will see if I can't at least draw a few drops of his impudent blood out of his posteriors, which Beatrice may wipe off with her handkerchief as a memento of the outrage she has so easily forgiven."

The hall was a large house, and our apartments were the

only ones occupied in that corridor, the rooms abutting on which were all in reserve for visitors expected to arrive in a few days, to spend Christmas with us, so that there was not much fear of being heard by any of the other inmates of the house, and Alice was under no necessity of thinking what might be the result of her blows. With a flourish she brought down the bunch of twigs with a thundering whack on his plump, white bottom; the effect was startling to the culprit, who was evidently only anticipating some playful fun. "Ah! My God! Alice, you'll cut the skin; mind what you're about; I didn't bargain for that."

ALICE (with a smile of satisfaction).—"Ho! Ho! did you think I was going to play with you? But, you've soon found your mistake, sir. Will you? will you, again take such outrageous liberties with a young lady friend of mine?"

She cut him quite half-a-dozen times in rapid succession, as she thus lectured him, each blow leaving long red lines, to mark its visitation, and suffusing his fair bottom all over with a peach-like bloom. The victim, finding himself quite helpless, bit his lips and ground his teeth in fruitless rage. At last he burst forth: "Ah! Ah! You she-devil! Do you mean to skin my bum? Be careful, or I will take a rare revenge some day before long."

ALICE, with great calmness and determination, but with a most excited twinkle in her eyes.—"Oh! You show temper, do you? So you mean to be revenged on me for doing a simple act of justice, sir? I will keep you there, and cut away at your impudent bottom, till you fairly beg my pardon, and promise to forgo all such wicked revengefulness."

The victim writhed in agony and rage, but her blows only increased in force, beginning to raise great fiery-looking weals all over his buttocks. "Ah! Ha!" she continued. "How do you like it, Fred? Shall I put a little more steam in my blows?"

Frederick struggles desperately to get loose, but they have secured him too well for that! The tears of shame and mortification stand in his eyes, but he is still obstinate, and I could also observe a very perceptible rising in his manly instrument, which soon stood out from his belly in a rampant state of erection.

ALICE, with assumed fury.—"Look at the fellow, how he is insulting me, by the exhibition of his lustful weapon. I wish I

32

could cut it off with a blow of the rod," giving him a tearful cut across his belly and on the penis.

Frederick fairly howled with pain, and big tears rolled down his cheeks, as he gasped out: "Oh! Oh! Ah! Have mercy, Alice. I know I deserve it. Oh! Pity me now, dear!"

ALICE, without relaxing her blows.—"Oh! You are beginning to feel properly, are you? Are you sincerely penitent? Beg my pardon at once, sir, for the way you insulted me in the other room."

FREDERICK.—"Oh! Dear Alice! Stop! Stop! You don't let me get my breath. I will! I will beg your pardon. Oh! I can't help my affair sticking up as it does."

ALICE.—"Down sir! Down sir! Your master is ashamed of you," as she playfully whisks his pego with her rod.

Frederick is in agony; his writhing and contortions seemed excruciating in the extreme, he fairly groaned out: "Oh! Oh! Alice, let me down. On my word, I will do anything you order. Oh! Oh! Ah! You make me do it," as he shuts his eyes, and we saw quite a jet of sperm shoot from his virile member.

Alice dropped her rod, and we let down the culprit who was terribly crestfallen.

"Now, sir," she said, "down on your knees, and kiss the rod."

Without a word, he dropped down, and kissed the worn-out stump, saying: "Oh! Alice; the last few moments have been so heavenly. It has blotted out all sense of pain. My dear sister, I think you for punishing me, and will keep my promise to Beatrice."

I wiped the drops of blood from his slightly-bleeding rump, and then we gave him a couple of glasses of wine, and allowed him to sleep with Lucy, in her room, for the rest of the night, where they had a most luscious time of it, whilst Alice and myself indulged in our favourite touches.

You may be sure Frederick was not long before he renewed his pleasures with me, whilst his sister took pleasure in our happiness; but she seemed to have contracted a penchant for the use of the rod, and, once or twice a week, would have us all in her room, for a birch seance, as she called it, when Lucy or myself had to submit to be victims; but the heating of our bottoms only seemed to add to our enjoyment when we were afterwards allowed to soothe our raging passions in the arms of our mutual lover.

Christmas came, and with it arrived several visitors, all young ladies and gentlemen of about our own ages, to spend the festive season with us; our entire party consisted of five gentlemen and seven ladies, leaving out the aunt, who was too old to enter into youthful fun and contented herself with being a faithful housekeeper, and keeping good house, so that after supper every evening we could do almost as we liked; myself and Alice soon converted our five young lady friends into tribades like ourselves, ready for anything, whilst Frederick prepared his young male friends. New Year's Day was his eighteenth birthday, and we determined to hold a regular orgy that night in our corridor, with Lucy's help. Plenty of refreshments were laid in stock, ices, sandwiches, and champagne; the aunt strictly ordered us all to retire at one A.M. at latest, so we kept her commands, after spending a delicious evening in dancing and games, which only served to flush us with excitement for what all instinctively felt would be a most voluptuous entertainment upstairs.

The aunt was a heavy sleeper, and rather deaf, besides which Frederick, under the excuse of making them drink his health, plied the servants first with beer, then with wine, and afterwards with just a glass of brandy for a nightcap; so that we were assured they would also be sound enough, in fact two or three never got to bed at all.

Frederick was master of the ceremonies, with Alice as a most useful assistant. As I said before, all were flushed with excitement and ready for anything; they were all of the most aristocratic families, and our blue blood seemed fairly to course through our veins. When all had assembled in Alice's apartment they found her attired in a simple, long chemise de nuit. "Ladies and gentlemen," she said, "I believe we are all agreed for an out and out romp; you see my costume, how do you like it?" and a most wicked smile, "I hope it does not display the contour of my figure too much," drawing it tightly about her so as to show the outline of her beautiful buttocks, and also displaying a pair of ravishing legs in pink silk stockings.

"Bravo! Bravo! Bravo Alice! we will follow your example," burst from all sides. Each one skipped back to his or her room and reappeared in mufti; but the tails of the young gentlemen's shirts caused a deal of laughter, by being too short

ALICE.—"Well, I'm sure, gentlemen, I did not think your undergarments were so indecently short."

Frederick, with a laugh, caught hold of his sister's chemise, and tore a great piece off all around, so that she was in quite a short smock, which only half-covered her fair bottom

Alice was crimson with blushes, and half inclined to be angry, but recovering herself, she laughed, "Ah! Fred, what a shame to serve me so, but I don't mind if you make us all alike."

The girls screamed, and the gentlemen made a rush; it was a most exciting scene; the young ladies retaliated by tearing the shirts of their tormentors, and this first skirmish only ended when the whole company were reduced to a complete state of nudity; all were in blushes as they gazed upon the variety of male and female charms exposed to view.

FREDERICK, advancing with a bumper of champagne.— "We've all heard of Nuda Veritas, now let's drink to her health; the first time we are in her company, I'm sure she will be most charming and agreeable."

All joined in this toast, the wine inflamed our desires, there was not a male organ present but what was in a glorious state of erection.

ALICE.—"Look, ladies, what a lot of impudent fellows, they need not think we are going to surrender anyhow to their youthful lust; they shall be all blindfolded, and then we will arm ourselves with good birch rods, then let it be everyone for themselves and Cupid's dart for us all."

"Hear, hear," responded on all sides, and handkerchiefs were soon tied over their eyes, and seven good birch rods handed round to the ladies. "Now, gentlemen, catch who you can," laughed Alice, slashing right and left into the manly group, her example being followed by the other girls; the room was quite large enough and a fine romp ensued, the girls were as lithe and active as young fawns, and for a long time sorely tried the patience of their male friends, who tumbled about in all directions, only to get an extra dose of birch on their plump posteriors before they could regain their feet.

At last the Honble. Miss Vavasour stumbled over a prostrate gentleman, who happened to be the young Marquis of Bucktown, who grasped her firmly round the waist, and clung to his prize, as a shower of cuts greeted the writhing pair.

"Hold, hold," cried Alice, "she's fairly caught and must submit to be offered as a victim on the Altar of Love"

Lucy quickly wheeled a small soft couch into the centre of the room. The gentlemen pulled off their bandages, and all laughingly assisted to place the pair in position; the lady underneath with a pillow under her buttocks, and the young marquis, on his knees, fairly planted between her thighs. Both were novices, but a more beautiful couple it would be impossible to conceive; he was a fine young fellow of seventeen, with dark hair and eyes, whilst her brunette style of complexion was almost a counterpart of his; their eyes were similar also, and his instrument, as well as her cunny, were finely ornamented with soft curly black hair; with the skin drawn back, the firey purple head of his cock looked like a large ruby, as, by Frederick's suggestion, he presented it to her luscious-looking vermilion gap, the lips of which were just slightly open as she lay with her legs apart. The touch seemed to electrify her, the blushing face turned to a still deeper crimson as the dart of love slowly entered the outwarks of her virginity. Fred continued to act as mentor, by whispering in the young gallant's ear, who also was covered with blushes, but feeling his steed fairly in contact with the throbbing matrix of the lovely girl beneath him, he at once plunged forward to the attack, pushing, shoving, and clasping her round the body with all his strength, whilst he tried to stifle her cries of pain by glueing his lips to hers. It was a case of Veni, Vidi, Vici. His onset was too impetuous to be withstood, and she lay in such a passive favourable position that the network of her hymen was broken at the first charge, and he was soon in full possession up to the roots of his hair. He rested a moment, she opened her eyes, and with a faint smile said, "Ah! It was indeed sharp, but I can already begin to feel the pleasures of love. Go on now, dear boy, our example will soon fire the others to imitate us," heaving up her bottom as a challenge, and pressing him fondly to her bosom. They ran a delightful course, which filled us all with voluptuous excitement, and as they died away in a mutual spend, someone put out the lights. All was laughing confusion, gentlemen trying to catch a prize, kissing and sighing.

I felt myself seized by a strong arm, a hand groped for my cunny, whilst a whisper in my ear said: "How delightful! It's you, dear little Beatrice. I can't make a mistake, as yours is the only hairless thing in the company. Kiss me, dear, I'm bursting to be into your tight little affair." Lips met lips in a luscious kiss. We found ourselves close to Alice's bed, my companion put me back on it, and taking my legs under his arms, was soon pushing his way up my longing cunny. I nipped him as tightly as possible; he was in ecstasies and spent almost directly, but keeping his place, he put me, by his vigorous action, into a perfect frenzy of love. Spend seemed to follow spend, till we had each of us done it six times, and the last time I so forgot myself as to fairly bite his shoulder in delight. At length he withdrew, without telling his name. The room was still in darkness, and love engagements were going on all round. I had two more partners after that, but only one go with each. I shall never forget that night as long as a breath remains in my body.

Next day I found out, through Fred, that Charlie Vavasour had been my first partner, and that he himself believed he had had his sister in the melee, which she afterwards admitted to me was a fact, although she thought he did not know it, and the temptation to enjoy her brother was too much for her.

This orgie has been the means of establishing a kind of secret society amongst the circle of our friends. Anyone who gives a pressure of the hand and asks: "Do you remember Fred's birthday?" is free to indulge in love with those who understand it, and I have since been present at many repetitions of that birthday fun.

Part III.

We returned to school, and I kept up a regular correspondence with Frederick, the letters to and fro being enclosed in those of Alice. Time crept on, but as you can imagine as well or better than I can relate all the kinds of salacious amusements we girls used to indulge in, I shall skip over the next few years till I arrived at the age of seventeen; my guardians were in a hurry to present me at Court, and have me brought out in hopes that I might soon marry and relieve them of their trust.

Alice was so attached to me that since my first visit to her home, she had solicited her aunt to arrange with my guardians for my permanent residence with her during my minority, which quite fell in with their views, as it enabled me to see more society, and often meet gentlemen who might perhaps fall in love with my pretty face.

Lady St. Jerome undertook to present both Alice and myself; she was an aunt, and mentioned in her letter that unfortunately a star of the first magnitude would also be presented at the same drawing room, but still we might have a faint chance of picking up young Lothair, the great matrimonial prize of the season, if he did not immediately fall in love with the beautiful Lady Corisande, and that we should meet them both at Crecy House, at the Duchess's ball, in celebration of the presentation of her favourite daughter, for which she had obtained invitations for us. For nearly three weeks we were in a flutter of excitement, making the necessary preparations for our debut. My mother's jewels were re-set to suit the fashion of the day, and every three or four days we went to town to see our Court milliner.

In company with Alice and her aunt, we arrived at Lord St. Jerome's town residence in St. James' Square, the evening before the eventful day; her ladyship was a most charming person of about thirty, without family, who introduced us before dinner to her niece, Miss Clare Arundel, Father Coleman, the family confessor, and Monsignore Berwick, the chamberlain of Pio Nono. The dinner was exquisite, and we passed a delightful evening, amused by the quiet humour of the confessor, and the sparkling wit of Monsignore, who seemed to studiously avoid religious subjects. Miss Arundel, with her beautiful, pensive, violet eyes, and dark brown golden hair, seemed particularly fascinated by the sallies of the latter, whilst there was a something remarked by both Alice and myself, which led us to suspect the existence of some curious tie between the two ecclesiastics and the ladies of the household.

Lord St. Jerome was not in town. At our special request, Alice and myself shared the same room, which opened into a spacious corridor, at one end of which was a small chapel or oratory. Our minds were so unsettled by the thoughts of the morrow, and also hopes of meeting some of our old friends in town, especially the Vavasours, that sleep was quite banished from our eyes; suddenly Alice started up in bed, with, "Hist! there's someone moving about the corridor." She sprang out of bed, and softly opened our door, whilst I followed and stood close behind her. "They're gone into the oratory," she said. "I saw a figure just in the act of passing in; I will know what is going on; we can easily slip into some of the empty rooms, if we hear anyone coming."

So saying, she put on her slippers and threw a shawl over her shoulders, and I followed her example; ready for any kind of adventure, we cautiously advanced along the corridor, soon we arrived at the door of the oratory, and could hear several low voices inside, but were afraid to push the door ajar for fear of being observed.

"Hush!" whispered Alice, "I was here when quite a little girl, and now remember that old Lady St. Jerome, who has been dead some time, used to use this room next to the chapel, and had a private entrance made for herself direct from the room into the oratory. If we can get in here," she said, turning the handle, "we shall be in a fine place to see everything, as the room is never used, and said to be haunted by the old lady." The door yielded to her pressure, and we slipped into a gloomy room, just able to see a little by the light of the moon.

Alice led me by the hand, having closed the door behind us; a cold shiver passed over my frame, but plucking up courage, I never faltered, and we soon found a little green baize door, bolted on our side. "Hush!" she said, "this opens into quite a dark corner, behind the confessional box," as she gently withdrew the bolt, and we then noiselessly entered the chapel into a little kind of passage, between the box and the wall, and fortunately protected from observation by a large open-work screen, which completely hid us, but afforded quite a good view of the interior of the chapel. Guess our astonishment when we beheld both Lady St. Jerome and her niece in earnest conference with the two priests and overheard what passed.

FATHER COLEMAN.—"Well, Sister Clare, the Cardinal has ordered that you are to seduce Lothair, by all the arts in your power; every venial sin you may commit is already forgiven."

MONSIGNORE, addressing Lady St. Jerome.—"Yes, and Sister Agatha here will assist you all she can; you know she is a nun, but by the modern policy of Holy Church, we allow certain of the sisters to marry when their union with influential men tends to further the interests of the Church; the secret sisterhood of St. Bridget is one of the most powerful political institutions in the world, because unsuspected, and its members have all sworn to obey with both body and soul; in fact, Sister Clare, this holy sisterhood into which we have just admitted you, by this special faculty from his Eminence, will permit you to enjoy every possible sensual pleasure here upon earth, and insure your heavenly reward as well."

The bright light shows us plainly the blushing face of Clare Arundel, which is turned almost crimson, as the confessor whispers something to her. "Ah! No! No! No! not now," she cried out.

MONSIGNORE.—"The first act of sisterhood is always to do penance directly after admission, and you have taken the oaths to obey both in body and mind, sister Agatha will blindfold you, throw off your robe, and submit your body to the mortification of the flesh."

Lady St. Jerome quickly removed the dressing-gown in which her niece was enveloped, and left the fair girl with nothing but her chemise to cover her beautiful figure; the bandage was speedily adjusted over her lovely eyes, and she was made to kneel on a cushion, and rest her arms and face on the rails of the altar. Father Coleman armed himself with a light scourge of small cords, fixed in a handle, whilst her ladyship turned up the chemise of the victim so as to expose her bottom, thighs, legs and back to his castigation; then she withdrew, and seated herself on the knee of Monsignore, who had made himself comfortable in a large chair close to the victim; he clasped her round the waist, and pressed his lips to hers, whilst their hands seemed to indulge in a mutual groping about each other's private parts.

The scourge fell upon the lovely bottom; each stroke drawing a painful sigh from the victim, and leaving long red weals on the tender flesh.

The confessor continually lectured her on her future duties, and made her promise to do all his commands.

The poor girl's bottom was soon scored all over, and dripping with blood; the sight of which seemed to inflame the others, so that the confessor's affair stood out between the opening of his cassock, whilst Lady St. Jerome spitted herself on the pego of Monsignore, and rode a most gallant St.

George as he sat in the chair.

THE CONFESSOR.—"Now, sister, for the last mortification of your flesh, you must surrender your virginity to the Church." Saying which, he produced several fine large cushions, took the bandage from her eyes, and laid her comfortably on her back for his attack, with an extra cushion under her buttocks, in the most approved fashion. Then kneeling down between her thighs, he opened his cassock, and we could see he was almost naked underneath. He laid himself forward on her lovely body, and whispered something in her ear, which was apparently a command to her to take hold of his lustful weapon, for she immediately put down her hand, and seemed (as far as we could see) to direct it to her crack herself. She was evidently fired with lust, and longing to allay the raging heat of the part which had been so cruelly whipped, for she heaved up her bottom to meet his attack, and so seconded his efforts that he speedily forced his way in, and the only evidence of pain on her part was a rather sharp little cry, just as he entered to break through the hymen. They lay for a moment in the enjoyment of the loving conjunction of their parts, but she was impatient, putting her hands on the cheeks of his bottom, and pressing him to herself in a most lascivious manner, and just then Monsignore and Sister Agatha, who had finished their course, got up, and one with the scourge, and the other with a thin cane (after first lifting up his cassock and exposing a brown hairy-looking bottom), began to lay on to Father Coleman in good earnest. Thus stimulated, and begging and crying for them to let him alone, he rammed furiously into Miss Clare, to her evident delight; she wriggled, writhed, and screamed in ecstasy, and gave us such a sight of sensual delirium as I have never seen before or since. At last he seemed to spend into her, and, after a while, withdrew himself from her reluctant embrace, as she seemed to try hard to get him to go on again.

We could see they were preparing to leave the chapel, so thought it time to make our retreat.

Next day we were presented, and nothing in the manner of the lively Lady St. Jerome, or the demure Miss Clare Arundel, would have led anyone to imagine the scene that we had witnessed in the small hours of the morning.

In the evening we were all at the Duchess's ball. Lord Carisbrooke, to whom I was specially introduced, was my partner in the set, in which danced Lothair and Miss Arundel as *vis-à-vis* to Lady Corisande and the Duke of Brecon.

Bye-and-bye the hero of the evening led me out for the Lancers, and afterwards we strolled into the conservatory, quite unobserved; his conversation was much livelier than I had expected, for Lady St. Jerome had represented to us that he was seriously bent on religion, and about to join the Romish Church. The conservatory was large, and we strolled on till the music and laughter seemed quite at a distance, and coming to a seat with a delightful fountain in front of us we sat down, but just as he was observing, "How delightful it was to withdraw from the whirl of gaiety for a few minutes," we heard some light footsteps approaching, and evidently a very loving couple, the lady exclaiming, with a saucy laugh, "Ah! No! How dare you presume so; I would never be unfaithful to Montairy even in a kiss"; there was a slight struggle, and, "Ah, Monster, what a liberty!" and we heard the smack of lips upon a soft cheek, and then, "Oh! No! Let me go back," but the gentleman evidently remonstrated, as I could hear him say, "Come, come, compose yourself, dear Victoria, a little, there is a seat here by the fountain, you must rest a moment."

LOTHAIR, with a start, whispered—"They must not catch us here, they'd think we had been eavesdropping; let's hide ourselves and never say a word about it," dragging me by the hand around a corner, where we were well screened by the foliage of the delicious exotics.

My heart was in a flutter, and I could perceive he was greatly moved. We stood motionless, hand in hand, as the lady and gentleman took possession of the cool seat we had just vacated; the latter proved to be the Duke of Brecon. I could see them plainly, and have no doubt Lothair did also.

LADY MONTAIRY.—"Now, sir, no more of your impudent pranks. Pray let me recover my serenity."

The Duke knelt down and took her hand, which she affectedly tried to withdraw, but he retained it, saying:

"Dearest Victoria, pity my passion. How can I help loving those killing eyes, and luscious pouting lips. That very fact of its being wrong makes my determination the greater to enjoy you the first opportunity. It is useless to resist our fate. Why has the God of Love given me such a chance as this?"

She turns away her head with affected prudery; but not a

42

blush rises to assert her horror at his speech. One hand presses her fingers to his lips; but where is the other? Under her clothes. He first touches her ankle, and slowly steals it up her leg. She fidgets on the seat, but he is impetuous, and soon has possession of her most secret charms. Her languishing eyes are turned on him, and in an instant, he is on his legs, and pushing her clothes up, displays a lovely pair of legs in white silk stockings, beautiful blue garters with gold buckles, her thighs encased in rather tight–fitting drawers, beautifully trimmed with Valenciennes lace. His lips are glued to hers at the same instant, and his hands gently part her yielding thighs, as he placed himself well between them. It is but the work of an instant. He places her hand on the shaft of love, which he has just let out, and it is guided into the haven of love. Both are evidently too hot and impetuous, for it seems to be over in a minute.

She hastily kisses him, and puts down her clothes as she says: "How awful; but I could not resist Your Grace without disordering all my dress. It's been quite a rape, sir," with a smile. "Now, let's make haste back before we are missed." He kisses her, and makes her agree to an assignation, somewhere in South Belgravia, for the morrow, to enjoy each other more at leisure, and then they were gone.

It would be impossible to describe the agitation of my partner during this short scene; Lothair seemed to shiver and shudder with emotion, I was also all of a tremble, and nestled close to him, my arm designedly touching the bunch in his trousers, always so interesting to me; I could feel it swell and seem ready to burst from its confinement; he nervously clasped my hand, and was speechless with emotion all during the scene which I have described; as soon as they were gone he seemed to give a gasp of relief, and led me out of our hiding place. "Poor girl," he said, "what a sight for you, how I trembled for my own honour, lest the scene should make me lose my self-control. Ah! wretched woman, to betray your husband so!" Then looking at me for the first time he said, "Do you not think it is best for a man never to marry?"

Used as I had been to such things, his terrible emotion made me quite sympathize with him, and my own agitation was quite natural, as I replied, "Ah! my Lord, you little know the ways of the world; I saw a more awful scene than what we have witnessed, only last night, enacted by men sworn to perpetual celibacy, and you yourself were mentioned as a victim to their infernal plot."

"My God! Lady, pray tell me what it was," he ejaculated.

"Not now, we shall be missed, do you know any place where I can have a private conference with your lordship? If so, meet me to-morrow afternoon at two o'clock, in the Burlington Arcade. I shall come disguised," I answered.

He hastily wrote the assignation on his tablets, and we made haste to return to the saloons from which we had been absent quite twenty minutes. A little while after, as I was sitting by the side of Alice, whispering my adventure in her ear, Lady Montairy, to whom I had previously been introduced, came and seated herself by my side. "Ah!" she said, with a sly look, "you're in a fair way to carry off the great prize; my sister Corisande will stand no chance."

"I've only danced one set with him," I replied, demurely.

"Ah!" she laughed, "it was not the Lancers I referred to, but your quiet stroll into the recesses of the conservatory. You had quite a lover's *tête-à-tête*."

"But we did not indulge in a *Pas Seul*, as you did with His Grace," I laughed, enjoying her confusion. She was speechless with surprise, her eyes fairly started with affright, and I hastened to reassure her, "I'm your friend, dear Lady Montairy, your secret is safe with me, and I hope you will not make any remarks in connection with myself and Lothair."

She squeezed my hand nervously, and asked, "Do you remember Fred's birthday? I was not there, but my brother Bertram was with his cousins the Vavasours, and passed as their brother Charlie, who happened to be too ill to go with them. I'm initiated into your society. We shall meet again," she added with a smile; "I must go now to keep my engagements."

The supper was a fairy feast, except for its substantial reality, and we returned home to Lady St. Jerome's charmed with everything, and especially with the fine prospect we seemed to have of future enjoyment.

Next day I made an excuse to go out alone to pay a visit to an old schoolfellow, and two o'clock found me sauntering through Burlington Arcade. Lothair was there to the minute, and gently whispered in my ear, as I was looking in a doll-shop, "Now, this is really kind of Your Ladyship, and proves you can be depended on; I have made a most excellent arrangement, we have only to step across the road to the Bristol Hotel in Burlington Gardens, where I have ordered luncheon for myself and cousin, in a private apartment, and they know me too well to pry into my affairs."

The chamber-maid attended me in the bedroom, and as soon as I had laid aside my cloak, hat, &c., I rejoined Lothar in the adjoining apartment, where a sumptuous luncheon was set out.

Lothair, whose shyness of the previous evening seemed considerably dispelled, most gallantly insisted upon my partaking of refreshment, before a word of my communication should be uttered. "Besides," he said, "a little champagne will give you courage, if it is at all disagreeable; the scene last night was such a shock to both of us that if you now prefer to be silent I won't press you about what you mentioned in the excitement of such a moment."

His conversation was very lively all through the repast, and when we had nearly finished I asked him to ring for a little milk, which was brought to me; he was at the moment abstractedly examining the debris of a *pâté de foie gras*. I poured part of the milk into two champagne glasses, and slyly added about ten drops of tincture of cantharides, with which Alice had provided me, to his portion. "Now, my Lord," I said, "I challenge you to pledge me in a glass of my favourite beverage, champagne and milk, I think it is delicious," pouring out the fizzing wine, and handing him the glass, which I first touched with my lips.

His eyes sparkled with delight as he drained it to the bottom, and flung the empty glass over his shoulder, exclaiming, "No one shall ever put their lips to that again, it was indeed a challenge, Lady Beatrice, after which nothing but the reality will satisfy me," then rising, he persisted in claiming the kiss I had, as he alleged, challenged him to take.

"Now," he continued, drawing me to a sofa, "let us sit down and hear the awful communication you hinted at; who were those wretched men?"

"Monsignore Berwick and Father Coleman," I replied; "did you ever hear of a secret sisterhood of St. Bridget, the nuns belonging to which devote both soul and person to the service of the Church?"

"No, never, go on," said Lothair, so I continued: "These nuns are all aristocratic ladies, who devote themselves, as I

45

said, implicitly to the interests of Holy Mother Church, to satisfy and appease the lusts of her priests, as well as marry any influential man they think they can lead by the silken tie of matrimony; such, my Lord, are Lady St. Jerome and Miss Arundel.'

"Incredible," exclaimed Lothair, "but I cannot doubt your word, dear Beatrice—permit me to call you," his eyes looking amorously at me, and evidently already slightly moved by the exciting dose I had given him. I took his hand in mine, it was feverishly warm, then looking him full in the face: "My dear Lord, I would not have been here if for one moment I had thought you could doubt my word."

"Call me Lothair, darling, throw away all awkward reserve," he said, putting his arm around my waist, and giving another kiss on my cheek, "go on; tell me all about those fiendish priests who have been plotting to ensnare me."

"Take my advice, Lothair," I went on, "you will find Miss Clare quite changed, her demure and reserved aspect turned to alluring and captivating glances; the Cardinal's orders are positive that she is not to spare even her honour if necessary, but that is an article I saw her surrender to the confessor." Then I described to him the scene we had witnessed in the chapel, which, added to the effects of the tincture, seemed quite to work him up to a state of amorous excitement.

"Honour! Honour!" he exclaimed, excitedly. "Alas! dear Beatrice, last night I felt able to lose life rather than that, and now it's gone, fled like a shadow, but what is it after all, but a mean, mistrustful shame; you must be mine, I can't restrain the fire of love which is consuming me; the very sin makes the idea more delicious." My faint efforts were useless, he was a fine strong young fellow; in an instant I was thrown backwards on the sofa, and his hands took possession of my longing cunny; the furor of lust was upon him, but I made a fair show of resistance, and seemed only to yield to force, shutting my eyes as if afraid to see how he was exposing himself.

He roughly forced my thighs apart, and throwing himself upon me, I could feel the hot soft head of his cock forcing its way between the lips of my vagina. I struggled and contracted myself as much as possible, and having previously well bathed the parts in a strong solution of alum and water, he experienced as great tightness and difficulty in penetration as if I

46

had really been a virgin. My subdued cries of pain were real, for his big affair hurt me very much, but he gradually won his way, which was at the last moment facilitated by a copious spend.

"Ah! Darling; how delightful," he cried, as he lay with his weapon up to the hilt, throbbing and enjoying the lascivious contractions to which I now treated him.

His lips were fixed to mine, the soft velvety tip of his tongue was a titbit I could not refuse, and I sucked it till I almost choked for want of breath. He spent again under the stimulating emotions with which I inspired him. He lay still for a few moments as we recovered our breath, then, with an upward motion of my buttocks, I challenged him to go on.

It was a most erotically voluptuous love engagement. I could not exhaust him; he was continually shooting his love juice into my very insatiable womb, and it was more than an hour before either of us would consent to a cessation of the game.

All that time we had been as closely joined together as the Siamese twins, only one heart and one soul seemed to animate us, whilst we were constantly returning the flow of sperm one after the other in the most thrilling manner.

After we had washed and refreshed ourselves, he begged my forgiveness for his impulsiveness, and promised to make me his wife, but I recalled to him his words of the previous evening: "That it was better for a man never to marry," and that for my part I thought that such sweet liaisons could never be enjoyed by "married people."

"Ha! Ha!" I laughed. "You have the two nuns of St. Bridget to enjoy. Be advised by me, and seem to fall into their traps. I will introduce you to another secret society which you have little idea of. It is devoted to the pleasure of love, without being under the control of a lustful priesthood. You shall meet me again this day week and tell me how you get on."

He parted from me very lovingly; and on my return to St. James' Square, I found that Lady Montairy had brought an invitation from the Duchess for us to spend a few days at Crecy House before our return to the country.

"How delightful," said Alice. "The Duke has gone to Paris on business, and the Duchess is often indisposed; we shall find ourselves in Paphian bowers."

47

Lothair dined with us that evening, but neither of us betrayed, by word or look, the new link between us.

Miss Arundel was attractive, and even alluring, in her manner towards him. Her face was all smiles as she addressed him in tones of sympathy, even of tenderness. Bewitching enough to turn the head of any less susceptible (even than Lothair) to the influence of the softer sex. She looked divine, dressed in a wondrous white robe, garlanded with violets just arrived from Paris; on her head a violet wreath, deep and radiant as her eyes, and which admirably contrasted with her dark golden brown hair.

I could see he was fascinated. He asked us all to drive down to Richmond and dine with him the next day, but Alice declined for me and herself, alleging as a reason the short time we had to stay in town, and that we should at once have to avail ourselves of the Duchess's invitation, and with Lady Jerome's permission would remove to Crecy House early in the morning.

I could see this plan afforded them infinite satisfaction. So next day saw us welcomed at Crecy House by Lady Bertha St. Aldegonde on behalf of the Duchess, who was confined to her room. Lady Montairy conducted us to our apartments, and dismissing the attendants as soon as possible, she embraced me first, and then Alice, saying: "How nice of you two dears to come so soon. You're just in time for a most important ceremony. To-morrow Mama thinks we are all going to the Academy, but in reality it is quite a different place. The fact is, Corisande is going to be received as a member of the Paphian Circle, as we call the society which you helped to originate. St. Aldegonde, indifferent and 'ne'er do well' as he seems, is the life and soul of it; Bertha indulges him in everything. Jealousy is unknown in our family. You will meet Bertram, Carisbrooke, and Brecon all there. We only want Lothair to make it perfection, as Corisande means to taste and try which she likes best."

ALICE.—"But surely we're not obliged to wait till to-morrow. Can't you, Victoria, give us a little party in your room to-night?"

"Yes," she answered. "But only a hen party; ourselves and Corisande. My room is the next to yours. The gentlemen will be at the clubs. St. Aldegonde never will have a woman at

48

night, and says the morning is the proper time, because his cock always stands best on an empty stomach before breakfast."

The indisposition of the Duchess was a good excuse for all the ladies of the family to retire early, and after having dispensed with the lady's-maids, we met in Lady Montairy's chamber, all attired "en robes de nuit."

Bertha St. Aldegonde was a really splendid woman, a dark brunette of a fully developed figure, prominent dark flashing eyes, and a most sensual chin. Victoria Montairy was also a fine woman, with a very beautiful classic cast of countenance, whilst the darling Corisande seemed more beautiful than ever, for want of ornament, in her spotless chemise de nuit.

Alice and I both kissed her with rapture, which she lovingly responded to.

"Now, what is the programme?" said Alice to Lady Bertha.

"St. Aldegonde and Montairy are both keeping themselves in reserve for the grand ceremony of to-morrow," she replied; "what weak things these men are; as if we wanted to be kept in reserve. Why Victoria and myself never get enough; the more we have the more we seem to require, and the less able they become to satisfy us. Talk about women's rights, they ought to compel husbands to find substitutes, when they can't do it for us."

"Well, if you have a pair of good godemiches, Beatrice and myself will try and satisfy you a little, whilst dear Corisande shall keep us up to the work with a good rod," said Alice.

The godemiches were brought forth, and proved to be of monstrous size, to our ideas; they were made of the finest vulcanized india rubber, beautifully moulded and finished, with all appendages complete; we strapped them on as soon as they were charged with a creamy compound of gelatine and milk. All were stripped to the buff.

Lady Bertha took me on her knee, kissing me lusciously, and handling the dildoe as if it had been alive. "What a fine fellow," she laughed, "but not a bit too large to please me." Meanwhile my fingers were busy, nipping and pinching her clitoris; she glued her lips to mine and fairly sucked my breath away, excited by my touches which had caused quite an erection of her finely developed clitoris. She drew me on to a couch, and I thrust the affair into her already spending cunny; her bottom responded to every shove, whilst I felt

49

the smarting cuts of the birch, which Corisande was applying alternately to myself and Alice; it was most delicious. I responded with all my ardour to the loving caresses of Lady Bertha, who clasped me firmly by the buttocks, whilst with two fingers of the right hand she frigged both my bottom and cunny at once; Alice and her partner were quite forgotten; I thought I had never experienced anything so delicious in my life. The combination of emotions quite carried me away, the lovely woman bounding under me in rapture, our luscious kisses, the warmth and exquisite titillations of my fundament arrangements seemed such an acme of bliss that when I made the godemiche spend into her my own nature seemed to melt into a sea of lubricity.

After a few moments I entreated her to be the gentleman, and let me have her stiff clitoris, which I was sure could give me great pleasure. "Certainly, dear," she said, "I often do it to Victoria; throw off the dildoe." As quickly as possible we change places, and I begged her first to bring herself forward over my mouth that I might kiss her pussey, and caress that exciting clitoris of hers. It was done at once, and I had a glorious view of the paraphernalia of love. A splendid mount covered with glossy black hair; the serrated vermilion lips of her cunny slightly parted, from which projected quite four inches a stiff fleshy clitoris as big as a man's thumb. I opened the lips with my fingers, passed my tongue lasciviously about the most sensitive parts, took that glorious clitoris in my mouth, rolling my tongue around it, and playfully biting with my teeth; it was too much for her; with a cry of "Oh! Oh! you make me come, darling!" she spent profusely all over my mouth and chin.

She sank down upon me, and I opened my legs to admit her. "Now it's my turn to repay the delicious pleasure I owe you," she sighed, kissing me rapturously, and sucking my tongue into her mouth, so that I could scarcely catch my breath; with her fingers she opened my slit as wide as possible, then directing her clitoris to the passage she seemed to stuff lips and all in, then closed my affair upon it, holding them together tightly with her hand. I can't express to you how novel and delightful this conjunction was to me; we were both so heated and excited, our spendings seemed to mingle together and add to our erotic fury; without separating for a moment she rubbed and pushed about inside of me,

50

the lips and hair of her cunny titillating the sensitive parts in a most thrilling way. We swam in a sea of lubricity, whilst Corisande added to her sister's enjoyment by the stimulating effect of her rod.

At last all was over, and we retired to rest, and did not rise till late next morning. Refreshed by a cold bath we had only just time to breakfast and prepare for our visit to the Academy. We drove to Burlington House, but only stayed half-an-hour, entered the carriage again and were driven to a large house facing the Thames, in Cheyne Walk; it was detached, and stood back in its own grounds.

We were received at the door by a quiet-looking old lady, who was the housekeeper and manager to the Paphian Circle; she ushered us into a large drawing-room, which occupied nearly all the space of the first floor, being supported in the centre by elegant fluted columns of black and gold, and the whole apartment looked like a hall of the veritable Alhambra, the windows closed by gorgeous black and gold curtains, and although it was daylight outside, lighted up by a constellation of wax lights, artistically arranged all round the walls.

The Duke of Brecon was there as a novice, with Bertram and Lord Carisbrooke as sponsors; Lords Montairy and St. Aldegonde, with several other gentlemen and ladies, were also present. Alice and myself were overwhelmed with compliments as being two of the original founders of the society.

Lord St. Aldegonde, as president, now asked Corisande and the Duke if they pledged their words to keep all the secrets of the Paphian Circle, remarking that oaths were quite useless, as he felt sure those who introduced them had every faith in their honourable intentions. Being answered in the affirmative, and having shaken hands with them, he requested all to prepare for dancing, as no one else was expected.

The company retired to the dressing rooms, and in a few minutes we were all back in the drawing-room, everyone in a state of nudity with the exception of silk stockings, garters, and elegant dancing shoes. To prevent jealousy or any undue preference there was a deep box on a sideboard, where the refreshments stood; in this box were deposited slips of parchment, each bearing the name of one of the gentlemen present, and the ladies had each to draw for her partner in the first waltz, and the *pas de deux* after it. Corisande drew Lord Carisbrooke, and my prize was St. Aldegonde.

I must not omit to mention that one of the ladies would get a slip with "Piano" on it, and the last gentleman had to turn over the music for her. This fell to Lady Bertha, who was a brilliant pianist, and at once struck up a well-known favourite from the Argyll Rooms, and we were instantly in motion. It was far more exciting than the blindfold romp on Fred's birthday; she kept us going till one by one, the couples subsided on the inviting couches, which stood around the room; my partner was in a brilliant state of erection, but he whispered to me, "Not yet, Beatrice dear, we must see to Corisande." Everyone seemed to act without the necessity of orders; all the couples ranged up in a semi-circle, round the couch where Carisbrooke was caressing and kissing her, whilst the beautiful girl, her eyes languishing with love, was sighing and looking at his fine cock, which she held in her hand. "Now, love," said the gallant, "as a novice you must kiss every gentleman's affair, and then we will initiate you into the mysteries of Venus." Corisande, all blushes, took each throbbing pego tenderly in her hand, and softly kissed the velvet heads. "Now, Brecon," said my partner, "you do the same to the ladies, and that part of the ceremony will be over."

"With pleasure, on my knees," said the Duke, and we each presented our cunnies to his lips. Carisbrooke now gently inclined Corisande backwards, and put a soft pillow under her bottom, then proceeded to place himself in position, but unable to restrain his excitability, he spent all over her lovely mossy mount and belly, some of the sperm going quite up to the alabaster globes which adorned her heaving bosom.

He blushed with shame and vexation, whilst Corisande was crimson, and gasping with excited expectation.

Lady Bertha, who was the coolest of the company, at once wiped all the sperm off her sister's belly with her fingers, with which she lubricated her crack; then taking hold of His Lordship's affair, directed it properly to the longing gap of love.

"Shove away. Shove, my boy. Heave up your bottom to meet him, dear," she laughed, giving Corisande a good sounding slap on the side of her buttocks with her other hand.

With a furious plunge, the dart of love made its effort just at the right moment. The collision with her hymen was most destructive, the virgin defences gave way as with an awful shriek of pain, she lost all consciousness. He completed the conquest of his victim's virginity, and then lay soaking, and trying to revive her sensibility by his lascivious throbbing inside of her, whilst we applied salts and restoratives to bring her round.

She very speedily came to herself, evidently forgetting the fearful pain of her ravishment; there was a delightful languor in her eyes, as she patted his bottom and hugged him to her bosom. He responded to the gentle challenge, making her revel in all the delights of coition, and never withdrew his blood-stained priapus till they had mutually spent several times.

My partner now led me to a couch, as the others dispersed on the same kind of business. He was still as stiff as ever, and I longed to feel him within me, but, to my surprise, he mounted the reverse way upon me, presenting his bottom to my face and asked me to press my firm bubbies together, so that his cock might spend between them whilst he gama-huched me. It was a luscious position, and I lent all my ardour to second his fancy, and his lascivious tongue made me spend in delight just as his sperm deluged my bosom and belly.

Alice had had Lord Montairy.

After this, the gentlemen's names were replaced in the box, and the ladies made another selection, but in case of anyone drawing the same partner a second time, she had to return the slip and draw another.

Thus we passed a most delicious afternoon, refreshing ourselves from time to time with champagne and ices, or something more substantial, for the worship of Venus and Priapus requires continual stimulating with the most invigorating viands.

In this short sketch of my adventures it would be impossible to describe everything at great length, but I can assure you the ladies fairly exhausted the gentlemen before they allowed themselves to be driven home to dinner.

Part IV.

I must now return to my liaison with Lothair; he had promised to meet me again in a week, when I hoped to hear the particulars of his drive to Richmond.

We lunched again at the Bristol Hotel, and without having recourse to the tincture, I found him almost as hot and impulsive as before. "Ah! Beatrice," he said, as we lay exhausted on the sofa, after a series of delicious encounters, "I cannot express half the gratitude and devotion I ought to have; for you, not satisfied with making me happy yourself, quite unselfishly advised me how to enjoy the two nuns. But first tell me of that Society of Love, which you promised to introduce me to, and then you shall have my adventure."

So briefly I described to him the Paphian Circle, and took his promise to allow me to introduce him at the next séance.

"I know," he said, "you thought me quite captivated by Miss Arundel, but I never forgot your advice, and resolved to seem to lend myself as a proselyte, accept all the advantages they might offer as baits, and get a thorough insight into all the plans of the Jesuits before I open their eyes, but it is a game that will last a long time. Now, as to the Richmond drive. Lády St. Jerome and Miss Arundel were most vivacious and alluring, as we drove down by road; then we had a beautiful row on the river whilst waiting for dinner, which we sat down to with excellent appetites. I plied the two ladies with wine, and requested them as a special favour not to leave me to myself at dessert, as I did not smoke, and there were no other gentlemen present. Everything was sparkling and agreeable, religion seemed to be avoided by mutual consent, the ladies had withdrawn from the table to a sofa in a recess, where their faces were screened from the light of the brilliant chandelier; they had each had two or three glasses of champagne and seemed very careful not to exceed the limits of decorum, when, taking a fresh bottle, I challenged them to drink to the prosperity of the Christian Church.

" 'Ah!' said Miss Arundel, with flashing eyes, 'but what Church do you refer to?'

" 'Dear ladies,' I replied, 'you shall word the toast as you please, and I will drain a real bumper to it in your company.'

" 'Then,' said Clare, 'we drink to the prosperity of the Holy Roman Catholic Church, and long life to His Holiness Pius IX.'

"Their eyes sparkled, and both seemed unusually excited

" 'What would we not do to assure your conversion, dear Lothair,' said Lady St. Jerome. 'Come and sit between us whilst we talk seriously to you.'

54

"I sat down on the sofa, and being well flushed with wine, impudently put an arm round each of their waists, and said, without thinking, 'Ah! that's mere nonsense; but in truth, I would sell both body and soul for the happiness you and your niece could confer on me.'

"Miss Arundel drew a deep sigh, but Lady St. Jerome softly whispered, as she laid one hand on my thigh, most awkwardly near to an important member, 'Ah! what do you mean? Join our Church, and there is nothing we will deny to you.'

" 'Nothing! nothing! you will get indulgences and dispensations for everything then,' whispered Clare, as she laid her head on my shoulder.

" 'No! no traffic with priests; I want my indulgence from you, dear ladies, if you care for my soul, now's the time to save me; drive me away in unsatisfied desperation, and such a chance will never occur again. Ah! how awfully I am tempted by the proximity of such charms!' I exclaimed, falling on my knees, and clasping their legs, as I hid my face in Clare's lap.

"They were both trembling with emotion, and I was equally agitated, but I seemed to guess from their looks and manner towards me, the present moment was too favourable for them to let slip.

"Lady St. Jerome was the first to speak. 'Dear Lothair, we do indeed pity your distress. Oh! Oh! for shame, sir, what liberties! Will you? Will you, promise us?' as she fidgeted about in confusion, feeling my hand slowly advancing up her legs beneath the clothes; both my hands were busy, but Clare had closed her thighs, and firmly stopped my advance in silence, whilst her aunt's ejaculations seemed to encourage me more and more.

" 'By all that's sacred, I promise everything you may demand of me, they shall receive me into the Church, as soon as they please, if you two will but be ministering angels to my impulsive passions,' I cried, taking advantage of her confusion to gain complete possession of the grotto of love.

" 'Clare, dear,' sighed Her Ladyship, 'can we possibly sacrifice ourselves for a nobler purpose; by now subduing his carnal lusts, we shall also draw a lost sheep to the foot of the cross.'

"I felt Miss Arundel's tightly compressed thighs relax in

their resistance, and she gave a spasmodic sigh as I victoriously advanced my rude hand also to her mossy retreat. 'Ah! how delicious to have possession of a double set of the loveliest charms, I will kiss you, and enjoy you by turns,' I said in rapture, at the prospect before me.

LADY ST. JEROME.—'Excuse me a moment, dear Lothair, Clare is all blushing confusion, let me spare her modesty as much as possible,' as she rose and locked the door, then almost turned out the gas.

"Pulling up her skirts, I threw Miss Arundel backwards on the sofa, and releasing my bursting weapon, threw myself between her yielding thighs, as I exclaimed, 'You have indeed relieved me of making an invidious selection, as I cannot restrain the heat of my passion, Clare must be the first victim to it.'

"It was almost, if not quite, dark in the recess where we were, but my lips sought those of the lovely girl, her entire frame seemed to quiver under me, and she gave a faint shriek as the head of my cock first touched the lips of her cunny. 'Courage, darling,' I whispered in her ear, 'I won't hurt you more than I can help; open your legs, and give way to me as much as you can, you suffer for a noble object.' As if I did not know she had already lost her virginity.

"Lady St. Jerome had now returned to the sofa, where she encouraged Clare to bear the dreadful pain with all her fortitude. Then Her Ladyship took my affair in her hand, saying, 'Let me, dear Lothair, direct you right. I'm a married woman, and know exactly how it ought to be done.' Her touch only added to my excitement. She kept drawing the foreskin back, and took care to present the head rather above the proper entrance to the vagina, to make me think the resistance I felt was genuine, but it gave me infinite pleasure, and made Mr. Pego spend all over the entrance of Clare's longing cunny. At last, after great difficulty, they let me fairly in, and I begged Her Ladyship to still keep her hand there and stimulate my exertions. I spent three times, each time more excitedly than the last, whilst the dear girl was a constant flood of lubricity, and seemed to melt with love, clinging to me with all the tenacity of her voluptuous furor.

"At last, notwithstanding her entreaties for me to go on, on, on, I managed to withdraw, as I told her she would leave nothing for me to repay all her dear aunt's kindness. 'But,

Clare darling,' I said, 'I will still give you pleasure with my tongue.' So I made her give way to Lady St. Jerome, who eagerly slipped off some of her skirts, as she said, to give me greater freedom, but in reality so that she might enjoy herself more. Her pussey was quite wet with spendings, which had flowed in sympathy with our enjoyment.

"Miss Clare was an apt pupil, and quickly arranged herself over her aunt's face, so as to present her excited cunny to my lips.

"Lady St. Jerome had an extraordinary gift of contraction in her vagina, it took hold of my cock, like a delicately soft hand with a frigging motion, as she wriggled and met my thrusts, of the most delicious kind. I grasped and moulded her lovely breasts with both hands, for she held me convulsively to her body, and I had no necessity to clasp her myself. Our conjunction was so exciting that I spent again immediately, under the touches of what I called her invisible hand, then steadying myself I revelled in love and lubricity for more than half-an-hour, both the dear ladies gasping, sighing, and sometimes when they spent giving vent to subdued shrieks of pleasure and dearment. Clare seemed quite as excited as her aunt, who I found was frigging her bottom-hole, and rousing all her lustful propensities to the utmost, with a disengaged hand, as soon as she found I was so safely rooted in herself that one arm could hold me.

"I can't tell you how we finished, for there seemed to be no end to it; however, about eleven o'clock we apparently awoke from a kind of delicious lethargy, into which we had all fallen, and we soon sufficiently composed ourselves to ring for the carriage and start for town; on the plea of keeping out the chilly night air, the windows were put up, and I had one or the other of them astride of my lap and spitted on the shaft of love till the noise of granite pavement under the wheels of the carriage warned us of the near approach to St. James' Square.

"I have promised not to marry, but expressed my wish to be received into the Church by the Holy Father himself soon after Christmas, when I will visit Rome on purpose; this will give me plenty of time to carry on my game, and prove to the Jesuits that I am now quite equal to the tricks they played on me, when they had me down at Vauxe before, and imposed on the weak senses of a poor boy, quite green to the

57

ways of the world. I can love Clare, when I don't think of it, but if I do I should hate her even in the midst of our love transports."

Our time in town was getting short, so at my suggestion Bertram and St. Aldegonde arranged an early day with Lothair, for his initiation to the Paphian Circle.

We were still at Crecy House, and this time the affair was managed under cover of a small private party at the Duke of Brecon's, where we dismissed our carriages, and then drove out in those of his Grace for a country excursion, which of course only extended to Cheyne Walk. Everything was in readiness, and Lothair being admitted as usual, we quickly appeared in the garb of Madre Natura as before. Partners were drawn for the first dance, my lot fell to the Duke of Brecon, whilst Lothair was drawn by Alice, and Lady Corisande presided at the piano, where her brilliant execution helped to add to the excitement engendered by the lascivious motions of the dance, in which, when the gentlemen and ladies changed partners as they went through the figure, they gave our bottoms a fine smarting spank, which we repaid by sharp little slaps on their extended cocks, soon getting tremendously warm and excited over our quadrille, and at the conclusion could scarcely restrain ourselves sufficiently to allow Lothair to give the usual kiss all round to our palpitating cunnies.

I noticed Lady Bertha very busy whispering to everyone, and soon found out that she was proposing a little bit of extra fun for us, of which the novice was of course to be the victim, whilst both pleasure and profit would accrue to the Paphian Circle.

The kissing ceremony was over, and then Alice told him he had yet another little penance to perform before he could be admitted to full rights of membership, pointing to a fine "Berkeley Horse," which was being wheeled into the centre of the drawing-room, a thing something like a common pair of steps, only covered with red baize, and provided with a cushioned footboard for the victim to stand on, whilst his hands were well stretched above his head, so as to only allow of his standing on tiptoe. Lothair in his simple ignorance stepped up gallantly and was instantly secured by his wrists to the topmost rings of the horse.

St. Aldegonde, grinning with delight, tightened the cords

unmercifully, making Lothair expostulate with him at the painful tension.

"That's nothing, my boy," said St. Aldegonde, "don't cry out before you're hurt. Wait until you feel the rods tickle and warm your posteriors, it will do you good, as it did me; it's the most invigorating thing in the world; ask Bertha if I did not give her all she required that night."

All the company were now furnished with beautiful bunches of long thin elegantly tied-up birch.

ALICE, stepping to the front.—"Now, sir, mind you answer all my questions under pain of severe punishment. In the first place none but orthodox members of the English Church can be admitted to the Paphian Circle, and a member has just hinted to me that you are going to Rome, and may be a Jesuit in disguise. Now, my Lord, what do you say to that?" giving his bottom a smart cut, which made him wince with pain, and left a long red mark across the white skin of his manly buttocks.

LOTHAIR.—"My God! you punish without waiting."

Before he could finish speaking all the ladies attacked him with their rods, raining a perfect shower of painful cuts on his helpless bottom, exclaiming, "Answer! Answer!! Answer!!! No prevarication! Don't spare him! &c.," whilst the gentlemen, who stood behind, cut into the fair bottoms of their partners, calling out, "Pass it on to him; cut away, ladies; he's a Jesuit, &c."

Lothair at first lost his breath, but soon shouted out lustily, "Hold! Hold!! It's not true! Don't kill me!"

His bottom and back were scored all over, and little drops of blood trickled down from places where the skin was broken.

ALICE.—"Well, my Lord, pray excuse our virtuous indignation, if you are not really a Jesuit. But how about a Cathedral you intend to build for them, eh?" cutting him several deliberate strokes as she was speaking, each one making him quiver under its smarting force.

LOTHAIR.—"Oh! My God! How do you know that? I've only had the plans drawn."

ALICE.—"But, my Lord, allow me to drive the thoughts of such a foolish thing from your mind. Can you not think of some better applications for your money? Will you promise me not to make yourself a fool?" cutting harder and harder every moment, till he fairly howled with pain, ejaculating,—

"Ah! Oh! Damme! How cruel of you Miss Marchmont! Ah—for God's sake let me off now. I—I—won't do it: I give my word for that."

ALICE.—"Beg my pardon instantly, my Lord, or you shall feel what cruelty really is like. Cruel indeed! to a young lady who is only doing a painful duty!" catching hold of a fresh rod, and slashing his bleeding bottom with all her might.

Lothair writhes his body about in dreadful pain, and his fine cock stands out rampantly in front, in a most outrageous state of stiffness, the head quite purple from the extraordinary pressure of blood which distended it. "Ah! ah! oh! oh! I do beg your pardon, I'm sure you will forgive me, and let me off now," he groaned in agony.

ALICE.—"I've only a trifling thing to ask you, now you have apologized. My duty is far more painful and disagreeable to me than it can possibly be to you; bodily suffering cannot for a moment be compared to anguish of mind," as she still cuts into his raw-looking posteriors, and looks round delightedly on the spectators for encouragement, then goes on again. "If you're not going to build that Cathedral, will you devote a fourth part of what it would have cost to the building of a proper temple for the meetings of our Paphian Circle?"

LOTHAIR, gasping in pain.—"Oh! Oh! Yes! That I will, £50,000, if you will let me down at once!"

There was a general clapping of hands all round, and cries of, "Enough! Enough! He's a good boy now," and then there was a scuffle all round to secure victims, which were mostly of the weaker sex, but Ladies Bertha and Victoria, by the aid of diplomacy, had got both their husbands prisoners on a sofa, and lashing into them most unmercifully, laughing and shrieking out, "Keep the game alive! Keep the game alive!"

Alice had meanwhile let down poor Lothair, who was into her in a moment, to the dear girl's great delight, both of them frequently spending and screaming with ecstasy.

My partner threw me across his knee, and made my bottom smart under his loud slaps. I screamed and struggled desperately, and at last equalized matters by grasping his stiff cock, and making him feel that two could play at the game of inflicting pain. He cried a truce, and I speedily righted myself, sitting up with my bottom in his lap, and his pego right up into my vitals. He clasped his arms round me, taking one globe of my bosom in each hand, which he moulded delightfully with his fingers as I rose and fell on his tight-fitting shaft, leaning back my head so as to meet his kisses and give him my tongue. This was a delicious position, his spendings seemed to shoot with extraordinary force into my womb, and my own helped to make quite a stream of sperm, which spurted all over his thighs at each insertion, and fairly drowned the hair round the roots of his pego.

St. Aldegonde and Montairy were having each other's wives for a change after their whipping, but cunt seemed decidedly at a discount with them, as each of them was indulging in a bottom-fuck, which those ladies seemed to relish immensely, and to add to the voluptuous excitement of the scene, the darling Corisande struck up "They a' Do't" to the tune of "A man's a man for a' that."

> The grit folk an' the puir do't,
> The blyte folk and the sour do't,
> > The black, the white,
> > Rude an' polite,
> Baith autocrat an' boor do't.
>
> > For they a' do't—they a' do't,
> > The beggars an' the braw do't,
> Folk that ance were, and folk that are—
> The folk that come will a' do't.
>
> The auld folk try't,
> The young ane's do't,
> > The blind, the lame,
> > The wild, the tame,
> In warm climes an' cauld do't,
> > For they a' do't, &c.
>
> The licensed by the law do't,
> Forbidden folk and a' do't,
> > And priest and nun
> > Enjoy the fun,
> > And never once say nay to't.
> > For they a' do't, &c.

The goulocks an' the snails do't
The cushie doos and quails do't,
    The dogs, the cats,
    The mice, the rats,
F'en elephants an' whales do't.
    For they a' do't, & c.

The wee bit cocks an' hens do't,
The robbins an' the wrens do't,
    The grizzly bears,
    The toads an' hares,
The puddocks in the fens do't.
    For they a' do't, &c.

The boars an' kangaroos do't,
The titlins an' cuckoos do't,
    While sparrows sma',
    An' rabbits a'
In countless swarms an' crews do't,
    For they a' do't, &c.

The midges, fleas, and bees do't,
The mawkes an' mites in cheese do't,
    An' cauld earthworms
    Crawl up in swarms,
An' underneath the trees do't,
    For they a' do't, &c.

The kings an' queens an' a' do't,
    The Sultan an' Pacha do't,
An' Spanish dons—loup off their thrones,
    Pu' doon their breeks, an' fa' to't.

For they a' do't, they a' do't
The grit as weel's the sma' do't,
    Frae crowned king
    To creeping thing,
'Tis just the same—they a' do't!

Her clear melodious voice sounding distinctly through the
apartment had such a thrilling effect that we all joined in the

chorus at the end of each verse, and never before felt so excited or saw such a scene of delicious wantonness as was displayed on every side, till at last exhaustion compelled us reluctantly to give up the engagement, and after a short rest we returned in the carriages to the Duke's mansion, as if we had only had an afternoon's drive.

This was altogether a memorable day, for as soon as we got back to Crecy House, Corisande whispered to me that as the gentlemen had all been fairly used up, her sisters had resolved to have an evening to ourselves whilst the gentlemen were in Parliament or at their clubs recruiting their enervated abilities by wine, smoke and cards. We might be sure of them till six A.M. at least, and the afternoon had left us all in such a burning unsatisfied state that they had impressed into our service four handsome young fellows, two footmen and two pages, who had never yet been admitted to any freedom with their mistresses, but Lady St. Aldegonde had already sworn them to secrecy as to what they might see in the evening, and given her instructions to have everything prepared in her own private drawing-room, so as to be ready as soon as the rest of the establishment had retired for the night.

It was past ten o'clock when we arrived home, but Bertha was so clever, it was all devised and ordered in a few minutes, the footmen, and pages little suspecting the scéne they were to be introduced to when taking their oaths of secrecy. Everything promised a deliciously enjoyable affair, especially as we had to undertake to seduce them to our purposes.

In less than an hour-and-a-half, it was all ready; the Duchess was still keeping her room, so Bertha dismissed all except John, James, Charles and Lucien (the latter a fine handsome French page) as well as two pretty lady's-maids, Fanny and Bridget. There were five of us ladies who sat down to a game of cards, for which the party was ostensibly designed, all of us very lightly attired in the most négligé style as if quite indifferent to any little exposures we might make of our charms.

"My luck is dead this evening," exclaimed Lady Montairy, throwing her cards down; "I shall be ruined if I sit here; what do you say to a dance; let's get the servants to join us for fun; come Lucien, have a waltz with me round the room, I feel so low spirited I don't care what I do to drive it away."

"Fie, sister! how you make the boy blush, but I wouldn't

mind a dance myself if it were not for the thing getting known," replied Corisande.

"Let's have a downright spree for once, John, James, and all of you will keep it secret, I should so like to know how you enjoy yourselves downstairs," laughed Bertha.

"Your Ladyship's slightest wish is binding upon us," replied John, most respectfully, speaking for the others, "and I am sure none of us would betray such a secret, when ladies condescend to a little familiar fun with their domestics."

Bertha seated herself at the piano, and everything was cleared out of the way for a waltz. Lady Montairy led off with Lucien, I proposed to Charles, a very handsome youth of seventeen, whilst Alice and Corisande had the two good-looking footmen, John and James for partners, Bridget and Fanny making a female couple.

What fun we had, how flushed and excited our partners looked as we clung to them in the voluptuous evolutions of this inspiriting waltz, as the strains of Lady Bertha's talented execution seemed to thrill through our souls; the young fellows quite delighted us by their easy graceful motions and manners, having evidently profited by their everyday experience in seeing their superiors conduct themselves in society.

At last we stopped from sheer exhaustion, Lady Montairy giving Lucien quite an amorous kiss, as she led him to a sofa, pretending she did it to put him at his ease, and we all followed her example, my partner excitedly returning my embrace with ample interest and ardour, his hot burning lips sending a thrill of desire through my frame.

Pretending to wish to cool myself a little I walked him into the next room, which was only lighted by the brilliant moon, and we opened the window, which looked out over a lovely garden, and then sat in a rather dark recess to enjoy the slight breeze which was loaded with perfume of flowers and had a soft sensuous effect on my excited nerves. I longed to enjoy my young partner, but did not exactly like the idea of being the first of the party to break through the slight barriers that still existed in favour of decency, although I knew perfectly well it was intended to be done by Lady Bertha and her sisters; still they seemed so slow in arriving at a thorough explanation with their company that I could wait no longer. "Charles," I whispered, "do you know what love is, have you ever had a sweetheart?"

"No, my Lady, I never had a chance yet, as I look at all the beautiful creatures, and think how hard it is that I dare not kiss one of them. Dear Lady, did you but know the intense pleasure your lips afforded me just now you not would think that kiss was thrown away, as I expect you did it in fun," he responded with emotion.

"Silly boy," I laughed in a whisper, "to think that should make you so happy, why I don't mind giving you another here in the dark, if it is such a pleasure, and costs me nothing," kissing him again in a very amorous manner. He clasped my heaving form to his bosom, and I could feel quite a shiver of delight rush through his trembling frame.

"What makes you tremble so, Charles?" I asked in the most innocent manner, laying my hand carelessly on his thigh just where I hoped to make an important discovery. Nor was I displeased to touch the engine of love which my hand gently prodded, as if quite unconscious of anything wrong. What a start he gave as he exclaimed, "I am so ashamed, oh lady, you have driven me mad," then suddenly letting his rampant love dart loose, it stood throbbing and spending over my hand, whilst I seemed to be unable to realize what I was doing.

"Oh; darling! Oh, Beatrice! Forgive me! What pleasure!" he seemed to gasp out, kissing me rapturously, and taking all sorts of liberties with my bosom, which he was moulding and pressing with his hands.

"What am I doing? Pray Charles, don't be so rude," I said hastily, dropping the hold of his affair, and pretending to want to free myself from his embrace, but the amorous lad had gone too far to realize his prize, and almost quicker than I can relate it, his hands were under my skirts, forcing their way to the very shrine of love itself.

My partner was far too impetuous to heed my faint remonstrances, and in spite of all I could do to keep my thighs closed his venturesome hand soon took possession of my heated cunny. "If I die I must have you, darling lady," he whispered in my ear, as he suddenly forced me quite back on the sofa, and tried to raise my clothes.

"Ah! No! No! I shall faint. How your violence frightens me!" I sighed, trying to smother my desires by simulating helplessness, and then feigning unconsciousness I promised myself a rare treat by allowing him to think I really had fainted, which, no doubt, would urge him to take advantage of the moment to riot unrestrained in the enjoyment of my most secret charms.

It was almost dark in the shadowy recess where the sofa on which we were was situated. "She's quite gone, the darling!" I heard him say to himself, as he gently parted my relaxing thighs, "I'll kiss it first." Then I knew he was kneeling between my legs, and I felt his fingers gently parting the lips of my cunt. "How I must have excited her, she's been spending!" he went on, then I felt his lips right between the nymphæ as he kissed me rapturously just on the excitable little clitoris. What a thrill of desire it sent through my frame, as it made me literally quiver all over with emotion, so that I could scarcely refrain from clasping his head with my hand, or nipping his dear face between my thighs.

This only lasted a few moments, which seemed awfully long in my excitable state, my cunt was spending and throbbing under the voluptuous titillations of his velvety tongue. Heavens how I wanted to feel his prick inside of me! and could not have feigned my fainting state another instant, but the moment my lips were in the act of parting to implore him to fuck me at once he started to his feet, pushing my thighs as wide apart as possible, and directly I felt the hot head of his cock placed to the mark; slowly and gradually he pushed his way in, as contracting my usually tight affair I made it as difficult as I could for him to achieve possession. How he kissed my lips, calling me, "Darling lady, dear Beatrice, oh, you love, what pleasure you give me!"

I felt him spend a torrent of his warm essence right up to my vitals, and then lay still upon me exhausted for the moment by the profuseness of his emission.

Still apparently in the state of inanimation, and without opening my eyes, I made my cunt nip and contract on his throbbing prick as it was soaking within me, in such a manner that he was almost immediately aroused from his delicious lethargy, and recommenced his movements, exclaiming to himself, "What a love of a girl, even in her fainting state, the love pressure of her cunt responds to the action of my prick. What pleasure it would be if I could but arouse her to sensibility!" as he kissed me over and over again rapturously, quickening his stroke till my blood was so fired I could no longer impose upon him, so I suddenly threw my arms around the dear boy's neck, whilst my amorous kisses responding to his silently assured him of the delight he was affording me.

"Here they are, the sly things, why Beatrice is the hottest of the lot, see she has got Charles well in her," laughed Lady Bertha, bringing a light into the room, and followed by all the others, looking very excited, and as if some of them at least had been doing the same; in fact I could see the front of John's trousers were undone, whilst the flushed face of Lady Montairy, and the delighted manner in which she clung to the handsome young French page, assured me that she at least was on the best of terms with her partner, added to which, in the background, Bridget and Fanny seemed as loving as any of them from their damask cheeks and sparkling eyes.

Charles was dreadfully confused, and I felt that the surprise was taking all the vigour out of him, so with the greatest presence of mind, I threw my legs over his buttocks and embraced him more firmly than ever, as I exclaimed, "It's this naughty fellow, my dear, has taken liberties with me, that I fainted from fear, and he is in complete possession of my virginity, and having aroused all my passions to the highest pitch he wants to withdraw, slap his bottom well for me, and make him now complete my pleasure, after satisfying his own greedy lustfulness!"

He struggled hard to get away but I held him tightly, whilst all of them slapped him without mercy, making him fairly bound in the saddle to my great delight, more especially when I soon found him swelling up quite an unnatural stiffness, till his prick was almost breaking my quim, and he was furiously fucking with all his might, as he cried out for them to leave off and let him do it properly.

The noise of the slaps on his bum seemed to give me intense delight and I never remember to have had a more delicious fucking, which as he had spent twice previously lasted a long good bout, till we both came together almost frantic with delight, as our mutual essences were commingled at the same moment.

"There, don't let me catch any two of you slipping away by themselves again," said Lady Montairy, as she gave a last tremendous slap, which fairly made the poor fellow bound under her hand, in spite of his exhaustive spend. "It spoils half the fun, when some are so sly, and pretend to be mock-modest when at the same time they are quite or more inclined for the sport than anyone."

All returned to the drawing-room and refreshed ourselves with champagne, jellies and other reinvigorating delicacies, as we laughed and bantered the four young fellows and the two lady's-maids about their sweethearts and love experiences, till Bertha wrote all the names of the female members of our party on slips of paper, which she said she would hold for the boys to draw their prizes, declaring that Bridget and Fanny, if drawn, should submit to be fucked, although they protested their virginity and determination to keep it for the present, much as they enjoyed the other fun.

First of all she asked us to assist her in stripping our cava-liers quite naked, in order that we might enjoy the sight of their adolescent beauties (John, the eldest, being only nine-teen). They were finely formed young fellows, but the splen-did proportions of Master Charlie's penis carried off the honours of the evening, being more than eight inches long and very thick. My lady friends were in ecstasies at the sight, and almost made the other three young fellows jealous by each wishing he might draw them for a partner.

"Now there shall be no deception or cheating; I've a novel idea how the lots shall be drawn," said Bertha, drawing up her clothes till she showed the beautiful lips of her luscious cunt, just peeping out between the slit in her drawers as her legs were wide apart; then drawing me close to her side she gave me the slips of paper and whispered in my ear to arrange them in her cunt with the seven ends just sticking out. It was soon done, then our gentlemen had to kneel down in front and each one drew his paper with his mouth.

This was a jolly bit of fun, Bertha looked as if she would have liked to be fucked by all four instead of merely having them draw lots from her gap, which was so tickled as they drew out the papers that she actually spent under the novel excitement.

John drew Bridget; James, Lady Montairy; Charles, Bertha, whilst I was lucky enough to get the handsome Lucien, who had been eyeing me with a most amorous leer, which you may be sure did not in the least offend me.

Corisande and Fanny were told to fit themselves with a couple of most artistically moulded india-rubber dildoes of a very natural size and not too large, which Lady St. Alde-gonde said her husband had procured for the purpose of having his lady bottom-fuck himself occasionally, when he wanted extra stimulation. "And now my dear, they will be very useful in enabling you to give these nice youths the double pleasure as they enjoy their partners."

The ladies were now also divested of everything, till the complete party were in a state of buff, excepting the pretty boots and stockings, which I always think look far sweeter than naked legs and feet.

The interest centred in the engagement between Bertha and Charles, as the others were all anxious to see the working of his fine prick in her splendid cunt. He was in a very rampant state of anticipation, so she laid him at full length on his back on a soft springy couch, then stretching across his legs she first bent down her head to kiss and lubricate the fine prick with her mouth, then placing herself right over him gradually sheathed his grand instrument within her long-ing cunt, pressing down upon him, with her lips glued to his, as she seemed to enjoy the sense of possessing it all. I mo-tioned to her bottom with my finger, and Fanny, understand-ing my ideas, at once mounted up behind her mistress and brought the head of her well-cold-creamed dildoe to the charge against her brown-wrinkled bottom-hole, at the same time clasping her hands round Bertha, one hand feeling Charlie's fine prick, whilst the fingers of her other were tick-ling the fine clitoris of our mistress of the ceremonies. It was a delightful tableau, and it awfully excited us all when they at once plunged into a course of most delicious fucking. Fanny was as excited as either of them as she vigorously dildoed her mistress, and kept her hands stimulating them in front. Corisande now attacked Fanny behind with her dildoe, delighting her with frigging combined.

How they screamed with delight, and spent over and over again; it is impossible to describe, but I had got Lucien's fine prick in my hand as we were kissing and indulging in every possible caress. It throbbed in my grasp as I repeatedly drew back the foreskin, till at length fearing he would spend over my hand, I sank back on a sofa, and drew him upon me, guiding his affair to my longing cunt, whilst he clasped me round the body and kissed more ardently than ever. I could see all that was going on round the room, Lady Bertha still riding furiously on Charles, stimulated by the double exertions of Fanny and Corisande, and watched with delight the frenzied enjoyment of the lady's-maid, as she handled and felt how Charles was going on in front, whilst her young mistress's dildoe almost drove her to distraction by its exciting movements in her bottom. Lady Montairy was riding James as he sat on a chair, but John was being quite baffled by his partner Bridget, who wriggled and avoided every attempt of his cock to get into her, as she kissed and allowed him any liberty except the last favour of love.

At last we all finished. "Now," said Lady Bertha, "we will rest and refresh ourselves a little, and then we will see to Bridget and Fanny having their maidenheads properly taken; meanwhile I will tell you a little adventure I once had down at Brentham a few months after my marriage. Well, you must know St. Aldegonde wanted to represent the county in parliament, and a general election was expected very soon, indeed it was rumoured the dissolution would occur almost immediately, so no time was to be lost, and there was one great landowner, who if we could but secure him to our side we were sure of carrying the day. He had been an old admirer of mine, and had been much chagrined at my lordship's success in obtaining my hand, and we both knew he was almost certain to throw all his influence into the opposite scale. We were just going to bed one night, and about to fall asleep after a beautiful fuck (it is nice when first married) when a sudden idea made me quite laugh, it seemed so good.

"St. Aldegonde was quite anxious to know what I had been thinking of, 'My love,' I said, kissing him (I don't often do that now, except when I want to wheedle him out of something) 'would you mind giving a bit of my cunt to secure your return for the county?' 'Why, Bertha darling, just at this moment nothing would make me jealous, as you've sucked the last drop of spend from my cock,' he said, with a yawn, and then realising my idea, he continued, 'Do you mean Mr. Stiffington, my love; it's a bright idea, if you do, and damned cheap way of buying him, besides cunt could never be reckoned bribery.'

"The prospect of adventure, added to the good I might do for my husband, made me volunteer to do it, and as secrecy was everything, we determined that I should go down to Brentham disguised as a servant.

"Next day we started apparently to go to Paris, but I left St. Aldegonde at the railway station, and started off to Brentham by myself after changing my dress at a hotel. The housekeeper at Brentham was the only person whom I took into my confidence, but of course she did not know all.

"She passed me off as a niece from town, who had a holiday for a few days, and I mixed with the servants as one of themselves; the idea that I could be Lady Bertha never entered their heads, as I was supposed to be gone abroad for a tour.

"Without delay she got the coachmen to drive me over to Mr. Stiffington's place, Manly Hall, with a note to that gentleman on some special business, which I must deliver with my own hands.

"The gentleman was at home, and I was soon ushered into the library, where he was attending to his letters or other business, after breakfast, about 11 o'clock in the morning.

"'Well, young woman, let me have the particular letter you brought from Brentham; why couldn't a groom have done as messenger? By Jove! you're a nice looking girl though!' he said suddenly, seeming to notice my appearance.

"'If you please, sir,' I said, blushing, 'I'm Lady Bertha's maid, and bring a very important note from Lord St. Aldegonde.'

"He was a fine handsome fellow of about thirty-five, full of life and vigour in every limb; his eyes looked me through and through, then suddenly he penetrated my disguise, as he exclaimed, 'Ah, no, you're Lady Bertha herself, what is the cause of this mystery?'

"I was all confusion, but he told me to sit down and tell him without reserve what I wanted, as he drew to a sofa and seated himself by my side.

"'Your vote and interest to secure my husband's return for the county,' I said in a low voice, 'we know you can turn the scale, so I ventured to solicit your influence in person.'

"'But how can you expect me to be otherwise than hostile to a man who deprived me of your beautiful self,' he replied, 'why did you jilt me for a lordling?'

"I looked down in pretended distress, as I answered with an almost inaudible voice, 'If you only knew our family necessities, it would soothe your wounded self-respect, noth-

71

ing but his dukedom in perspective sealed my fate against my own feeble will, and now it is my duty to further his interests in every way.'

"'Dear Bertha,' he exclaimed excitedly, 'do I really hear right, would you have preferred me, can you not pity my unrequited love, won't you even favour me with a smile as I look in your face?' taking my hand and covering it with impassioned kisses. 'I would support your husband, but—but I must be bribed—let me think what you shall give me, dearest; of course he's had your first virginity, but I must have the second, it will cost him nothing, and no one need know.'

"He was growing quite impetuous; with one arm around my waist, whilst he covered my blushing face with the most ardent kisses, I could feel his other hand wandering over my bosom or my thighs, as he felt them through my dress, then taking one of my hands he forced me to feel his standing cock which he had let out of his breeches; the mere touch sent a thrill of desire through my whole frame as I sank backwards in an assumed faint.

"He jumped up, fastened the door, then went to a drawer, from which he took a small book and a little box, then kneeling down by my side he gently raised my clothes, kissing my legs all the way up, inside or outside of my drawers as he could get at them, and parting my thighs opened the slit in my drawers, till he had a fair view of my pussey. 'What a sweet little slit, what soft silky down it is ornamented with,' I could hear him say as he pressed his lips to my Mons Veneris, then I could feel his fingers parting the lips of my cunt with the greatest tenderness to enable him to kiss the little button of love. This was too much, I pressed his head down with my hands, as I spent over his tongue with a deep drawn sign of pleasure. 'She's mine, how she likes it, the touches of my tongue have made her come!'

"'Look, darling,' he continued, as he rose to his feet, 'I thought a few delicate kisses would revive you if properly bestowed in the most sensitive place, but I don't mean to have you there; this book will show you the most delightful avenue of bliss, and open up to your ravished senses heavenly bliss you have hither had no conception of.'

"Keeping my clothes up, and making me retain hold of his priapus in one hand, he showed me a series of splendid little drawings in the book, all illustrating the way to enjoy bottom-fucking. He could see I was tremendously excited, so lost no

72

time in placing me on my hands and knees on the sofa, then anointing my tight little bum-hole with some ointment from the box, and putting some also on the shaft of his prick, he made me push my bottom well out behind, with my legs wide apart so as to give him every facility, but 'Ah! Ah! No, no, I can't bear it!' I exclaimed, the tears fairly starting to my eyes as I felt the first advance of his lovely engine, forcing its way through the tightened orifice; the pain was like a number of needles pricking the part all at once. I can describe the sensation as the sphincter muscle gradually relaxed in no other way. He frigged me deliciously in front all the while, pushing so firmly and getting in in such a gentle manner behind that I seemed to love him more and more every moment, and long for him to accomplish his task, and complete my enjoyment, as the very pain seemed a percursor to some extraordinary bliss, nor was I disappointed; the pain was soon succeeded by the most delicious sensations as his movements stirred me up to the highest pitch of excitement, and he never withdrew till we had spent thrice in rapturous ecstasies, screaming with delight and almost losing our lives from excess of enjoyment.

"Thus my mission was successful, and his lordship became a Member of Parliament."

This tale had worked us all up, so that we were mutually groping each other's privates, and as soon as Bertha had finished we seized Fanny and Bridget, but too much of the same thing being rather tedious to read I will only say that John and Charles took their virginities in splendid style, when the girls really found no more nonsense would be tolerated.

This was my last adventure in town, and in the next part I shall go on to relate what happened after my marriage with Lord Crim-Con, which took place shortly afterwards.

Part V.

I now come to a most important epoch of my life, which at once sealed my matrimonial fate.

We were to leave town the next day, and were taking a morning walk in Kensington Gardens with Lady St. Jerome, when who should suddenly meet Her Ladyship, and demand an introduction to her charming young friends (meaning myself and Alice), but a tall handsome-looking old fellow of thirty, with the most wicked pair of dark eyes I had ever seen.

Lady St. Jerome appeared to have a most sinister smile upon her face, as turning to us she said, "My dears, allow me to present you to the Earl of Crim-Con, the most gallant gentleman of the day, but be careful how you accept his attentions." Then seeing a rather savage look cross his countenance—"Pardon me, my Lord, if in introducing you to Lady Beatrice Pokingham and Miss Alice Marchmont, I caution them to beware of such a dangerous lover; they are under my protection at the moment, and I should fail in my duty if I did not."

The angry flush was but momentary, being instantly replaced by a most agreeable smile, as he replied, "Thanks, thanks, my dear cousin, but your piety always makes you so hard on my little foibles. Will nothing ever make you believe I have honourable intentions; you know how often I have asked you to try and find me a nice little darling wifey-pifey, who would lead me with her little finger, and keep me out of mischief."

"You might have found a good wife long ago, you miserable hypocrite," retorted Her Ladyship, "you know that a certain place is said to be paved with good intentions, and that is where all yours will go to, my lord, I fear, but I only just cautioned my young innocent friends here."

"Ah, hem, I think I know that warm place you allude to, just between the thighs, is it not my Lady?"

Lady St. Jerome blushed up to her eyes as she exclaimed, in an apparently angry tone, "Now, this is really unbearable, that Your Lordship should at once commence with your obscene inuendoes; my dears, I am so ashamed of having introduced you to such a horrible specimen of modern society."

"A truce, I will really be on my best behaviour, and try not to offend the most delicate ideas again," he said with great seeming earnestness, "but really cousin, I do want to be married and kept out of harm. Now I suppose these two young ladies are eligible parties, do you think either of them would have a worn-out roué like me?"

"Really, my Lord, you are incorrigible to go on so and talk like that before two young ladies at once," expostulated our cicerone.

"Ha, you don't believe me, cousin, but, by God, I am not jesting, you shall see presently, just wait a moment," he said, then taking out his pocket-book, pencilled something on two slips of paper which he held in his hand, with the ends slightly projecting. "Now, cousin, just draw one and see which it is to be."

"Only for the fun of the thing, to see what you mean"; then she pulled one of the slips from his hand, exclaiming with a laugh as she looked at it, "Beatrice, you are to be Lady Crim-Con if you will take such a scapegrace for better or worse."

His Lordship.—"I really mean it, if you will have me dear lady; may I call you Beatrice? What a happy name, especially if you would make me happy."

It is impossible to write how I felt at that moment; I knew that he was rich, with a great title, and despite his bad reputation, that was a most tempting bait to a comparatively portionless girl.

Somehow he took my arm, and Lady St. Jerome, with Alice, walking in front, seemed to go any way but direct home, in order to give His Lordship every facility to urge upon me his sudden courtship. I can't tell you how it happened, but before we reached the house, I had promised to have him, and in less than a month we were married.

I need not trouble about the wedding ceremony, but at once give some account of the first night I had with my spouse. When I first mentioned him, I spoke of an old man of thirty; that is exactly what he was, and although still a handsome fellow, one would have guessed him to be fifty at least.

His youthful vigour had been expended long ago, by constant and enervating debauchery, and now instead of being able to enter the lists of love in a genuine manner, he had a perfect plethora of disgusting leches, which he required to be enacted before he could experience sensual excitement.

Our first night was passed at the Lord Warden Hotel, Dover, as we were on our way for a continental tour.

During our short courtship I had never allowed him the slightest liberty, as my common sense told me that such a man would discard the most beautiful girl if he could but take advantage of her before marriage.

Well, then, the ceremony at St. George's, Hanover Square,

where the nuptial knot was tied, was scarcely over, and we had just taken our seats in the carriage to return to Lady St. Jerome's house, from which I was married, when he gave me a rude kiss, and thrusting his hands up my clothes, seized upon my cunt in a very rough manner, as he laughingly told me not to pretend to be prudish, as "he knew I was a little whore, and had had Lothair and lots of other fellows, in fact that was the reason he had married me, and meant I should be a damned little bitch to him, and do everything he required, which a virtuous girl might object to; besides," he added, "I always looked out for an orphan who had no blasted parents to complain to. There, don't cry like a fool," as he saw the tears of mortification run down my crimson face, "you have only to pander to my curious tastes a bit, and we shall be happy enough."

I felt his advice the best I could take at the moment; his evident knowledge of my intrigues gave him such an advantage that I dried up my tears and resolved to make the best of a bad bargain, as I returned his kiss as lovingly as possible, and begged him "not to be a bad boy before other people, and he would find me everything he could wish."

I must have been very nearly screwed that night before I retired to bed to await His Lordship's coming. I got in between the sheets perfectly naked in accordance with his orders, and commenced frigging myself at once, the many bumpers of champagne he had made me drink in his company, to various obscene toasts, which he constantly proposed, such as—

"A stiff prick for a randy cunt." "Here's to a girl who would rather be buggered, than not fucked at all," and one in particular, which awfully excited my ideas, viz.: "Here's to the girl who likes to frig herself before you till she spends, then suck your prick to a stand, and prefers to have you in her tight wrinkled bum-hole rather than anywhere else."

Presently he entered the room, with a hiccup; as he pulled the bed-clothes off me, he exclaimed, "You're a damned pretty little bitch, Beatrice, and being nearly drunk, my dear, you see my cock happens to stand for once, we will make the best of it. I had the whites of a dozen raw eggs in some milk this morning, and just now a cup of chocolate with half-a-dozen drops of the tincture of cantharides to make me randy for once."

His coat, trousers, and everything were thrown off in a

76

trice, till he was as naked as myself, whilst his eyes had an almost demoniac kind of glare, so unnaturally brilliant did they look just then.

Springing on the bed, "Ha," he exclaimed in a husky voice, "my little beauty has been frigging herself and spending. Suck my prick or I'll kill you, you little bitch!" he said savagely, as he reversed himself over me, and plunged his head between my thighs, where he at once commenced to suck my quim most deliciously, whilst I nestled his rather long prick (it was not very thick), between my bubbies, pressing them together with my hands so as to make him fuck me there, whilst I was so excited that I readily kissed and took his balls in my mouth.

He was so furious in his gamahuching that he continually made me feel his teeth quite sharply, as he bit the clitoris and nymphæ, growling out, "Spend, spend, why don't you come, you little bitch?" getting more outrageous and cruel every moment, till his bites made me shriek with agony as I writhed about, and deluged his mouth with quite a profusion of my creamy emission.

"A devilish good spend that," he murmured between my thighs, "but I have made your poor cunny bleed a little!" as he seemed to enjoy licking up the sanguineous mixture.

"Now suck my prick," he said with renewed fierceness, turning round and presenting it full in my face. "You're a cheating little bitch, and I mean to have you dog fashion."

I took that long prick in my hands, frigging the shaft as hard as I could, whilst I just titillated the ruby head with my tongue, till I felt it was tremendously distended and as hard as iron.

"Jump up quick, on your hands and knees, you little whore," as he gave me a couple of tremendously smarting smacks on my buttocks, loud enough to have been heard a long way off, only our bedroom was at the end of a corridor, the whole of the rooms in that part of the hotel having been taken en suite for us.

Turning up my rump as desired, I thought it was only a fancy of his for entering my cunt that way, but he suddenly spit on the head of his long stiff affair, and presented it to my astonished bum-hole, as he exclaimed with a chuckle of delight, "I'm going to fancy you're a boy, and take the only maidenhead you have left, your cunt will do another time, but it must be a virginity on a wedding night!"

"Ah, no, no, no, you shan't do that to me!" I cried out in fright.

"Nonsense, you little randy bitch, shove your arse out, and let me get in, or I'll serve you out dreadfully, and pitch you out of the window into the sea, and say you committed suicide through overexcitement!"

My fright increased, I was really afraid he would murder me, so I resigned myself to my fate, and clenched my teeth as I felt the head of his prick like a hundred little pins forcing its way within my tightly contracted vent hole. At last he got in, then withdrawing his hands from my mount where he had been tearing and pulling the hair to increase my pain, he placed both arms round my neck, and beginning slowly, fucked my bottom most voluptuously, till with a scream of delight I spent again in perfect ecstasy as I felt the delicious warmth of his spendings shooting up my fundament.

Being so overexcited by the means he had taken to prepare himself for our noces, he retained his stiffness, and never gave up possession of my bottom till we had come together a third time.

As soon as he withdrew his long limp cock, now reeking with a mixture of spendings and soil, he at once secured me to the bedposts with some silken cords before I could get away, or was well aware of his purpose.

"Now, my pretty boy, I have got you nicely, and will whip another cockstand out of you as soon as I have sponged off all the effects of our late enculade," he said, bringing some cold water and a sponge in a basin; he laved and cooled my heated parts, till I began to feel quite grateful to him. At last he sponged himself, and wiping himself and me with a fine soft towel, proceeded to select his instruments of flagellation from a small long leather case, which I had supposed only held a gun.

He showed them to me delightedly, then selecting a fine switch of horse hair mounted on a cane handle, he began to whip me with it between my thighs, and on the lips of my cunt in a most exciting manner, till I was so carried away with emotion that I begged he would fuck me properly to allay the longing irritation of my burning cunt.

"My prick isn't stiff enough yet, but I'll suck your spendings for you, my beautiful randy little tit," he cried out, fall-

78

ing on his knees and twisting my body round so that he could get at my cunt. How delightful the thrusts of his tongue were to me in my excited state. I wriggled about in ecstasy, and getting one foot on his prick gently rolled it on his thigh under my sole, till I felt it was getting enormously stiff again, and at the same moment almost fainted away from excess of emotion, as I delighted my lecherous husband by another copious spend.

I thought he was going to fuck me properly now, his engine was so rampant, but instead of that he turned my back to him once more, and selecting a fine light birch rod, made of three or four twigs only, elegantly tied up with blue and crimson velvet ribbons, he commenced to flagellate my tender bottom; how his light switch seemed to cut and weal the flesh at every stroke; it was in vain that I cried for mercy as the tears of real agony rolled down my cheeks; he only seemed the more delighted, and jeered me upon the effects of every cut, telling me first how rosy my bottom looked, then, "now you bitch, it's getting fine, and red, and raw, it's bleeding deliciously!" till at last the rod was used up, the splinters lying all about the floor and bed, then throwing it aside he again assaulted my poor bottom-hole, apparently more and more delighted as he gave me pain, in again forcing his entrance as roughly as possible; however, when he was fairly in I soon forgot everything under the influence of his ecstatic moves, till I could remember no more, and suppose I fainted; he must have released my bonds and allowed me to sink on the bed, for when I awoke the sun was streaming in at the window, and His Lordship was snoring by my side.

His treatment on my wedding night was comparatively mild to what he afterwards made me go through, but his penchant for getting pleasure out of me soon seemed to wear off, although now and then he would fit me with a dildoe and make me bugger him behind, whilst I frigged him with my hands in front till he spent.

Another of his amusements, and which seemed to afford him particular delight, was to show me all his collection of bawdy books, drawings, and photographs, till he could see I was awfully excited, and then he would jeer me about being married to a used-up old fellow, like himself, didn't I wish I could have Lothair now, &c.

One day having amused himself this way with me for some

time he made me lie down on a sofa, and tied a bandage over my eyes, fastened my hands and feet so that I could not move, then throwing my clothes all up he tickled and frigged me with his fingers till I was quite beside myself with unsatisfied desire and begged him to fuck me, or at least to fetch his dildoe and give me some kind of satisfaction.

"It really is a damned shame to tease you so, my little whore," he laughed, "so I will get the dildoe out of my cabinet in the next room."

He was scarcely gone many seconds before he returned, and I felt his fingers opening the lips of my cunt, as I thought to insert the dildoe, but instead of that it was his prick, and throwing his arms around me he seemed to be more vigorous than ever, his cock swelling and filling my longing gap in a manner I had never felt it before. I spent in an ecstasy of bliss, as I murmured my thanks in endearing terms for the pleasure he had afforded me by such a delicious proof of his manliness.

Presently a strange hand seemed to be feeling his prick, and thrusting a pair of fingers into my cunt alongside of his still vigorous engine.

"Ah! Oh! ! Oh! ! ! Who is that?" I screamed from under my skirts, which were thrown over my face.

"Ha! Ha! ! Ha! ! ! She pretends to think I've been fucking her when she must have known it was James all the time!" I heard him laugh, as at the same moment all the obstructions were removed from my face so that I could really see it was the young butler on the top of me, with his prick still in full possession, and just beginning to run a second course.

"Kiss her, put your tongue in her mouth, my boy! Fuck! Fuck away! or it will be the worse for your arse!" exclaimed His Lordship, who was handling his balls with one hand, and slapping his rump furiously with the other. "See how she pretends to be ashamed; it's quite delightful Lady Beatrice, to see you can still blush."

I screamed and protested against the outrage, but James's delicious motions soon made me forget everything, and recalled to my mind the orgie we had with the servants at Crecy House, and in imagination I was again in the arms of the wondrously developed Charlie.

We spent a second time, but he kept his place and continued the love combat with unabated vigour, and His Lordship seeing that I was quite carried away by my feelings, and responding to his man's attack with all my naturally voluptuous ardour, released both my hands and feet so that I might thoroughly enjoy myself.

"Hold tight James," he cried out, "she's so high spirited, you'll get unseated, but the little devil needn't think she's to have this treat all to herself!"

Saying which he mounted on the sofa behind the young butler, and I could see his long prick was now as stiff as possible, and he seemed to have a rather easy task in getting into his man's bottom, no doubt having often been there before, but wanted some extra excitement on this occasion, so he sacrificed me to his catamite, in order to bring himself to the necessary pitch by seeing all our lascivious movements.

You may be sure that after this James and I were upon the best of terms, His Lordship introducing him to our bedroom at night, and joining us in every kind of wantonness; he even once contrived to get his long thin prick into my cunt alongside of James's as I was riding a St. George; it gave me the most intense pleasure, and immensely delighted them both by the novel sensation, besides the idea of having achieved an apparent impossibility.

After this Crim-Con seemed to get quite blasé and indifferent to everything we did, and even insisted on sleeping by himself in another room, leaving us to ourselves. However, both myself and paramour were not so blind as to believe he was quite used up, but onsulting together we came to the conclusion that His Lordship had fallen in love with my young page, a youth of fifteen, who had only recently entered my service, and slept in a small room at the end of a long corridor in which both our bedrooms were situate.

He always locked himself in when going to bed, as he said, for fear I would not let him alone, so to determine the mystery one night we floured the whole length of the corridor, and in the morning were rewarded by seeing the marks of His Lordship's footsteps, both going and returning from the page's room.

We did not want to spoil his fun, only to enjoy the sight of it, and reap a little extra excitement if possible from the scene, so next day we examined the ground, and found that a small room next to that occupied by the page exactly suited our purpose, and being furnished as an extra bedroom for visitors we had only to make some good peepholes to enable us to sit or kneel on the bed and see everything.

After retiring to bed at night (James and myself had been in the drawing-room all evening going through the most exciting and lascivious ideas, to amuse His Lordship, who contented himself by leisurely watching our love gambols, smoking his cigar, and evidently keeping himself in reserve for something bye-and-bye), instead of settling ourselves between the sheets we adjoined to the spare room, next to that in which Reuben, the page, slept.

We were too soon for His Lordship, as on applying our eyes to the peepholes, the boy's room was yet in the most profound darkness, so as the night was warm, and there was no necessity for covering, we reclined upon the bed to await the coming of Crim-Con; meanwhile we amused ourselves by kissing and toying with each other's parts, till my handsome butler, notwithstanding the previous hard work of the evening, was in a most rampant, impatient state, and would fain have cooled his ardour within my longing cunt but that would have spoilt all, as our transport would have been certain to be overheard by the page, and thus prevent all our anticipated sight-seeing.

Just as I was whispering to him to keep quiet, we heard a match struck in the next room, and applying ourselves to the holes, were much astonished to find Reuben was not alone, there was the butler's assistant, a rather tall fair youth of sixteen, for whom we had never reckoned in our calculations; he had always such a cold, reserved respectful manner, even to James, that we never for a moment gave him a thought as likely to be mixed up with His Lordship's amusements.

Reuben lighted a couple of the candles, then turning to his companion, who was lying on the bed frigging slowly his standing prick, as if keeping it in a state ready for use, said, "Will, it's time His Lordship was here now, what a good job I broke away from you just now, or you would have spent and spoilt all; he likes to see us looking ready and randy, but if he thinks we have been fucking or frigging by ourselves he would damn us, and bolt off in a rage."

Reuben and Will were both quite naked, and there was a great contrast between the youths, for while the latter was rather slim, tall and fair, the former was a regular Adonis in figure, beautifully plump rosy face, dark hair, and dark fiery impetuous eyes his prick was also in a fine state of erection, and neither of them had more than a suspicion of downy hair around the root of their pricks.

"What a fine fellow you look Rube, no wonder His Lordship seduced you; besides, you are a dear unselfish chap for introducing me into the fun, won't I fuck you gloriously when he is here to see us. I love you warmer, hotter than ever I could the prettiest girl in the world! And then, too, think of how well it pays!"

Here the two boys lay down on the bed fondling each other's pricks and kissing mouth to mouth, sucking tongues, and twining about in the most amorous manner, till I fully expected every moment to see them spend, but they stopped suddenly, a step was heard outside, the door creaked on its hinges, and His Lordship appeared with a large table lamp in his hand.

"Hold, hold hard, you randy rascals!" he exclaimed, "I believe you've been and had your fun already. If you have, you buggers— ," he hissed between his teeth, in a frightfully suggestive manner, which seemed almost to terrify the boys, who paled slightly for a moment, and then both of their faces flushed crimson.

Rube was the first to answer. "Oh no, my Lord, we have been too careful only Will was just telling me his love, and how gloriously you should see him fuck me."

"Bravo! So he shall my dear, and I will suck your darling pego, and find out if you have been deceiving me."

He placed his lamp on a small table at the foot of the bed, so that the room was now excellently well lighted, then seating himself on the bed he opened his dressing-gown, showing his long limp prick, and taking the pair of them on his lap, they sat on his naked thighs, whilst he kissed them, thrusting his tongue into their mouths, or handled and compared their two charming pricks.

This was only a little preliminary toying, then presently asking Rube if the cold cream was under the pillow, he threw aside his only vestige of a garment, and stretched himself on his back on the bed.

"Now my plump little beauty," he said, addressing the page, "kneel over my breast, and give me your prick to suck, and now Will, mount behind him, and I will put your tool to his arsehole."

James's assistant was too ready to need a repetition of the welcome order, he was there in a moment, his hard cock quite eight inches long, battering against the tight dark wrinkled nether hole of his love.

His Lordship was so eager for work that he scarcely had taken Rube's seven inches between his lips before his fingers were busy with the lubricant on Will's prick and the page's bottom, directing the former's delighted tool so cleverly to the mark that almost immediately he completed his insertion up to the roots of the hair, and was revelling in the delicious sensations and pressures to which his love treated him.

His Lordship sucked excitedly at the morsel in his mouth, and we could just hear him mumbling out, in a half-choked voice, "Beautiful! Fuck! Go on quick. Spend, spend! Ah—r—r—," as we could see Rube's dark eyes full of fire, and his prick stiffen and shoot its juice into Crim-Con's mouth, till the drops of thick creamy spend fairly oozed from his lips, as he still sucked and smacked his lips with great gusto; besides, we could see his own prick rising into quite a manly state.

Will fucked into his love's bottom with fury, and seemed to spend almost at the same time, and so exhaustively that he must have fallen backwards had he not clung round Rube's neck.

We were not idle whilst this exciting scene was enacted under our eyes. James instinctively wetted the head of his prick and my bum-hole with spittle, and soon drove his great machine through the narrowest gate of Paradise. Its movements were indeed heavenly, blissful. I never before felt such an acme of pleasure, the sight before me, the soul stirring movements behind, and our mutual emissions almost made me groan in an agony of delight.

A perfect frenzy of lust seemed to take possession of my body, I could see His Lordship's prick was now finely erect, and the two boys were alternately kissing and sucking him.

Whispering my paramour to follow me, I quickly rushed from our concealment into the room where they were. As the door was not locked and before they could recover from their surprise, I threw myself on my back, on His Lordship's belly, almost taking the breath out of him by my sudden weight on his stomach, regardless of his "Damned Hellish Bitch" and other exclamations of displeasure. I fixed his stiff prick in my bottom-hole in triumph, nipping and squeezing, and wrig-

84

gling my bum about on him as James with his tool in an awfully excited and distended state took possession of my hot raging cunt.

The boys seemed to quite understand my ideas, as they each of them knelt and presented their pricks for me to fondle, whilst Crim-Con, still cursing and swearing at me for a "Damned Hellish Bitch, &c." groaned under our weight, but I could feel he was thoroughly enjoying it, as his prick stiffened more and more every moment, under the delightful movements and pressures to which I treated him; besides, the membrane between his prick and James's was so slight that it was almost like two cocks rubbing together in my cunt.

I frigged the boys till their eyes almost started from their heads from excess of emotion, they spent over the firm round globes of my bosom, but I still kept them stiff, alternately kissing the head of one or the other prick whilst Crim-Con's hands tickled their balls, and frigged their a..seholes till we made them nearly mad.

I had never felt my husband's long thin prick so well before, and James's affair was so distended by the excess of lustful excitement that I was gorged to repletion, and yet felt that I wanted more, more, more! Had I been cunt all over I should have wanted every hole well filled by a good stiff one. What a delicious moment. Ah! ah! if I could but die like that! I seemed transported to another world, my senses were leaving me, I was indeed in Paradise!

I remember no more of this extraordinary scene, but James told me next day they were frightened, I went off into such a death-like faint, they had to carry me to my room, and use restoratives till I gradually breathed a little, and sank into a restless kind of sleep, that I had bitten both the boys' pricks till they were sore and bleeding. "As for His Lordship," he added, "I am afraid he is as good as dead, he was so exhausted Dr. Spendlove had to be fetched, and he fears the worst."

This was too true, His Lordship only lived forty-eight hours, whilst I have never been well since. The extraordinary excess of lubricity that night seemed to have quite undermined my constitution, and I have gradually declined from that time. I was advised to be very careful how I indulged in venereal pleasures in future, but in spite of my weak, nervous, excitable nature, I have found it impossible to quite abandon those pleasures which seem to me to give the only real foretaste of the future Paradise; regardless of declining strength, whenever the opportunity offered I have indulged in the delights of love myself, or in seeing others do it.

The executors settled everything, whilst the incoming earl, to show his appreciation of their services in furthering his interest, made most lavish provision for James and the two youths, as he afterwards told me that he considered they helped him to the title and estates a good five or ten years before he could reasonably expect to have come into them.

"And do you not think, my Lord," I asked him when he told me this, "that I also deserve your thanks, where is your gratitude to little Beatrice?"

He looked at me in a curious kind of way. He was a handsome young fellow of eight and twenty, but married to death by a fair fat wife, who besides having a fortune of her own, had already blessed him with nine children, and a prospect of blessing him with many more.

"I can't make you out Robert," I went on to say, "you're so different to your poor brother, and so content with the same thing every day; every look, every smile you have is for that splendid wife of yours. He was for flirting with and having every pretty woman he came across; what sort of a heart can you have, you have never seemed to pity me for my loss?"

He was so handsome, and I so disliked the new Lady Crim-Con, that I resolved to seduce him, and gratify both pique and passion at the same time.

"What are you driving at, Beatrice dear, I'm sure you puzzle me?"

"Ah! you know how delicate and how lonely I am, and never even to give a brotherly kiss of sympathy. I know Her Ladyship hates me, but I shall be gone to Hastings in a few days," I said, bursting out into sobs as if my heart would break, the tears from my downcast eyes dropping upon one of his hands which he had placed in a deprecating kind of way on my lap as he sat by my side.

He kissed me tenderly on the forehead, more like a father, as he said, "I'm sure I only wish I knew how to cheer you up, my dear."

"My dear," that sounded quite a little affectionate and as

if the ice was breaking, so throwing my arms round his neck, I kissed him passionately in return for his fatherly salute, sobbing out in a low broken voice, "Oh, Robert, you do not know what it is to be left dull, miserable, and all alone in the cold, cold world, can you not spare me a little, only a little of those loving smiles your wife must be quite surfeited with?"

He gave a soft sigh, and I felt an arm steal round my waist, as he very tenderly drew me close to him, and did not seem at all loath to receive my kisses, which were getting yet more impassioned.

"If you do give me a kiss, what will Her Ladyship lose?" I whispered.

A perceptible tremulousness seemed to vibrate through his form as our lips at last met in a long, loving kiss. It was quite plain I had at last excited his amorous sensuality, which had previously been so dormant in his respectable married bosom.

"Now, I love you Robert, dear, and you needn't mention such an indifferent thing to Lady Cecilia," I whispered, when at last our lips parted.

"A slice from a cut loaf is never missed, you know Beatrice," he said, as he smilingly held me at arm's length, and gazed into my blushing face, and continued, "besides, I can easily make it up to her, so she will lose nothing."

"Your loaf is pretty well sliced dear," I replied, "considering how many children you have to eat bread and butter, Robert."

Again he drew me to him, and we exchanged the most lascivious kisses as I sat on his lap. This billing and cooing being so effective that I very soon felt his prick stiffening quite perceptibly under my bottom. His face flushed, and an extraordinary fire beamed in his usually quiet eyes; we understood each other at once. Without a word he inclined my unresisting form backwards on the couch, and as I closed my eyes, I felt him raising my clothes, his hands stole up my thighs till he gained the seat of joy. My legs mechanically opened to give him every facility, in a moment he took advantage of my tacit invitation, and I felt the nose of a fine battering ram at the entrance of my widowed cunt.

The desire for a really good fuck had been consuming me for some days, and I could not resist the impulse, however immodest it might seem to him, of putting my hand upon his glorious engine of love, and directing it into love's harbour myself. It was in, I was gorged to repletion, spending, sighing with delight, almost before he could make a move.

Opening my eyes, I could see he was delighted at my ecstasy. "Ah, you darling man, my darling Robert, you don't know what it is for a young widow to be deprived of the natural solace of her sex. Now, push on my boy, and let us be thoroughly happy, let us mix our very souls in love's emission, and then tell me if you can spare one a few crumbs of your cut loaf now and then."

A very few thrusts brought down my love juice again, and I also felt him shoot a tremendously warm flood of his essence into my longing cunt. Our lips were joined in fierce loving, tongue-sucking kisses, whilst I threw my legs over his buttocks, and heaved up my bottom to meet his manly action with the most libidinous abandon.

Her Ladyship was out with the carriage, and we were quite safe for a couple of hours at least; still, considering his family duties, I made him keep a shot or two in reserve for the night, as he contented himself by kneeling down and worshiping at the shrine of love, where he had just been paying his tribute to Venus, exclaiming in ecstasy, as he examined or kissed the various charms, "What a love of a cunt! How small and tight! What a charming chevelure, &c.!"

A day or two after this, to our mutual delight, Lady Cecilia was summoned into the country, to attend on her mother's sick bed.

My room was next to theirs, so at night it was a very simple thing for him to slip into bed with me. I found he knew very little about ornamental fucking, himself and wife had strictly adhered to the plain family style, which had produced such fruitful results. My ridicule of his ignorance made him quite ashamed of his want of knowledge, especially when I introduced him to the delights of bum-fucking, and he faithfully promised me that when Her Ladyship returned, he would insist upon his marital rights over every part of her person, and so steer clear of babies in future, and that if I only made a good peephole I might see all his fun with Lady Cecilia.

Delighted with my conquest, I determined to persuade him to degrade his wife in every possible way, that I might enjoy the sight of it. So I initiated him into every possible style of enjoyment, till I had the satisfaction of knowing that the hitherto respectable husband was completely changed into a lustful libertine.

The Earl was as good as his promise. "My Robert," as I called him in our loving intercourse, was so well schooled that he was quite equal to the assertion of all his rights as a husband by the time Lady Cecilia returned home.

After dinner, on the evening of her arrival from the country, he found me sitting alone in the conservatory, and sitting down by my side, whispered in my ear how delighted he was at being able to have a last word of advice with me before retiring to rest with his, no doubt, rather expectant spouse.

"You have so drained me, last night and early this morning, dear Beatrice," he said, putting his arm round my waist, and meeting my ready lips in a long breathless kiss, and then continued, "Nothing but some extraordinary excitement will enable me to do justice to her expectations. I must fuck her at least three or four times after such a long absence; how shall I be equal to the occasion?"

"Have me first," I replied, "whilst she is seeing the children put to bed, there is plenty of time; it will give you zest for the fun to come, the idea of taking the virginity of her maiden bottom-hole will excite you enough, and the more she resists and gets indignant, the more you will enjoy it."

I had been gently stroking his prick outside his trousers; my touch was magical, it stiffened immediately, and when I let the impatient prisoner out of his confinement, I thought I had never before seen his priapus so distended and inflamed with lust as at that moment.

Rising up, I first stooped to give the engine of love a warm kiss, and keeping it in my hand, raised my clothes, and turning my bottom to his belly, spitted myself on the loving object, opening my legs and straddling over his lap, so as to get the very last fraction of its length into my heated cunt. We sat still for a moment or two, enjoying the mutual sensations of repletion and possession so delightful to each of the participators in a loving fuck, before commencing those soul-stirring movements which gradually work our heated desires to that state of frenzied madness which can only be allayed by the divinely beneficent ecstasy of spending, and mingling the very essences of our nature.

The idea that I was robbing his hated wife of her just expectations added such piquancy to our loving conjunction that I literally moaned or whined with delight, as I twisted my head round in the act of emission, so as not to lose the luscious kiss which is such an extra pleasure in those supreme moments of our happiness.

He did not come at the same time, but stopped and rested a moment or two, then rising, and keeping me still impaled on his dear prick, without losing place even for a single second, he laid my body face downwards on a little table which stood handy, and then recommenced his delicious moves, with his hands under me in front, frigging and tickling my cunt, till I almost wrenched myself away from him by the violence of my convulsive contortions. Suddenly drawing quite out, with another plunge he drove the head of his tool into the smaller orifice, which is so delightfully near and convenient when in the position in which he had me.

"Ah! Oh—oh—oh—oh—o—o—o—oe!!" I screamed, swimming in lubricity as I felt him so gorging my bottom, whilst his busy fingers were adding to my erotic madness by the artistic way in which they groped within my spending cunt. "Oh, heavens, Robert, Robert! Do, do come darling! There, ah—re, I feel it, how deliciously warm!" I murmured excitedly, as his flood of boiling seed inundated the gratified and sensitive sheath which enclosed him so tightly.

After recovering from our transports, we conversed about how he should proceed with his wife, his prick all the while as stiff as a policeman's truncheon, till at last fearing Lady Cecilia might surprise us, I went into the drawing-room and played the piano whilst he smoked his cigarette amongst the flowers in the conservatory outside the window.

Her Ladyship pretending fatigue (we knew what she was in a hurry for), the family retired rather earlier than usual to rest, but I took care to be at my peephole before Cecilia and Robert entered their bedroom.

As it was a habit of his to go over the lower part of the house, and see everything safe for himself before going to bed, his lady came first and at once commenced to undress.

She was about the same age as her husband, a vastly fine, fair woman, rather above the medium height, light auburn hair, slightly golden in tint, deep blue eyes, set off by dark eyebrows and long dark lashe a full mouth, richly pouting cherry lips, and a brilliant se. of pearly teeth; then as she gradually unrobed herself, her various and luscious charms quite fired my lascivious blood, as one by one they stood revealed to my earnest gaze. What magnificent swelling breasts still round and firm, and then as she lifted her chemise over her head, and exposed the lovely whiteness of her belly (still without a wrinkle, as she had easy confinements and never suckled her children, for fear of spoiling her figure), set off below by a bushy Mons Veneris, covered with light curly silken red hair, through which I could just perceive the outline of her slit.

Now she stood before a cheval glass, surveying herself at full length, I could see a blush cross her beautiful face, as she seemed almost ashamed to look at her own nakedness. Then a self-satisfied smile parted those cherry lips, and displayed the sparkling pearls of teeth, as she patted the shiny marble skin of her belly and bottom (evidently thinking of the effect of the sight upon Robert when he should enter the room), then she playfully parted the lips of her cunt and examined it closely in the glass. The titillation of her fingers brought another blush, and she seemed as if she could not resist the temptation to frig herself a little, moving a couple of digits in a restless kind of way backwards and forwards between the vermilion lips of love.

My blood was on fire, and much as I hated her, I would have liked to gamahuche her there and then. But suddenly the door opened, and Robert stood transfixed, as he exclaimed in surprise, "Surely, Cecilia, you have lost all modesty; why have you never exposed yourself to me like that before?"

"Oh, Robert dear, how you startle me, you came up so soon and I was only just looking at the love I know you are longing to caress as soon as the light is out."

"I really did not know you were such a charming figure, Cecilia, but now you are naked I will feast on the sight, but we won't put out the lights, my dear. I must now examine in detail every charm. By the way, I may tell you that during your absence I found some bad books of my late brother's and they so fired my imagination by the extraordinary descriptions of various modes of sexual enjoyments that I quite blushed to think of our innocent ignorance, and long to try some of them with you."

91

He had almost torn his clothes off whilst speaking, and I could see his prick as rampant as possible, in fact I believe it had never lost its stiffness since our excitable bout a short time before

Throwing himself into her arms, they hugged and kissed, whilst she, taking hold of his pego, slowly backed towards the bed as she tried to bring its head to the mark.

"Not there, Cecilia, love, you have another maidenhead I mean to take to-night; our plain silly way of doing it only leads to getting a lot of children, and surely my quiver is full enough of them. I'll have no more, it's positive ruination, however rich a father may be. No, no, the French style in future, do you understand, I mean to get into your bottom," he said, as seriously as possible, yet with evident excitement.

"What a nasty idea! You shall never do that, Robert, to me!" she exclaimed, crimsoning with shame to the roots of her hair.

"But I must and will, Cecilia. Look at this book, here are all the different ways of 'doing it.' Why they suck each other, fuck—ah—you start at the vulgar word—but it's fuck—fuck—fuck—that's the name for it. They fuck in bottoms, under armpits, between the bubbies—another nasty name for titties —anywhere—everywhere—it's all the same to a man, all what they call C U N T, a word I am sure you have seen somewhere in your lifetime written on shutters, doors, or even on the pavement—a deliciously vulgar word, Cecilia, but the universal toast of men when they meet in company (I could see he was trying to make her look at a little French book, called *La Science Pratique*, with its forty pretty little plates), how my blood has been fired by fancying all these delightful ideas remained to be enjoyed when you came home."

"Why Robert you are mad, I'll burn that horrible book, I won't learn their filthy ways!" snatching at the book.

"You're my wife, every bit of your body is mine to do as I please with it; don't drive me to extremities, Cecilia, or I may be rough, for I'm determined to put my prick in your arse, now at once!" trying to turn her over.

"Robert, Robert, for shame, Beatrice will hear your disgusting language. You shall never abuse me that way!" hiding her face in her hands and beginning to sob.

"But I will, and you may blubber like a child. Your tears

only urge me on, if you resist I'll smack and beat you, till you are obedient!"

She struggled, but a woman's strength is soon exhausted, and at last he got her face down on the bed, with her bottom on the edge and her feet on the floor, then giving her a tremendously painful smack on her bum, he spread her legs wide apart, opened the cheeks of that glorious bottom, anointed the head of his bursting prick with spittle, also the tight-looking brown hole he was about to attack, and then pushed on to the assault of the virgin fortress.

I could hear her moan with pain as the head gradually forced its way within the sphincter muscle. "Ah—it's pricking—oh, oh—you'll rend me, Robert—oh, pray—Ah—r—r—re.—Oh! Oh!"

At last he was in, and rested a moment or two, then slowly began his fucking motions.

Presently I could tell by the wriggling of her bottom that she enjoyed it. His hands were busy frigging her cunt in front. How excited they got, each seeming to spend at the same moment, but he kept his place, and the second finish was so excitable that they screamed quite loudly in the frenzy of emission, whilst Cecilia actually fainted away with Robert fallen exhausted on her senseless body.

Presently he recovered sufficiently to be able to apply restoratives to his fainting wife, and as soon as he had brought her round, so that she could understand what he said, proceeded to tell her "that in future they would enjoy all the novel ideas he had found in that nice French book, no more big bellies for you Cecilia, or the anxiety of children for either of us. You must now suck my prick, till it is stiff enough again," he said, presenting it to her mouth.

"No, no, I never can do such a dirty trick, besides, it's doubly disgusting, you have not even washed since you outraged my bottom," she sobbed, as her eyes filled with tears, seeing no signs of compassion in his face.

"What's that to me, you've got to suck it, so go on, my dear, without all those wry faces, which only add to my fun, it's rare sport to make you submit to my fancies. I find I've been a fool ever since I was married, not to have asserted my right to do as I please with every bit of you. person, cunt, arse, mouth, or bubbies; they can all afford me intense pleasure, without getting in the family way. Now go on, and I will fuck you with a fine large dildoe. Mind you must swallow every drop of my spendings when it comes."

He forced his prick between her reluctant lips, all slimy and soiled as it was from the previous enculade, then producing an enormous dildoe, nearly twelve inches long, and big in proportion, he put a little cold cream on it, and presented the head to her notch, trying to force it in.

"Ah! No! no!! that's so awfully large!" she almost screamed, but the head was partly in, and despite her sobs, and moans of pains, he soon succeeded in passing at least ten inches of it into her distended vagina.

Her cunt was exposed towards me, so that I could see how gorged it was with that big india-rubber tool, and the sight of her slit so stretched to its utmost capacity caused quite a thrill of desire to shoot through my veins; it was almost impossible for me to prevent myself making some kind of demonstration. How I longed to be with them and join in the orgie of lust. Each shove of that tremendous affair now seemed to afford her the most intense delight. She sucked his prick in a kind of delirium, her highly wrought feelings banishing every sense of delicacy, shame, or disgust that might have previously deterred her from doing so. I frigged myself furiously, they screamed and spent, till at last both spectatrix and actors were thoroughly exhausted.

When I awoke next morning, and applied my eye to the peephole, it was just in time to see Her Ladyship awake. First she felt her cunt to see if it was all right, and not ruined by the giant dildoe she had taken in the previous night. Her eyes sparkled with desire, and she repeatedly blushed as I suppose the recollection flashed through her mind. Presently throwing the sheet entirely off her husband's body, she handled his limp affair for a few moments, then putting her face down, took the head of his prick in between her lovely lips, and sucked away with evident relish, till she had him in a glorious state of fitness, and was about to treat herself to a proper St. George, when Robert, who had only been feigning sleep to see what his randy wife would do, suddenly woke up, and insisted upon her applying it to her arse-hole instead of her cunt, wetting it with spittle.

Slowly but surely she achieved its insertion, although to judge by her face it was evidently a painful operation. But when once in how they enjoyed that glorious bottom-fuck.

94

Even after he had spent she rode on till he met her again, and both seemed to come at the same time, kissing each other in a frenzy of erotic madness.

My peephole afforded me the sight of many more luscious scenes between Lady Cecilia and her husband before I left town to take up my residence at Hastings for the benefit of my health.

My agent had secured and furnished for me a pretty little detached residence of thirteen or fourteen rooms, surrounded by gardens and orchards, so as to be delightfully free from the prying curiosity of my neighbours.

The household consisted of a cook and housekeeper, both young persons, not exceeding twenty-four or -five years of age, the latter being the daughter of a decayed merchant, a most pleasant and intelligent companion, but up to the time I engaged her, strictly prudish, virtuous.

Being naturally fond of young boys and girls, we had also two very pretty page-boys of about the age of fifteen or sixteen and two beautiful young girls about the same age, instead of housemaid and lady's-maid.

At first I felt considerably enervated by the little excesses I had been a party to, or witnessed, whilst staying with the new Earl, but the soft bracing air of the southern coast soon made me feel more like myself again, and long to indulge in the delicious dalliances of love, to which my warm temperament made me always so inclined.

The result was that I determined to seduce every member of my virgin household, each one of whom I believed to be thoroughly virtuous up to their entering my service.

The two youngest girls, as my special attendants, slept in the next room to mine, and had a door of communication by which the two rooms entered into the other without the necessity of going into the corridor.

I had quite a passion come over me to gamahuche these two pretty young things, and make them thoroughly subservient to my purposes.

You may be sure I was not long in putting my plans in operation as soon as I had sketched them all out in my brain. That very same evening, after my two pretty demoiselles had put the finishing touches to my toilet and left me sitting in my chemise de nuit, in front of a cosy fire with my feet resting on the fender, as I pretended to be reading a thrilling

95

romance:

"Leave that door open, my dears," I said, as they respectfully bid me good night. "I feel so dull perhaps I shall call for you to keep me company, if I feel that I cannot go to sleep."

In a few minutes I heard them tittering and laughing.

"Now, girls," I cried, "come here this moment. I want to know what you are having such fun about. Come just as you are, no putting anything more on or waiting to hide your blushes. Annie! Patty! Do you hear?"

Afraid of making me angry, the two girls came blushing into my room just as they were, in their nightgowns.

"Well now, what is it that is amusing you so?"

"Please, my Lady, it was Patty," said Annie with a wicked look at her companion.

"Ah, no, you fibber! My Lady, it was Annie began it," retorted the other, looking quite abashed.

Nothing could be got out of them, each saying it was the other.

At last I said: "I can guess pretty well what you two girls were amusing yourselves about; now tell me truly, were you looking at each other's privates in the glass?"

This question hit the mark, and seeing how shame-faced and blushing they both were, I went on: "No doubt, examining to see which one showed most signs of hair on her little pussey. Let me see Annie," as I suddenly caught the bottom of her nightdress and in an instant had it reversed over her head, so as to cover up her face and expose all the rest of her beautiful little figure. "Why, the impudent little thing hasn't a hair to boast of! Give her bottom a good slapping, Patty!"

Patty was only too pleased to do it, and the slaps fairly echoed through the room, mingling with Annie's piteous cries to let her go.

My blood was up. The sight of her beautiful bum, all flushed and rosy under the sharply administered slaps, made me fairly lust to take further liberties. So I let the little victim go, whispering in her ear, and her tearful eyes were brightened in a moment. She darted at Patty and sooner than it takes to write was dragging her about the room fully exposed, with her head and arms secured in her reversed nightdress.

I amused myself by slapping poor Patty's pretty posteriors

till they were almost black and blue, regardless of her sobbing and crying for mercy.

At last we let her go, and I took her on my lap to kiss away her tears. She soon smiled again and nestled herself to my body quite lovingly. This seemed to make her companion almost jealous as she appealed to me with a flushed face to kiss her also, which I readily did in the most loving manner, and I asked her to fetch a decanter of wine and some glasses from a cabinet, saying I felt so dull and sleepless I must have something to cheer me.

"Ah, my dear lady," exclaimed Patty, kissing me again and again, "you don't know how we all love you and feel for you, being left alone and unhappy. There is nothing we wouldn't do to bring a smile to your pale face."

"Then we'll sleep together and have a romp on the bed. Only mind, you are good girls, and never tell your mistress's doings," I replied, taking a glass of wine, and ordering them to do the same.

A second and a third glass seemed to open their eyes immensely; the least touch or joke sent them into fits of laughter. They blushed and seemed quite excited. In fact Patty, who had remained on my knee, was almost ready to faint with emotion as she caressed my face and bosom, the cause being a hand I had managed to slip under her night-dress, so that one finger had been tickling and playing with her almost hairless slit and gradually working her up to a state of excitement she was at a loss to comprehend.

"Let us all be naked. Throw off every rag, my dear ones, I want to feel your soft warm flesh next to mine, to cuddle you and feel you all over. Shall I read a pretty little piece of poetry about a potter who married your namesake, Patty?" I said, and seeing they were ready for anything, told Annie to bring me a manuscript called "The Haunted House" from a drawer in the cabinet.

"Now listen to 'The Tale of a Potter' and don't laugh till it is finished. You will find it rather free but nothing more than big girls like you ought to know." Then I commenced:

> Young Hodge, he was a worthy wise,
>   A potter he by trade;
> He fell in love with Martha Price,
>   She was a parson's maid.

This Hodge worked amongst his pans,
    His pots, his mugs, his delf;
He said: "A sad fate is a man's
    When he is by himself.

Now soon I'll marry Martha Price,
    A nice snug home I've got;
The parson soon the knot shall splice,
    And we'll both piss in one pot."

Then Hodge he made a pretty pot,
    And took it to his love;
Said he: "I've brought this pot to show,
    I mean your love to prove.

Now name the day, the happy day,
    Whose night shall bring me bliss;
When your sweet cunt and my stiff prick
    Shall mingle in this their piss."

They married were within a week,
    And Hodge he was in luck;
He took sweet Patty's maidenhead
    With his first vigorous fuck.

Then in her arms he fell asleep,
    But started with affright;
And in the middle of the bed
    He sat up bold and white.

"Oh, love! oh, love! I've had a dream,
    A dream to cause me fright;
I dreamed we both were in my shop
    And there I hugged you tight.

I dreamed I went your cheek to kiss,
    We romped with hugs and squeezes;
When down I knocked the pots and pans
    And broke them all in pieces."

Then Martha answered with a laugh:
    "No pots you've broke, good man;

But much I fear this very night,
   You've cracked a Patty Pan."

And from that night unto this day
   Hodge in that crack would pop,
A prick as thick as any brick,
   But the crack he cannot stop.

So maids beware, heed well your pans.
   With this my tale is ended;
If your pan's cracked by prick of man,
   It never can be mended.

Throwing down the manuscript, I had a finger in each of their cracks sooner than it takes to write. "What darling little pans each of you has! I long to throw you on the bed and kiss them. What do you think of mine with its soft curly hair? Only it's a broken pan, you know, my dears, as I've of course had my husband."

"La, and was that really so nice, dear lady? Oh, I love you so, do let me look," exclaimed Patty, slipping off my knee and kneeling between my legs to get a better sight of the object of her curiosity, which she first kissed most lovingly, and then, parting the hair, put a couple of fingers right up my cunt. This so tickled and delighted me that I leant back in the chair and pulled Annie close to my bosom as I hugged and kissed her, whilst I still had a finger in her little slit, as far as it would go. My legs also mechanically opened to facilitate inspection, as Patty exclaimed, "How deep my two fingers can go right up and it is so warm and moist. It makes me feel I could eat it!"

In a few minutes we were all tossing on my bed in a state of nature. They laughed, screamed and blushed as I excitedly examined and kissed their respective cunnies. How my tongue revelled around their budding clitorises till they rewarded me with those first virgin emissions which are always so deliciously thick and creamy. How lovingly they both repaid all my caresses, Patty paying the most ardent attentions to my cunt, which delighted her more and more every moment, whilst Annie seemed to prefer sucking my bubbies as I gamahuched her.

"What a treat it would be to see you both lose your

maidenheads at once," I exclaimed.

"Ah! couldn't the pages do it for us, dear lady? I do love that Charlie so!" appealed Patty without consideration in her excitement.

"I'll try and manage it; but we must be careful not to let them into our secrets before I can find out how they are disposed," I replied.

"Oh, I know Charlie is a rude, bold little fellow, wicked enough for anything if he had the chance. What do you think, I once actually caught him handling his affair in the pantry when he thought no one was looking and when I happened to enter suddenly; it was sticking out straight and red-looking at the top. His face was quite red and he seemed rather short of breath; but the impudent fellow, like the dare-devil he is, shook it fairly in my face as he asked me to give him a kiss, saying: 'What do you think of this, Patty? That's how it gets, when'—oh, mistress I can't tell you all he said."

But I pressed her and at last she told me: "It was when we had been waiting on his mistress. 'Oh, Patty,' he said, 'isn't she lovely, such mouth and teeth and loving eyes, I feel as if I could jump at her, I do!'"

"Very well, Master Charlie," I laughed, "perhaps I shouldn't so much mind if you did, when we are alone some-day I will give him the chance and let you two dears know all about it. But I will first read you another song from 'The Haunted House' and to-morrow I will give you a copy, and I expect both to be able to sing it soon."

"LIVE AND LEARN."
Tune:—Drops of Brandy

When I was little and good,
    A long time ago 'm afraid, Miss;
A stiff prick was not understood,
    I was a quiet little, shy little maid, Miss.
I knew but one use for my cunt,
    I knew not what joy 'twould afford me,
The sight of a cock would affront,
    And talk about fucking have bored me.
But now, oh, much wiser I've grown!
    I'll stretch my legs open for any,
My modest shy feelings have flown,

And fucks, why, I can't get too many!
I like a stiff prick up my arse,
　　Though too much of that makes you bandy.
When I look at my quim in the glass,
　　It always pouts red and looks randy.
I like a fuck—morn, noon, and night,
　　On every weekday and Sunday:
If I'm fucked on the Sabbath, all right!
　　But I want to be buggered on Monday.
Oh! Let it be hot or be cold,
　　I'm always alive for a cock, Miss;
Men, fair, dark, young or old,
　　Here's a hole that'll take in their jock, Miss!
I can spend for an hour at a time,
　　My cunt is as hot as fire, Sir;
The man that says: "Fucking is crime,"
　　I say to his face, he's a liar, Sir.
Then give me a prick in each hand,
　　Turn my arse north, my cunt to the south;
And get all your jocks well to stand,
　　One in each hole and one in my mouth;
I'll fuck and I'll suck and I'll frig,
　　Until you're all quite bloody well spent, Sir!
Then I'll take in the lodgers again,
　　And never once ask them for rent, Sir!
Hurrah! for my cunt, my best friend,
　　Hurrah! for a cock to kiss, Sir;
I'll fuck till this life comes to end,
　　I hope too, there's fucking in bliss, Sir!"

When we awoke in the morning it was too late for a repetition of our tribadism, so I made them get up quickly and bring in breakfast, promising to look after Master Charlie during the day.

Part VI.

After luncheon I ordered Charles to take several shawls and a floor-stool into the summer-house of the garden, as I wished to take a nap, and was sure the open air was more conducive to refreshing sleep than the close atmosphere of a room on a warm sunny day.

Annie and Patty exchanged significant glances as I gave the

order, but my uplifted finger stopped any further manifestation of intelligence.

We had a fine large garden at the back of the house, in some parts beautifully shaded by umbrageous elms of a venerable age, especially on the banks of a small circular pond about twenty yards in diameter, where, facing the south, the summer-house stood under the trees by the side of the small lakelet.

I followed Charles as he carried out my orders, and arriving at our destination, ordered him to spread the shawls over a sofa which stood there, for fear the leather might be damp. Then he fetched a pillow, and placed the foot-stool at my feet.

I had nothing on but a loose morning-wrapper, with my chemise and drawers underneath.

"How very oppressive it is," I exclaimed, as I languidly sank back on the couch as soon as he had prepared it, allowing as I did so, a most negligent exposure of my neck and a slight glimpse of the orbs of love beneath.

"Ah! Oh, oh! My goodness; the dreadful cramp!" I almost screamed, as bending down in great apparent pain, I pulled up the robe to rub the calf of my right leg. "Ah, oh! what torture!"

Charles was on his knees at my feet in a moment.

"Oh, my Lady, is it so very bad? Let me bend up your toes!"

"No, no, not there, rub the calf, as hard as you can, Charles, there's a good boy!" I replied, my face wincing under the pain. "Higher, rub along my leg, the foot's no use!"

Somehow the toe of my bad foot touched his trousers just outside the most interesting part of his anatomy; the slipper had fallen off and I could feel his prick quickly harden and throb under my toes, whilst his face flushed all over, and I thought quite a perceptible tremor passed through his frame, as he went on rubbing my leg below the knee, and I need not say how my own lustful temperament was affected by the contact.

My robe had opened down the front so that he had a full view of legs, drawers and bosom, perhaps the wrinkle of love itself.

My blood was in a boil and I could no longer resist the

impulse to enjoy such a beautiful Adonis.

"Get up, Charles, it's better now," I said in a low voice, "and pray don't tell what you've seen by accident. That cramp threw me into such an awful agony I did not know how I tossed about!"

"Dear Lady, your secrets are always safe with me," he replied, looking down bashfully as he rose to his feet. "I could kiss the ground under your feet to prove my devotion!"

"No, you are such a kind boy that just for this once, Charles, only this once, mind, I will give you a kiss myself instead. Come closer to me! What a fine boy you are. Now don't be bashful, really I mean to kiss you, if you promise never to tell."

"Ah, Madame, how kind of a great lady to a poor page-boy like me! I shall never forget such a favour and would die for you any time!" he said with bashful excitement.

"Come then," and I took his handsome face between my hands and kissed him repeatedly. "Why don't you kiss me, Charles?"

"Oh, Lady, and may I take that liberty?" he asked, his warm lips almost sucking the breath from me, so earnest was his kissing.

"Yes, yes," I murmured, "you may kiss me now, dear boy! And would you be faithful, Charles, if I trusted my life, my honour to your keeping?"

"Those kisses have made me your slave forever, dear Lady. Nothing could ever wring a secret of yours from me."

"Then, Charles, I will tell you I'm in love with your figure! I know you must be a perfect Cupid, and should you like to strip quite naked, that I may enjoy the sight of a living statue? Will you do so, no one will ever know?" I asked.

His face was crimson and I could see that he actually trembled under my gaze. "Now Charles, make haste, and if you do that for me I'll give you a sovereign and a new suit of clothes."

Slipping off his jacket I began to unbutton his trousers. Turning them down, my eager hands wandered under his shirt, feeling the firmness of the ivory-like flesh of his deliciously rounded buttocks whilst my eyes did not fail to detect how his linen stood out in front and was saturated with his spendings.

He seemed to understand me now and almost quicker than

I can write it, he was naked as Adam in Paradise.

My roving hands took possession of his beautiful little prick, quite six inches long, and ornamented round the tight-looking balls by just a shade of curly brown hair.

"What's this, Charles, are you often wet like this?" as I called his attention to the glistening sperm on my fingers. "What a big fellow this is, quite enough for a man. Did you ever make love with a girl?"

"No, my Lady, but I wanted to try it with Patty, only she never would."

"Then you shall with me, Charles, now. And I'll try to get Patty for you afterwards, I should so like to see you two together," I said, drawing his prick to my lips and sucking it deliciously for a moment or two till I felt he was getting near a second spend.

"Now, sir, kneel down and kiss me," I said, letting him go as I reclined on the sofa and opened my legs whilst his hands opened the slit in my drawers and exposed the lips of my cunt to view. His mouth was glued to it in a moment, and ah! oh! how his lascivious tongue made me spend in a second or two whilst my unslippered foot was rolling his prick on his thigh. But I was afraid of losing the next emission of his love juice, so I gently drew him over my body and directed his dart of love into my cunt.

He was hardly up to his business, but the instinct of nature seemed to prompt him to shove in.

What ecstasy as I felt the slow insertion of his virgin prick! How it seemed to swell inside the luscious sheath which received it lovingly.

At first we lay motionless, billing and cooing with our lips, till I began a slight motion with my buttocks, to which he was not slow to respond.

How I enjoyed that boy! The knowledge that I had a really virgin prick within me added such a piquancy to my enjoyment that I fairly screamed from excess of emotion as I spent and felt his balsam of life shoot into my longing womb.

He had to fuck me three times before I would let him dress and go about his business. He had been with me over two hours, but the time was well spent in making love and worming out of him all about himself and the other page who slept with him, Sam, who although good-looking had so much Indian blood in him that his complexion was almost black.

In answer to my questions Charlie informed me that they often played with each other, and rubbed their cocks together till the thick white stuff squirted out, and he added: "Dear Lady, would you believe it, his affair is two inches longer than mine; besides, it is the blackest part about him!"

"Do you think he would like a game with us?" I asked.

"Oh, certainly. He is just the fellow! It was he who taught me all I know, and I must tell you what he told me, that his last master, Colonel Culo, who had brought him over from Calcutta, had him sleep in his cabin all the way home and seduced him by handling and sucking his prick, which was so nice that at last Sam let the Colonel fuck him in the bottom-hole. The Colonel wasn't very big, you know, and easily got into him by using a little pomade. Then, when Sam left him because the Colonel was afraid he might get about his daughters if he kept him in his service, he was presented with a present of fifty pounds. He often wants me to let him get into my bottom as he said it felt very nice, but I never would go further than playing with cocks."

"Well then, this very night, about an hour after all the rest are in bed, bring him with you to the girls' door. You will find it ajar and mind only to come in your shirts and be sure not to disturb the cook and housekeeper."

With these orders I kissed and let him go, then went in to dress for dinner.

Just before we went to bed I treated Cookie and the housekeeper to a good glass of port in which I put a rather stiff narcotic to make them sleep well so that in case our revels with the two pages should prove noisy they would be too sound asleep to hear anything of it.

Patty and Annie were all nervous excitement and expectation after I told them of my arrangement. We were all naked and they hot as possible, and could not resist pressing their naked bodies against me, while with tears and blushes they expressed their fears of the pain of losing their troublesome virginities.

At last I heard a slight noise in their bedroom which so startled them that they flew to go and hide themselves underneath the bed, whilst I opened the door and entering their room, which was in darkness, found my two young men in the dark hesitating to tap at the door.

"Slip off your shirts and slippers," I whispered in a low voice "Feel, I am quite naked myself, all is to be free between us now," as my hands groped for their pricks. I found them to be as stiff as possible, and could not resist pressing their naked bodies against my own belly, where the contact of their throbbing pricks had such an effect on me that selecting Sam by the size of his affair, I backed towards the girls' bed and drew him upon me. What a luscious bit it was! So large that my cunt was fairly gorged with the delicious morsel, which spent almost before it was well into me. My arms held him firmly round the waist as my body rested against the edge of the bed so that without withdrawing he had to go on with the delicious fuck, and I begged Charlie to put his prick into Sam's behind, to make him do his work well with me. The latter was nothing loath, and although the want of lubricant was rather an obstacle, Charlie soon succeded in spite of his wincing and flinching a little.

The effect was to give my cavalier quite double energy. My hands passed behind him and played with Charlie's prick and appendages as he fucked Sam's bottom delightedly.

This was another virgin prick I was enjoying. Fancy taking the maidenheads of two handsome youths in one day. It fired me with the most lustful sensations! How my cunt throbbed on his glorious black prick. How we spent in torrents of that elixir of love which makes us die in ecstasy at each fresh emission. What heavenly joys to spend together, as we did, three times without withdrawing. I knew such excesses were only tending to shorten my life, but reason is powerless to resist the attraction of such Cytherian joys.

At last it was finished and we entered my room where the lights of a dozen candles showed everything to the best advantage. The figures of the two youths reflected in the looking-glasses round the room seemed to fill my apartment with lusty young fellows, half dark and half fair, all with limp and glistening pricks, just as they had withdrawn from the combat of love.

"Listen, my dears, cannot you hear the heavy breathing of the two girls under my bed? I'll wager they've been frigging each other whilst we had that glorious fuck in the other room!" I exclaimed. "But let us first refresh our affairs with a cold douche and have a glass of champagne! Then see if we won't drag them out in the light, my boys!"

106

We laved ourselves, and a couple of glasses apiece immensely revived our flagging energies. I had a nice little dog-whip with a long lash on it. So telling the boys to lift up the curtains of the bed, I slashed under on the surprised and timid beauties so effectually that I had only time to give about a half-dozen cuts before they sprang from their concealment and ran screaming round the room as I followed and plied my whip smartly over their tender bottoms. The sight of the thin weals which every cut drew on their tender skin, the shrieks of pain and the blushing effects on both faces and bums, so excited us that the boys' pricks stood again immediately and I longed to see the two pages ravish them as roughly as possible. Yes, I confess, that at that moment I felt awfully cruel and should have liked to see them suffer the most dreadful agonies under their defloration.

I know that with many men their delight is intensified if they can only inflict pain on the victims they ravish, but for a woman to gloat over such a sight is almost incomprehensible. Yet it is so, I was literally mad with lust of blood and torture!

At last I made them kneel down and kiss the boys' pricks as they begged of them to take their maidenheads.

Charlie had Patty and Sam had Annie. I ordered them to lay the girls on the soft Turkey carpet in the middle of the room with pillows under their buttocks. Then my two young champions, kneeling between their legs, opened the lips of the girls' spending cunts and proceeded to insert the heads of their pegos within the vermilion clefts of the victims.

It was a most delightful sight for me as I witnessed the blushes and enjoyed every painful contortion of their faces as the pricks were ruthlessly shoved into them under the influence of my whip, which I used without pity to push the boys on to victory. At last it was done and I could see that the boys had spent into them and I was sorry it was so soon over.

The tears of the girls were changed to loving smiles as by my directions they all had another wash. Then we sat down to jellies and wine, indulging in all manner of freedoms and jokes, till my young men began to feel their feet again and I could see that both of them were enjoying and eyeing me most amorously.

My blood was up and nothing would do but I must enjoy

107

them both at once with the girls joining in the best way they could.

Sam and Charles sat on either side of me, and I could feel both pricks ready for action. So I made the former sit on the edge of the bed and take me on his lap, and as soon as I felt properly sitted on the fine black prick, I called Charlie to shove his cock into me from behind, along with Sam's. This was not quite so easy to do, as Sam quite filled my sheath. Yet I was determined to have it so, and with the assistance of the girls, Charles succeeded in accomplishing my erotic fancy. Then by my orders, Annie and Patty tickled my clitoris and the lips of my distended cunt, as well as the cocks and balls of my two lovers.

Description fails me in endeavouring to picture the excessive voluptuousness of this conjunction, *trio in uno*. My profuse spendings so lubricated their pricks that they were soon quite comfortably rubbing together up and down, up and down inside my delighted cunt, and then: "Ah! Oh! Oh! I spend! I die in ecstasy! Where am I? Ah! heavens! Oh! God, what bliss!" That is how I screamed out and then almost fainted from excess of emotion, only to awaken directly to find them also in the frenzy of their emission.

The excitement was so great that my champions retained their stiffness and kept their place whilst the girls, not to be outdone, jumped up on the bed, and Patty, turning her bottom to my face, buried Sam's face between her thighs as she pressed her cunt to his mouth for a gamahuche; Annie straddling and lying over her to present her cunt and bottom to my lascivious tongue, which did not fail to seize the opportunity to revel both in her cunt and little wrinkled pink bum-hole.

This went on until sheer exhaustion compelled us to separate, and how I hugged and kissed them all, when at last I let them retire to their respective rooms.

Next day I was very ill and the day after that a medical man had to be called in, Patty going by my express desire to a doctor with very limited practice whom I thought would not be exhausted by his lady patients.

As soon as he arrived my servants all retired and left us alone.

"My dear lady," said Mr. Loveshaft, "what has brought you to this state of unnaturally prostrating excitement? Tell me all. Don't keep anything back if you wish me to do you any good."

"Oh, Doctor," I replied in a whisper, "pray, put out the light, the fire is quite enough to see by, and put out your ears close to my lips. I can only whisper my confession, and don't want you to see my blushes."

This was done and his face was close to mine when I threw my arms nervously round his neck and drew his face to my feverish lips and I kissed him more wantonly, saying:

"I want love; there's no one to love me. Oh! Oh! Fuck me first and physic me afterwards. I know you must be a gallant man, and mine's a real case of nymphomania!"

Whilst one hand still held him in a most amorous embrace, the other wandered to his prick, which my impassioned appeal had brought to a sense of its duty in a moment. What a fine fellow he was too, both long and thick, as opening his trousers without resistance he let me take it.

"Throw off your clothes, there's a love of a man, and let me have this first, and the medicine afterwards," I exclaimed, thrusting my tongue into his mouth.

He was a most amiable doctor and it was nearly an hour before the consultation was over.

I rapidly declined after this and in spite of the doctor's unremitting attentions, both to my health as well as my cunt, I grew worse and worse and had to be sent to Madeira for the winter. So I shall conclude my long tale with my adventure on shipboard on the voyage out.

My housekeeper, whom I shall call Miss Prude, went with me as companion. We had arranged to have a fine large state-cabin in the stern of the steamer, with sleeping beds, or more strictly speaking, berths for four, as I engaged Patty and Annie to accompany us as servants. At any rate, Miss Prude thought so, but I had a deep design to seduce that virtuous young lady in spite of herself. So, by a little bribery, Annie was induced to stay behind and let my dear Charlie take her place in female attire.

As you journey to Southampton at night, we embarked at a very early hour before daylight, my companion being with me in a first-class carriage whilst the servants travelled in another part of the train and looked after the shipment of our luggage. Miss Prude never for a moment suspected the change while she and I retired to our berths as soon as we got on board, leaving everything to the girls.

For the first two days sea-sickness quite prostrated us all, especially my companion, but on the third day she was quite lively and the supposed Annie kept as much as possible out of sight till we all retired to rest. The servants had got into their berths and appeared to be asleep. Miss Prude and myself were both undressed and sitting side by side on the ottoman. I asked her to put out the lamp and as she did so I put my arm around her waist and drew her gently down by my side.

"Isn't it lovely now we've got over the sickness? What a beautiful sensation the motion of the vessel gives. Oh, if you were but a nice young man now, my dear!" I said kissing her most amorously and thrusting my tongue into her mouth whilst one of my hands wandered under her nightdress and invaded all those delicious hairy parts, so sacred to virginity.

"Oh, for shame, my Lady! How can you be so rude?" she exclaimed in a loud whisper.

Still I found she did not repulse me and from the heaving of her bosom she was evidently in considerable confusion.

"What is your Christian name, darling? Miss Prude is so cold," I asked, between my lascivious kisses.

"Selina, but pray, don't, my Lady!" she said almost with a sigh as my fingers found out her little clitoris between the pouting lips which her yielding legs had allowed me to titillate.

"What a love of a name; Selina! and you must call me Beatrice, will you—there's a darling? And we must sleep together in the same berth, there's room for both. I must kiss you all over to prove my love—even there, darling," I said indicating her pussey with my finger, which was on the spot at the time, "and you shall do the same to me. Or, if you don't like, you shall see how Patty loves to kiss my crack. Ah! Ah! you'll soon learn Selina, to know what is nice, even if it seems horribly rude to think of."

"Did you never guess, my dear," I continued, "why some girls are so awfully fond of each other? Well, I will tell you —it is because they are in the habit of procuring from each other all those forbidden joys which married people alone are supposed to enjoy."

She was all atremble. My fingers were fairly buried in her slit, as far as they would go, and making her spend deliciously.

"Oh! Oh! I must suck it, every pearly drop that distills from your virgin recess is worth its weight in diamonds!" I said excitedly, throwing her back at full length on the otto-man, whilst I fell on my knees between her yielding thighs and glued my lips to her cunt. My tongue revelled in that thick creamy emission which only real virgins give down, for when their love-juices have not secreted so long, they are far more creamy than the spending of a woman is after often being fucked or frigged.

She enjoyed it immensely. How she wriggled and twisted in the excess of her excitement.

At last I got up and woke Patty. Then returning to my ladylove, I whispered in her ear: "Selina, darling, I am going to give you a real taste of what a man is like. Patty is going to put on my dildoe and fuck you with it, while she tickles my bottom-hole and you gamahuche my cunt. Won't that be a delightful conjunction, my love?"

"You frighten me, Beatrice dear. What is a dildoe, will it hurt?" she whispered in a low tone.

"Exactly like a man's affair, Selina! And although it can shoot a delicious soothing emission into you at the ecstatic moment, there is no fear of getting in the family way," I softly replied. "Now Patty is ready; let me straddle over your face and present my cunny to your sweet lips for a sucking kiss. You will like it. It will excite you so, to the unmistak-able joy the dildoe will give when it once gets in," suiting the action to the word by placing myself over her.

Her blood was in a boil. She eagerly thrust her tongue into my longing cunt which almost instantly rewarded it by a copious spend which Selina seemed to relish as much as any epicurean gamahucher would have done; her legs lasciviously wide apart, which Master Charlie was not slow to avail him-self of; the position in which I was over her effectually pre-venting the longing virgin from seeing the impending ruin.

Opening the lips of her spending cunt gently with his fingers, the fellow cunningly frigged her with the ruby head of his prick, until poor Selina got so excited that she began to bite me and wriggle about in such an extraordinary way, as well as moan and sob out: "Oh! Ah! shove, shove! Do push it in further, Patty dear! I feel I must have it. Oh! Oh! Ah-h! It hurts now! Pray, don't!" as he commenced to force the

111

maidenhead in earnest. I pressed my cunt upon her mouth so that she could not scream and intensely enjoyed the pain we put her to; for she was awfully tight and Charlie was not to be denied. He pushed and rammed at her in lustful fury, spending, but still going on, till he got the whole of his manhood fairly into her sheath, then he rested for a few moments, making his prick throb in its tight receptacle till all sense of pain seemed to be lost to our victim; and the natural lubricity of her nature asserted itself once more, and answered with a wanton heave of her bottom to every thrust of her partner. There seemed no satisfying her greedy cunt, now it had once got a taste of the real thing.

At last we got off her, and lighted the lamps once again, let her see the dildoe for herself and guess! How astonished she was to find it was real life, instead of a hateful substitute, but she forgave us for the deception which had afforded her such exquisite pleasure.

After refreshing our parts with cold water, she thoroughly enjoyed the sight of Charlie fucking the amorous Patty, and with her own hands handled his balls and tickled them as well as Patty's cunt during their encounter.

As we could not expect to have more than another two nights on board ship, I determined to make the best of the time, especially as I had a particular fancy for a good-looking youth in preference to men; and there were a couple of young middies on board I had quite fallen in love with as they had shown me many delicate attentions when I was so ill for the first few days.

A fine bright morning saw us on deck directly after breakfast.

"Good morning, my Lady," said young Simpson raising his cap with a knowing, wistful look.

"Come here, you impudent-looking boy," I laughed, and as he approached, said, in a whisper:

"Can you keep a secret?"

"My bosom is as safe as an iron chest, if Your Ladyship has anything to confide," was the reply.

"I am going to leave you soon, you know, and would like to give you and young William a treat in my cabin tonight, if you can manage to come after all are retired and you are off duty then, I think."

"Yes," he replied, "from 10 P.M. to 6 A.M. and you may

112

depend on us being very quiet."

Putting a finger to my lips as a sign of strict secrecy, I glided away from him and sat on the poop for the greater part of the day, looking at the water in a dream anticipation of the fun I hoped for at night.

I had made ample preparation for them and bribed the stewards not to take any notice if they heard noises in my cabin, as I was going to give a little party to two or three young lady passengers before going ashore at Funchal, the port of Madeira.

After supper, myself and companions lay down to rest in our clothes, leaving the lamps burning and the refreshments all ready to hand. After a while, when all was quiet, our cabin door opened softly and the two handsome boys in their best uniforms quietly saluted us as they entered, both of them kissing me before I could rise from the couch. The door was bolted by Patty, who laughingly told them to mind how they behaved, or they would get served out. In reply to which both of them caught her and kissed her in spite of her pretended resistance.

The middies were hungry and soon did ample justice to a game-pie washed down with several bumpers of champagne as they toasted us, from the servants to myself.

I drank glass for glass with them. My veins were on fire, consumed by my lustful longings to enjoy two such handsome youths, and as soon as they had finished their repast, I begged them to sit by my side on the ottoman. And just as Simpson was in the act of sitting down I drew him upon my lap, saying with a laugh:

"What a nice baby he was to nurse, what a pretty little dear; kiss its dear mama."

My lips met his in a long-drawn osculation which seemed to make him quiver all over with emotion as he lay on my bosom.

"Did you ever have a sweetheart, dear boy?" I asked.

"Yes; such a pretty girl at the Cape. I have rare fun with her when I go ashore."

"What! Are you impudent enough to take liberties with her?"

"Yes, she even let me get into bed with her."

"You impertinent little fellow to mention such a thing to me! Here, Miss Prude, and you girls, tie him up and pull down his breeches! I've got a tickler that will make his bottom smart for this!" I exclaimed, pushing him from me with great apparent disgust.

"What a lark! I should like to see them do it. Here, Peter, old boy, help us or these girls will really master me," and he began to find himself rather overmatched.

A smile and a gesture from me only turned his chum Peter Williams to our side and it was fun to see how foolish he looked when he found himself really tied up to one of the berths and his breeches pulled down in spite of all he could do. How he blushed as they tucked up the tail of his shirt and exposed a very pretty white-skinned bum which was soon rosy enough under the hand-slapping he got from the whole party, thoroughly enjoying the joke.

"Stand aside all of you," I said sternly, "and let me pay him the desserts for his impudence," advancing birch in hand.

He was a plucky little fellow and distained to cry out although I saw two or three big tears roll down his crimson face under my infliction, and I could also see that his cock was as stiff as a poker. He was released, and without even waiting to pull his breeches up, rushed forward to help us as we stretched his friend Peter on the ottoman, and then by my direction he sat on his back, whilst I gleefully let him have a due share of the birch till he begged hard to be let off.

When they thought to adjust their clothes we all began to laugh and joke them about the beautiful red weals we could see, pulling up their shirt-tails and taking such liberties that in a short time they were quite undressed and we had two youths in a state of nature with standing pricks to look at.

"Well, I wouldn't give much for those toys of yours if that is all you have to show the girls!" I said laughingly, as I switched the parts indicated with my rod. "Why Annie here has a better cock than any of you. We'll all strip and you shall see."

This was the expected signal and all further restraint on our impulsive passions was thrown aside in a moment.

I think those two handsome middies had never really had a girl before and that I really took their maidenheads. In fact, I indulged in my letch for having two pricks in my cunt at once, whilst Charlie fucked Miss Prude before our eyes, till she had hysterics from excessive lubricity.

We kept it up till nearly five o'clock, fucking, gamahuch-ing and indulging in every fancy we could think of. I even made Charlie get into my bottom with Simpson in him. Peter Williams also postillioning her companion with his prick in his fundament, whilst Miss Prude and Patty tickled and helped to excite us the very best way they could.

At last they were obliged to leave us and I may say that was the last lustful orgy I was ever able to indulge in, for my constitution broke down rapidly even during my stay at Madeira and I returned to England in the following May, since when, dear Walter, you have been my constant and lov-ing attendant, and seen how rapidly this consumption is carrying me to my grave. Oh! I would that I had strength to do it once more and that you were my manly champion in that combat of bliss which I shall never taste again. Would to Heaven I might die in spending as I felt your very soul shoot into my vitals, but, alas! it cannot be! Still, if there is bliss in the world to be, I feel assured of an everlasting fuck.

Amen! I am unable to hold my pen any longer.

CONCLUSION.

THE ORIGIN SPECIES.

Air.—"Derry Down."

When Adam and Eve were first put into Eden,
They never once thought of that pleasant thing—breeding
Though they had not a rag to cover their front,
Adam sported his prick, and Eve sported her cunt.
Derry down.

Adam's prick was so thick and so long—such a teaser;
Eve's cunt was so hairy and fat—such a breezer;
Adam's thing was just formed any maiden to please,
And his bollocks hung down very near to his knees.
Derry down.

Eve played with his balls, and thought it no harm:
He fingered her quim and ne'er felt alarm;
He tickled her bubbies, she rubbed up his yard,
And yet for a fuck, why they felt no regard.
Derry down.

But when Mrs. Eve did taste of the fruit,
It was then that her eyes first beheld Adam's root;
Then he ate an apple, and after he had done't,
Why then he first found out the value of cunt.
Derry down.

Then they say they made fig leaves, that's fiddle-de-dee.
He wanted a quim, and quite ready was she;
They gazed on their privates with mutual delight,
And she soon found a hole to put jock out of sight!
Derry down.

Then Adam soon laid Mrs. Eve on the grass,
He pop't in his prick, she heaved up her arse;
He wriggled, she wiggled, they both stuck to one tether
And she tickled his balls, till they both came together!
Derry down.

Since then, all her children are filled with desire,
And the women a stiff-standing prick all require!

And no son of Adam will e'er take affront,
For where is the man that can live without cunt.

Derry down.

THE WANTON LASS.

Air.—"Derry Down."

There was a lass they called bonny Bet,
With a jolly fat arse, and a cunt black as jet;
Her quim had long itched, and she wanted, I vow,
A jolly good fucking, but couldn't tell how.

Derry down.

She thought of a plan that might serve as the same,
That herself she might shag without any shame;
So a carrot she got, with a point rather blunt,
And she ramm'd it and jamm'd it three parts up her cunt.

Derry down.

She liked it so well that she oft used to do it,
Till at length the poor girl had occasion to rue it;
For one day, when amusing herself with this whim,
The carrot it snapped, and part stuck in her quim.

Derry down.

She went almost mad with vexation at this,
Indeed it was time, the poor girl couldn't piss.
The lass was in torture, no rest had poor Bet,
So at last an old doctor she was forced to get.

Derry down.

The doctor he came, and she told him the case,
Then with spectacles on, and a very long face,
He bid her turn up, though she scarcely was able,
And pull up her petticoats over her navel.

Derry down.

Her clouts she held up, round her belly so plump,
And he gave her fat arse such a hell of a thump,
That he made her cry out, tho' he did it so neat,
And away flew the carrot bang into the street.

Derry down.

Now a sweep passing by, he saw it come down,
Picked it up and he ate it, and said with a frown,
By God! it's not right, it's a damned shame, I say,
That people should throw buttered carrots away.

Derry down.

NURSERY RHYMES.

There was a young man of Bombay,
Who fashioned a cunt out of clay;
    But the heat of his prick
    Turned it into a brick,
And chafed all his foreskin away.

There was a young man of Peru,
Who had nothing whatever to do;
    So he took out his carrot
    And buggered his parrot,
And sent the result to the Zoo.

There was a young girl of Ostend,
Who her maidenhead tried to defend,
    But a Chasseur d'Afrique
    Inserted his prick,
And taught that ex-maid how to spend.

There was a young man of Calcutta,
Who tried to write "Cunt" on a shutter.
    When he got to C-U,
    A pious Hindoo
Knocked him arse over head in the gutter.

There was a young man of Ostend,
Whose wife caught him fucking her friend;
    "It's no use, my duck,
    Interrupting our fuck,
For I'm damned if I draw till I spend."

There was a young man of Wood Green,
Who tried to fart "God Save the Queen."
    When he reached the soprano,
    He shot his guano,
And his breeches weren't fit to be seen.

There was a young man of Dundee,
Who one night went out on the spree;
    He wound up his clock
    With the tip of his cock,
And buggered himself with the key.

There was a young lady of Troy,
Who invented a new kind of joy:
    She sugared her thing
    Both outside and in,
And then had it sucked by a boy.

There was a young man of Santander,
Who tried hard to bugger a gander;
    But the virtuous bird
    Plugged his arse with a turd,
And refused to such low tastes to pander.

There was a young lady of Hitchin,
Who was skrotching her cunt in the kitchen;
    Her father said "Rose,
    It's the crabs, I suppose."
"You're right, pa, the buggers are itching."

There was an old person of Sark,
Who buggered a pig in the dark;
    The swine, in surprise,
    Murmured "God blast your eyes,
Do you take me for Boulton or Park?"

———————

QUEEN BATHSHEBA.

A Temperance Ballad.
(Attributed to Sir Wilfrid Lawson.)

Grass widows and princes! a warning I sing,
Of the sad wicked doing of David, the King;
With Bathsheba, wife of poor Major Uriah,
Who was bathing one day, when the King chanc'd to spy

He was drinking up-stairs, and the weather was hot;
And her window was open (a thing she forgot);
And the stark-naked beauty had not an idea,
That while she was washing, a creature could see her!

She and her little sister were sporting together,
Enjoying the heat of the bright summer weather;
They bath'd in the fountain, and while they were washing,
Were romping all naked, and leaping and splashing.

What man could resist such an awful temptation?
He forgot he was King of the sanctified nation;
He was fill'd with delight, and lewd admiration,
And was mad for the raptures of fierce fornication.

Beware of the Devil, who seldom lies sleeping!
So while she was washing, and while he was peeping,
The King's living sceptre grew stiff as a rod,
"Nice mutton!" cried David, "I'll fuck her, by G——!"

So calling a page, he desir'd him to go,
And enquire all about her.—He answered, "I know

The lady your Majesty's pleas'd to admire,
Is the wife of the valorous Major Uriah."

His Majesty answer'd: "Go, fetch her! Be quick!
Much conscience, indeed, has a stiff-standing prick!"
The page ran to call her; she put on her smock,
And hurried to wait on his Majesty's cock.

One touch to her hand, and one word in her ear,
And she fell on her back, like a sweet willing dear;
He was frantic with lust, but she seiz'd his erection,
And put it at once in the proper direction.

She was girlish and lively, a heavenly figure,
With the cunt of an angel, and fucking with vigour;
He got her at once with child of a son,
And he said a long grace when the swiving was done.

So the lady went home, and she very soon found
Her belly was growing unluckily round.
"This an honour," said she, "I could hardly expect,
Your Majesty now must your handmaid protect."

"Never fear," cried the King, "I'll be your adviser,
I'll send for the Major, and no one's the wiser."
So he sent for Uriah, who speedily came.
But unluckily never laid hands on the dame.

King David was puzzled, he made the man tipsy,
But still he avoided the lewd little gipsy;
David laid a new plot, and his wish was fulfill'd,
In the front of the battle Uriah was kill'd.

———————————

THE HORRIBLE FRIGHT.

Poor Sally! I hear from your loving Mamma,
That you're in a horrible fright of Papa;
Take courage, dear girl, for the sweetest delight,
Is closely akin to a horrible fright.

In your dreams, did you ne'er see a horrible man,
Who crushes and conquers you, do all you can?
He treats your poor innocent mouse like a rat
That's touzled and claw'd, and devour'd by a cat.

He produces a horrible fright of a thing,
That fits like a finger in conjugal ring;
He thrusts, and he pokes, and he enters your belly,
Till the horrible monster is melted to jelly.

When you draw a new glove on your finger so tight,
The glove is, you know, in a horrible fright;
But soon it is taught your dear finger to love,
The man and the woman are finger and glove.

Away with your horrible fright, and away
With the wretch of a father, who hinders the play;
If he dares interfere, when you kiss on the sly,
Just pull up your petticoat, piss in his eye.

Ah! Sally, my darling, I wish that this night,
I might put you, my love, in a horrible fright;
You might lie down a maiden, in five minutes more,
I would open a secret, ne'er open'd before.

You then would behold, long, ruddy, and thick,
That horrible monster, a stiff-standing prick;
You'd cry out, "Oh, softly! Oh, gently! Ah! Ah!
Oh lordy, oh lordy, oh harder, la! la!"

At last, dearest Sally, your horrible fright
Would end in a shudder of tipsy delight;
You'll open your buttocks, as wide as you can,
To admit every inch of the dear cruel man.

You'll devour every inch of his horrible yard,
Till the testicles hit on your bottom so hard;
Your terrible fright, my dear girl, will be over,
You'll breathe out your soul, on the lips of your lover.

There's an end of this horrible fright of a song,
Your mother shall read it, and say if it's wrong;
No, she will approve it—her greatest delight
Is the prick which you fancy such a horrible fright.

PAYNE'S HILL (Mons Veneris).

In Middlesex a hill we meet,
  For beauty known to fame;
Where wealthy Payne has built his seat,
  Payne's Hill they call its name.

"Pray, Mr. Burke," said Lady Payne,
  "What Latin word is this?
(I've searched the dictionary in vain),
  Pray what's *Mons Veneris?*"

He look'd into her beauteous eyes,
  So innocent of ill;
And gave the happiest of replies,
  "It signifies *Payne's Hill!*"

There was a young lady of Gaza,
Who shaved her cunt clean with a razor;
    The crabs in a lump
    Made tracks to her rump,
Which proceeding did greatly amaze her.

There was a young lass of Surat,
The cheeks of whose arse were so fat
    That they had to be parted,
    Whenever she farted,
And also whenever she shat.

There was an old priest of Siberia,
Who of fucking grew wearier and wearier;
    So one night after prayers,
    He bolted upstairs,
And buggered the Lady Superior.

There was an old man of Natal,
Who was lazily fucking a gal,
    Says she, "You're a sluggard,"
    Said he, "You be buggered,
I like to fuck slowly, and shall."

There was a young farmer of Nant,
Whose conduct was gay and gallant,
    For he fucked all his dozens
    Of nieces and cousins,
In addition, of course, to his aunt.

There was an old man of Tantivy,
Who followed his son to the privy,
    He lifted the lid,
    To see what he did,
And found that it smelt of Capivi.

There was a young man of this Nation,
Who didn't much like fornication;
    When asked, "Do you fuck?"
    He said, "No, I suck
Women's quims, and I use Masturbation."

There was a young parson of Eltham,
Who seldom fucked whores, but oft felt 'em.
    In the lanes he would linger,
    And play at stick finger,
'Twas on the way home that he smelt 'em.

There was a young lady of Rheims,
Who was terribly plagued with wet dreams;
    She saved up a dozen,
    And sent to her cousin,
Who ate them and thought they were creams.

There was a gay parson of Tooting,
Whose roe he was frequently shooting;
    Till he married a lass,
    With a face like my arse,
And a cunt you could put a top-boot in.

A learned divine down at Buckingham,
Wrote a treatise on cunts and on fucking 'em;
    A learned Parsee,
    Taught him Gamahuchee,
So he added a chapter on sucking 'em.

———————————

THE LADY FREEMASON.

As a brother of old, from his lodge was returning,
He called on his sweetheart, with love he was burning,
He wanted some favours, says she, "Not so free,"
Unless you reveal your famed secrets to me."

"Agreed—'tis a bargain—you must be prepared,
Your legs well exposed, your bosom all bared."
Then hoodwinked and silent, says she, "I'll be mum,
In despite of the poker you'll clap on my bum."

To a chamber convenient his fair charge he bore,
Placed her in due form, having closed tight the door,
Then presented the point of his sharp *Instrumentis*,
And the Lady was soon made an "entered apprentice."

His working tools next to her gaze he presented,
To improve by them seriously she then consented,
And *handled* his *jewels* his *gavel* and *shaft*,
That she in a jiffey was passed "fellow craft."

She next wanted *raising*, says he, "There's no urgency,"
She pleaded that this was a case of emergency,
His *column* looked to her in no particular way,
But she very soon made it assume perpendicular.

He used all his efforts to raise the young elf,
But found he required much raising himself;
The task was beyond him. Oh! shame and disaster,
He broke down in his charge, and she became master.

Exhausted and faint, still no rest could betide him,
For she like a glutton soon mounted astride him,
"From refreshment to labour," says she, "let us march.
Says he, "You're exalted—you are now royal arch."

In her zeal for true knowledge, no labour, no shirking,
His jewels and furniture constantly working,
By night and by day, in the light or the dark,
With pleasure her lover she guides to the mark.

A FACT.

When tipsy Harry fumbled Kate,
  And felt her hairless belly;
"What's this," he cried, "thou's but a babe,
  This is no cunt, I tell ye!"

To whom the indignant lass replied,
  "Pray, why should you upbraid me?
It is not my fault, I am just
  As God Almighty made me."

"What's that to me?" replied the brute,
  "To stroke a child's unlucky;
If God Almighty made you so,
  Let Mr. Spurgeon fuck ye!"

TOASTS.

Gent:—The first four letters of the alphabet—A Big Cunt
Daily.
  Lady:—In with it, and out with it, and God work his will
with it.

MY GRANDMOTHER'S TALE OR MAY'S ACCOUNT OF HER INTRODUCTION TO THE ART OF LOVE.

From an unsophisticated Manuscript found amongst the old lady's papers, after her death, supposed to have been written about A.D. 1797.

CHAPTER I.

When I was sixteen years old I was a pupil teacher at the N. School. I had a bedroom to myself, but I always chose one of the elder girls to sleep with me. My favourite, Susey P——, was about my own age, and of a warm friendly disposition. We soon became very intimate, and promised to tell each other all our secrets.

We were both exceedingly curious to know all about the secret pleasures of love, and often talked over the subject at night, all the time fondling and playing with each other's cunts.

"Did you ever hear any name for this little chink, May?"

"Yes, dear, cunt. One of the girls wrote it the other day on her slate. She said that was what the boys called it."

"And what do they call their own things?"

"Pricks."

"Why do they call them pricks?"

"I suppose it is because they prick our cunts."

"Would you like to have your cunt pricked?"

"Yes, I think, I would like it now, for my cunt feels so very hot."

"So it is, and mine is just the same. O May! if my cunt could be turned into a prick what fun we would have."

She then got over me, and rubbed her cunt against mine, while I held the cheeks of her bottom and pressed her in be-

129

tween my thighs.

"May, did you ever notice the lump between the legs of Mr. T——, the resident tutor?"

"Yes, dear, that's his prick, every man has that, though some have it larger than others."

"O yes, I know that, but have you seen it swell out when he talks to us girls, and leans over us to make us hold our pens right?"

"Perhaps he is then thinking of our cunts."

"I am sure of it, and especially of yours, for you are his favourite. If he were here now I know what he would like to do."

"What?"

"Just to get on top of you, and shove his prick into your cunt, and fuck you."

I only laughed, and we soon fell asleep.

On Sunday, a short time after, having a headache, I remained at home. I was not aware that anyone was in the house, until happening to pass Mr. T——'s room, he suddenly sprang out, caught me in his arms, drew me in, and closed the door.

"Oh Mr. T——. Please let me go."

"Dearest May, let me tell you how dearly I love you." And while he half smothered me with kisses, he gently drew me towards the bed.

"No, I won't sit down—let me up—don't attempt to put your hands under my clothes."

But he forced his hand up, and I felt his eager fingers exploring all my secrets there.

"Mr. T——, take your hand—I cannot allow such liberties —let me up, or I'll scream."

"Don't, my pet, for there is no one to hear."

"Do let me up, and take your hand—oh my! how dare you lift my clothes."

He held me down, and soon, in spite of my struggles, he uncovered all my belly and thighs, and my cunt lay bare and exposed to view.

It was the first time it had been seen by man, and I felt horribly ashamed. But a peculiar sensation of pleasure quickly turned the idea of exposure into a source of delight.

His face flushed, and his eyes sparkled as he looked down, and exclaimed, "What a lovely cunt you have, May; this rising mound is covered with such a profusion of rich brown hair, and the swelling lips, how deliciously they pout, while the glowing red chink between is most luxurious and inviting. I must kiss it. Oh! how sweetly it smells."

He stooped and warmly kissed my cunt.

Then opening the lips he sucked the clitoris and pushed his tongue into the hot recess.

The touch of his mouth made my cunt thrill, and when I felt his tongue moving around the clitoris, and penetrating the sensitive folds inside, I could not help opening my thighs and raising myself a little, so as to afford him a freer access to that pleasurable spot.

When he stood up I saw that his trousers were down, and that his prick was sticking out pointed towards me, and nodding its great red head as if in proud defiance.

Holding it in his hand, he said, "Look at this poor fellow, May, he craves your kind indulgence, and only asks to hide his blushing head for a moment in this sweet nest; won't you take him in your hand?"

"O, for shame! Mr. T——. Put that horrid thing away. I won't look at it, or touch it. I won't let you put it in." And I covered my cunt with my hand. He pulled my hand away, and placing it on his prick, forced my fingers round it. It felt deliciously smooth and soft, but at the same time firm and stiff.

"Mr. T——, let me up. What do you mean?"

"I mean that I am going to fuck you May; to put my prick into your cunt and fuck you."

"I will never let you. It would harm me, and hurt me."

"No, my love, it will neither hurt you nor harm you. Let me put it in, do, my sweet pet."

He pushed the head of his prick in between the lips of my cunt, and moving it up and down the furrow, said, "There, that does not hurt you, I am sure." He then placed it at the inner opening, and with a sudden push forced it in.

"Oh! Mr. T——. Take it out. Oh! it is hurting me. You said you would not hurt me."

But he only pushed harder, then something gave away inside, and I felt the whole prick rush up into my belly. It had a startling effect at first, and almost took away my breath, but when he went on to work his tool in and out, and I felt it rubbing with a most delicious friction against the throbbing

131

folds of my cunt, the feeling became one of overpowering delight. I twisted about and heaved to meet his thrusts.

"There, darling, now don't you like that?"

"Yes, I like it now, that's very nice."

"Now say it's name."

I whispered, "Prick."

"Say it out."

"Prick."

"And yours?"

"Cunt."

"And doing this?"

"Fucking."

"Go on, say what it is you like."

"I like to feel your prick fucking my cunt."

"Oh, go on, it's just coming."

"Prick—cunt—fucking—belly—bottom."

Then, drawing his prick suddenly out of my cunt, he poured a torrent of hot seed over my belly, and up to my very breasts.

After this Mr. T—— and I lost no opportunity of performing the sweet rites of Venus, and he soon initiated me into all the various ways and modes of enjoyment. I found that I could fully trust him, as he was very discreet, and particularly careful to avoid doing me harm.

Susey and I too became more and more confidential. I acknowledged to her that I had been fucked, but did not name Mr. T——.

One night I prevailed on her to give me full particulars of some love scenes between her elder sister Jane and her intended, Mr. John C——.

"They used to take me out to walk with them. They generally went to a wood, where they had a favourite resting place, well sheltered among the trees. But when there they always sent me away to gather blackberries or flowers.

"I often saw him kiss her, and sometimes when no one was looking, push his hand up under her petticoats. This aroused my curiosity, and I resolved to watch them.

"So the next time when I went off with my basket, I made a circuit, and entered the wood behind them. I crept through the trees until I could both hear and see them plainly.

"He was lying on his back, his trousers all open, and a long fleshy thing with a purple head was standing up. She was stooping over it moving it up and down with her hand. Then she kissed it, and took it in her mouth and sucked it.

" 'How nicely you suck my prick, Jane. Kneel up now, I want to see your beautiful bottom and cunt at the same time.'

"As she did so he threw up her clothes over her back, uncovering the two round cheeks of her bottom, and the thick lips of her cunt jutting out like a huge hairy mouth between.

" 'My darling, you have a splendid backside, the sight of it would bring to life the prick of a dying man. Keep as you are, I'll fuck you this time from behind, in what is called dog fashion.'

"He then got up, and knelt between her legs, and drawing apart the white cheeks of her bottom, pushed his prick into her cunt.

"Then holding her hips, he worked his article rapidly in and out, telling her to push back her bottom to meet each thrust of his prick.

"She panted and pushed, while he grunted out, 'Do you feel it Jane? Do you feel my prick?'

" 'Yes, dear John, I do feel your prick, ever so far up my cunt—that's right—drive it in hard. Fuck—fuck—fuck.'

"Then they fell together on the grass, and I ran away."

"How did your cunt feel, Susey, when you saw his prick, and watched them fucking?"

"Oh, it used to get very hot, and then I would rub it and squeeze it as hard as I could."

"Did you often see them doing it, Susey?"

"Yes, many a time, and in every kind of way. Would you believe it, I saw him once fuck her in her bottom, and she did not mind it a bit."

"Did they ever find you out, Susey?"

"They did. I'll tell you how. One day I crept up very close to them, she was standing with her back against a tree, holding up her clothes. He was kneeling between her legs kissing her cunt. He looked up and she said:

" 'Well, to please you—there—watch.'

"And a stream of amber fluid spurted out with a hissing noise from between the hairy lips of her cunt. She had scarcely done before he kissed it again, and sipped up the drops that hung about the hairs.

133

" 'Now, John, it's my turn to see you spouting.'

" 'Well, if you hold my prick I'll try.'

"She held it while he pissed, rubbing it all the time, as if she was milking a cow's teat, and when he had done, she kissed and sucked it.

" 'Your prick is in grand order to-day. Look how stiff it is.'

"She bent it down, and let it go, when it sprang up erect as before.

" 'Lie on your back, John, and I'll get over you, I know it is a way you like.'

"So he lay down, his fine prick standing up in full erection.

" 'Now tuck up, and turn your bottom to my face.'

"She did so, and straddling over him with her great white bum jutting out, she stuffed his prick, neck and shoulders, into her gaping cunt.

"Then she bounded up and down like a jockey riding. When she rose up I could see the prick standing up, all red and inflamed. Then heaving down, the prick rushed up into her cunt, and her bottom came flap against his belly.

"This scene excited me greatly. I envied Jane. She seemed to enjoy it so thoroughly. And not thinking what I was doing, I forced my middle finger right up my cunt, the sudden pain made me cry. 'Oh!' They started, and quickly drawing aside the branches, saw me, my clothes up, and my finger in my cunt.

" 'Holloa, Susey! is that you?' cried John.

" 'You wicked little minx,' said Jane, 'how dare you steal upon us in that manner?'

"I said nothing, but covering my face with my hands, began to cry.

" 'Don't scold her, perhaps she could not help it. Come here, Susey, sit down and dry your tears. Now promise you will never speak of anything you may have seen.'

"I sat down, and earnestly promised all that they desired.

"John, passing his hand up under my clothes, and pinching the lips of my cunt, said: 'You have already given me a glimpse of this little nook, Susey. I want a closer and fuller view. Lean back. Open your legs. There. There. Hasn't she a nice innocent looking little cunt, Jane? I think the cunt of a young girl before the hair grows over it is particularly pleasant to look upon, and to kiss too,' he said, as he held up my bottom with his hands, and buried his face between my legs.

134

"I felt his whiskers brushing my thighs, and his soft tongue pushing into my cunt.

" 'Yes,' replied Jane, 'you may pet and kiss Susey's little plaything as much as you like, but remember that is all.'

" 'Tell me, Susey, what did you see?'

" 'I saw you pushing something into Jane.'

"He drew out his prick, and putting my hand on it, asked, 'Was this what you saw?'

" 'Yes.'

" 'Do you know what it is called?'

" 'Yes, I heard Jane call it prick.'

" 'And what's this little slit?'

" 'My cunt.'

" 'Would you like to see the prick going into Jane's cunt again, and fucking it?'

" 'Oh, yes, I would very much.'

" 'Well, Jane, my love, let us have another turn before we go, my prick is awfully excited.'

"He laid her back, and opening her legs, made me look at her cunt. I had often seen it before when she was bathing, but had never looked into it until now. I was surprised at its depth and extent. He put my hand on it, and said: 'See these fine thick lips, how they swell out. That's the sort of cunt a man loves to fuck. And this deep chink, how red and hot it is. Put your fingers in.'

"Three fingers entered easily. The soft warm folds inside closed on my fingers, and seemed to suck them in.

"Just like your own cunt, May. Oh! how hot it is! and how it throbs! And mine is throbbing too. Let us have a mutual suck before I proceed with my story."

I readily agreed, for my cunt felt all in a flame. We threw off our shifts, and lay naked on the bed. She got over me, and lifting up my thighs, sucked eagerly at my cunt, and twining her arms round my hips, tickled my bottom.

My tongue was equally busy about her sweet orifice, and as she felt it penetrating the heated parts inside, she wriggled about, and pressed her bottom on my face.

We were soon partially relieved by a copious discharge from our founts of pleasure.

Susey then resumed her exciting narrative:

"John knelt between Jane's thighs, and made me direct his prick into her open cunt. I held it by the root as it passed quickly up. He told me to stir his balls and pinch his bottom.

"Meanwhile, I watched the operation with the greatest interest and delight.

"As the prick went in, the lips enclosed it with a kind of eager suction, and when it came out they seemed to follow it, as if loath to part with such a pleasant morsel.

"John put his hands under her, and raised her up. As he warmed to the work, his great muscular bottom heaved backward and forward with increasing rapidity, making his prick plunge in and out of her hot receptacle.

" 'Are you pinching him, Susey? Pinch hard.'

"I pinched his bottom, and tickled the hole there with my finger.

" 'Push it in, Susey, oh, that is so nice. Tell us what you see, dear.'

" 'I see your bottom heaving backward and forward and your prick rushing in and out between the thick hairy lips of Jane's cunt.'

" 'What else do you see, Susey?'

" 'I see the bag below your prick, and feel two round things in it.'

" 'Stir them, Susey. What else do you see?'

" 'I see the round hole of your bottom.'

" 'Move your finger inside, Susey. Oh! Oh!!' he cried, as he drove his prick with great force into her cunt, and banged his balls against her bottom, while she clasped him in her arms."

All this time Susey had been frigging my cunt with her fingers, and now she sprang on top of me, and pounded her cunt against mine, until our cunts again overflowed with love's sweet juice, and we lay back to rest.

The next time I went to Mr. T——, after the usual preliminaries of petting, sucking, &c., he said he wished to try a new mode of enjoyment which he had seen in a picture. So he first set up a large mirror before us, and then sitting on the edge of a sofa, he lifted me up backwards, and placed my bottom on his belly. Then putting his hand under my thigh, he raised my knee up to his breast. So that, in the glass, we had a most exciting view of my open cunt, and his upstanding prick nestling its rubicund head between the hairy lips.

I rested my foot on his knee, and then pressing down,

watched it slowly disappearing in the pouting gap. As I rose up, the sweet instrument of pleasure again appeared, all red and shining with the moisture of my cunt, and when I pressed down it hastily returned, leaving nothing outside but the balls in close contact with the hairy lips.

Mr. T—— smiled, as he saw his tool absorbed in the crimson recess of my greedy cunt, and said:

"How beautifully plump and pouting your cunt is, my sweet May. With what delicious pressure it sucks in my bounding prick, while the soft cheeks of your bottom rub sweetly against my belly. But let us not hurry, it is so pleasant to talk together while my prick is soaking in your cunt. I want you to tell me something about your friend Susey. Does she know much of these matters?"

"Indeed, she does, everything in fact."

"Do you speak out the names? Prick, &c.?"

"Yes, she talks freely of pricks and cunts, and of fucking too."

"Was she ever fucked, do you think?"

"I think not, but she has often seen it done."

"How was she able to manage that?"

I told him how she had seen her sister fucked by her intended before their marriage.

"Do you often pet each other's cunts?"

"Yes, nearly every night."

"How?"

"When we are stripping for bed, she often asks me to lean back; and then she kisses and pets my cunt, and I do the same for her."

"Has she a nice cunt?"

"It is a nice little cunt, much tighter than mine; the lips are very plump, and well covered with light red hair. The skin round it is white, and smooth as satin, and the inside a bright pink."

"Why, May, you have quite excited me. Would you be awfully jealous if you saw me fucking her?"

"No, I would not be such a fool."

"May, you are the dearest girl, and have the sweetest cunt in the world. But I must take out my prick now. Hold it in your hand. There—see—how it spouts."

Before leaving I consented to let him hide in my wardrobe

the following evening, that he might hear and see how we got on together.

When the time came I detained Susey in the schoolroom, until I was sure that Mr. T—— was safely ensconced in his hiding place. Then we went to our room, and having carefully fastened the door, commenced undressing as usual right opposite my wardrobe. I stopped her as she was putting on her nightdress, and said:

"Susey, the night is warm, let us have some sport before we go to bed. And first give me a good peep at your nice little cunt."

I stretched open her thighs, as she leaned back on the bed, that Mr. T—— might have a better view.

I opened the soft pouting lips, and said:

"Your cunt is very red to-night, have you much feeling in it?"

"Yes, it is all aglow. Oh! pinch the clitoris—rub your finger—there—you may push it in if you like."

The door of the press opened a little further.

"Susey, my pet, I want to see you make water. I'll hold the pot between your legs, and you can do your pee into it."

I did so, and soon the hot piss came gurgling out.

I heard a stir in the press behind me.

"Now, May, it is my turn to see you perform, and I will hold the pot for you."

I spread my thighs and fired away.

"Lean back May, and let us tip cunts, for want of something better."

She got in between my thighs, and pushed hard against my cunt. Mr. T—— must have had a grand view of her peach-like bottom, as she heaved it up and down.

The door of the press opened further, and I could see the head of a prick sticking out.

"Tell me, May, once again, how you felt the first time you were fucked?"

"Well, you know, he pushed me back on the bed, pulled up my clothes, and in spite of all my efforts, laid bare my cunt. Then he forced himself in between my thighs, and with his naked prick standing up. He made me take it in my hand and rub it up and down. He praised my cunt, and sucked it, which I thought very nice, though I wondered at his doing it."

"I don't," said Susey. "I love to suck your cunt, darling May, but go on, tell me more."

"He said he wanted to fuck me. I said he shouldn't, but he forced the head of his prick into the mouth of my cunt. Then giving a great heave he drove it up. It smarted me a good deal at first, but when it got in altogether, and he commenced to work it in and out, the pleasure was so great that I could not help telling him, when he asked me, that I liked his fucking very much, and that his prick felt very nice in my cunt."

Here Susey commenced bounding between my thighs. "Oh! May! how I long for a prick. How I do wish that Mr. T—— was here. I could almost ask him to fuck me, my cunt is so burning hot."

The press door opened, and Mr. T—— stepped out perfectly naked. In a moment he was behind Susey, poking his prick against her cunt.

"Here I am then, ready and delighted to gratify each of my sweet pets."

Susey started, but when she looked back and saw Mr. T——, and felt the head of his prick in her cunt, she hid her blushing face in my neck, and resigned herself to his amorous attack.

I laughed and held her buttocks open while he drove his prick into her maiden cunt.

It did not hurt her much, as she had enlarged the opening when frigging it with her finger.

After a few strokes I asked her how she liked the feel of a prick in her cunt.

"Oh May," she replied, "why do you ask me. You know well yourself how a prick feels."

I slipped my hand between them, and felt her hot clitoris clinging to his prick, as it plunged in and out. While at every push she got behind, her belly and breasts heaved against mine.

Mr. T—— was too much excited by all that he had seen and heard to be able to prolong his fuck, so he had to draw out his prick to avoid harm.

I held it in my hand, as he rubbed it in the furrow between the cheeks of her bottom, and I soon felt the emitting spasm, as it poured a stream of hot sperm over her back.

Susey seemed disappointed, however, and asked why he

took it out.

"Just because I would not injure you."

Then he explained how that unless the seed was injected on the mouth of the womb, which lay at the end of the passage, there was no danger of any woman being put in the family way. And though the pleasure of both parties is lessened by the withdrawal of the prick at the moment of highest enjoyment, yet a man must be a selfish brute if on that account he would run the risk of doing such a grievous wrong to any girl whom he respected and loved.

He now placed his pendant tool in Susey's hand, and said if she would pet it a little that it would soon be in working order again.

She raised it up, and regarding it with interest, drew back the soft movable skin, and uncovered its rosy head.

"Kiss it Susey," I said bending her down.

She kissed the end of his prick, as she gently worked it up and down. Then as it gradually stiffened she let its head pass into her mouth, while her roving hands wandered over his bottom and balls.

Then he laid her back that he might inspect and kiss her pretty love chink.

"Is not this soft red hair very nice?" I said, passing my hand over her swelling mound.

"Yes it is exceedingly nice and exciting," and he buried his mouth in the pouting slit, while I caressed his prick and balls.

Rising up, he presented his prick, which had now regained its former size and strength, and asked, "Which of you will take it in?"

Susey said, "Fuck May, Mr. T——. I would so like to put your prick into her cunt, and see you fuck her."

He leaned over me as I lay back on the bed, and Susey, looking up between his legs, popped his tool into my cunt, and held his balls as he pushed it up.

Then, at his request, she laid down beside me, with her thighs up, and her pretty little cunt open before him. He leaned over and kissed it, at the same time softly working his prick in and out of my cunt, and not being so hot as before, he was able to prolong the pleasant exercise. After a minute or two he stopped and said, "I must take it out now, as I feel it coming. Hold it in your hand Susey, and you will soon see what a man's seed is like."

She held it over my belly, while he pressed his balls against my cunt. And the white seed, like fluid starch, spouted in spurts from his excited tool.

"Oh! isn't it funny," she said, stooping down, and touching with her lips the tip of his prick, when a fresh spurt darted into her mouth.

"Oh! there is very little taste. Will it do me any harm in my mouth?"

"None whatever, not even if you swallowed it all, indeed, it is considered most invigorating."

He told us afterwards how greatly he enjoyed seeing us playing together, and especially doing our pee, for, he added, nothing excites a man so much as seeing a woman doing her pee, the water streaming out of her hairy chink is most suggestive of love's delights.

We spent many nights after this when we sported and fucked in every possible way. His great delight was to have one of us sucking his prick and tickling his bottom, while he sucked and frigged the cunt of the other. He loved to make us spend in his mouth, at the same time that we swallowed his seed.

We let him fuck us in our bottoms too.

He said this gave him great pleasure, for our bottom-holes were smaller and tighter than our cunts. We did not like it so well, but we were so fond of him we could not refuse.

Mr. T—— often lent us pictures that were a great source of amusement. Among others, a set of scenes between a handsome white girl and a negro. In the first he is sitting on a chair, playing the banjo, his trousers open, and his great black tool sticking out. She has her eyes fixed on it, while she holds up her dress, and points to a most voluptuous cunt between a pair of widely extended fat thighs, as much as to say, "Look here, Sambo, here is a place that will soon take the stiffness out of your prick."

In the next behold him on his knees, between her thighs, holding open the thick furry lips of her cunt, while with his tongue he licks round the clitoris, and the red chink below it, muttering, "Oh, sweet cunt! how I lub to taste you, to suck you, and to fuck you."

In the next she is seen stooping forward, with the full orbs of her snowy bottom naked before him. With one hand he pats those delicious prominencies. With the other he directs his prick, now larger than ever, into her cunt.

It seems to quiver with delight, as the organ of bliss penetrated its soft folds.

Now Sambo, work your active bottom; drive home your noble tool, and make this willing fair one feel the vast pleasure that can be given by the sturdy prick of the despised negro.

CHAPTER II.

When vacation came, and the school broke up, I returned home to my father, who was a widower. And Susey went to keep house for her bachelor uncle in Scotland.

We promised to keep up a regular correspondence, and to write a full account to each other of everything interesting.

I felt very lonely after Susey had gone, and missed Mr. T—— more than I could tell.

My cunt demanded a large share of my attention. I did not know what to do with it. In vain I looked at it in the glass, I combed it, I petted it, I frigged it with my finger, I poked it with a candle until I spent, but it was a poor substitute, I panted for that reality.

About this time I noticed Tom, the gardener's son, a lad of eighteen. He was always eager to work in my garden, and never seemed so happy as when I commended him.

One morning I was sitting in the summer-house when he returned from his breakfast.

Not seeing me he came to a corner near the summer-house, and, taking out his prick, began to make water. I could see it through the leaves as he held it in his hand. It was a large, strong-looking prick, and I feasted my eyes on its fair proportions. He seemed in no hurry to put it up, but looked at it as he drew back the skin, making its red head swell and bound in his hand. Then, with difficulty, he forced it into its usual hiding place, and went to his work.

The sight of this prick set my cunt on fire, and I resolved to get possession of it if I could.

I returned to my room, and taking off my drawers, carefully washed and dressed my cunt.

Then going back to the garden I called Tom, and told him to set up the ladder against the pear tree by the wall, as I wanted to see if the fruit was ripe. He held the ladder as I climbed up. He was just below me, and as I moved my legs about, reaching to the pears, he must have had a full view of all I had between them.

I glanced down to observe the effect. His face was flushed, and he was gazing up with all his eyes.

"Take care, Miss, or your will fall."

"No fear, Tom," I replied, stretching out to one side, when my foot slipped, and I came sliding down, just over him, so that his head passed up between my thighs.

He caught me in his arms, and as he held me for a moment I felt him kiss my cunt.

"Oh, Miss, are you hurt?"

"Not much, only a little stunned. Carry me into the summer-house."

He took me in his arms, his hand still resting on my naked bottom, and laid me on a seat.

"Shall I call anyone, Miss? You seem very faint."

"No Tom. I shall be all right in a few mintues; it is only my knee."

I lay on my back with one leg up. He was kneeling on the ground at my side. I saw him peeping up under my dress.

"Is it here, Miss?" Putting his hand on my knee, "May I rub it?"

"Yes Tom, thank you, that makes it better."

He rubbed my knee, he touched my thigh above the stocking, he moved his hand gradually higher and higher, until at last he slightly touched the hair on my cunt. He looked up at my face. I lay with my eyes closed.

He grew bolder, he pressed the lips, he felt the chink between, he rubbed the clitoris.

"Tom, where are you putting your hand?" I said, in a languid tone.

"Oh Miss, I can't help it. You are so beautiful."

He convulsively grasped my cunt, and pushed his fingers into its glowing slit.

"Tom, I cannot allow this, let me up."

"Darling Miss May, don't be angry."

He forced his head under my clothes, and rapturously kissed

143

my cunt.

I trembled with delight as I felt the touch of his lips, and the soft probing of his tongue, yet for appearance' sake, I cried, "For shame, Tom, let me up, you are making me very angry."

I raised myself on my elbow, and saw that his prick was out and standing in fine condition.

"Tom, how dare you expose yourself in that manner. Go away."

"Miss May, I can't help it, indeed I can't."

He still kept his hand on my cunt, opening and closing the lips, and pinching the clitoris.

He drew me across the wide seat, and getting in between my thighs, pushed the head of his prick against the lips of my cunt.

"Sweet Miss May, do let me put it in, oh do."

"No Tom, I won't allow it. Let me up now, perhaps I may some other time."

He pushed again, the head entered, it passed up, the whole prick was in, it filled my cunt.

My hungry cunt, with what eagerness it sucked in a morsel so delicious! Oh! there is nothing to be compared to a standing prick for gratifying a girl who knows and understands the supreme delights of fucking.

So I lay back and let him work away.

"Tom, what are you doing?"

"I am only—fucking—fucking your cunt—Miss May. Oh! how good you are—ain't that nice!" he said, as he drove up his prick with most thrilling effect.

"It is, dear Tom, press up to my heart."

"Do you like my fucking you, Miss?"

"Yes, Tom, you have a very nice prick, but take care or you may do me harm."

The dear fellow understood me, and just before he spent drew out his prick. I took it in my hand, and held it while it poured forth a torrent of love's juice.

I need not say that after this many happy love scenes were enacted in the summer-house.

Tom proved very docile and prudent. He had a wonderful prick, always ready for its work, and eager for a fuck. He knew well how it use it with effect, and I soon found that he was no tyro in the art of love

He told me many curious things; among others, that papa was in the habit of fucking our milk-maid Sarah in the hay-loft. It was she herself told him, for he had been the first to open her maiden channel.

He offered to place me in a position where I could safely witness all that passed between them.

"Meet me early to-morrow morning. For it is after Sarah brings in the milk, and while Robert the groom is at his breakfast, that the master comes out."

So the next morning Tom conducted me to the hay-loft. He covered himself and me lightly with the hay.

We had not long to wait, for we soon heard papa talking in a low voice to Sarah as they came up the ladder.

They came down near us.

Papa then said: "Take him out, Sarah, I have been longing for a fuck all night."

She unbuttoned his trousers and drew out his prick. It was in good order, with a fine large ruby head.

The sight of my father's prick had a curious effect on me. At first I did not like to look at it, but at length the amorous feeling overpowered every other; and I almost envied Sarah as she held it admiringly in her hand, slowly moving it up and down. Then she took out his balls, and putting her hand underneath pushed it on to his bottom.

He had meanwhile pulled up her coats, and uncovered a fine thick-lipped cunt, which pouted in fleshy luxuriance.

"What a splendid affair you have, Sarah! It is the most lascivious cunt I ever looked at. Now tell me, who fucked you last?"

"La, sir, why do you ask me that?"

"Just because it excites me more to hear you tell. You know I don't care who fucks you, provided you hide nothing from me, and keep yourself from harm. Did not Robert fuck you last evening? Your face was so red when I met you after leaving him."

"Well, to tell the truth, sir, he did."

"Tell me how it happened."

"I went into the stable to borrow a lantern, he caught me in his arms and kissed me. Then he forced me back on a heap of straw, pushed his hand under my petticoats, and got hold of my cunt. I scolded him, and boxed his ears. He did not

145

mind, but squeezing in between my thighs, he thrust his big tool into my cunt, and fucked me like mad."

"Has he a big tool, Sarah?"

"Yes, it is very big and strong, but he does not use it so nicely as you do, he is always in too great a hurry."

Papa now got over her, she held his prick, and with her hand directed it into her cunt. He pushed it slowly up until his balls pressed her bottom. She grasped his buttocks, and vigorously heaved up to meet every thrust he gave, saying at every heave, "Dear sir, oh, how nice—push it in—drive it home—that's the way—how your prick fills my cunt—fuck me fast—fuck me hard."

I was leaning forward on the hay, and Tom over me, his prick and balls resting on my naked bottom; but as soon as papa commenced fucking Sarah, he lodged his prick in my cunt.

He then timed his strokes, so that each time papa pushed I felt Tom's prick driving up my cunt, and his hair tickling my bum.

I spread my thighs and raised my bottom, Tom suddenly drew out his prick, and holding open the cheeks of my bottom, popped it in there. As it was well moistened with the juice of my cunt, it slipped in easily. I dared not speak, so had to let him have his own way.

He pushed it home, and bending his arms round my hips he frigged my cunt. After a few strokes, which were far from disagreeable, he administered a warm and soothing enema, just as papa with a grunt of satisfaction poured his libation at the shrine of Sarah's cunt.

He then got up and went away, after telling her to remain until he was out of the yard.

He had not gone many minutes when Robert popped up his head.

"Holloa, Sarah, so master has been just oiling your notch. I heard him fucking you, and all you said too. And now I'll have my revenge."

He seized her in his arms, threw her on the hay, and pitched her clothes over her head.

She struggled and kicked her legs about in the air, but Robert held her down while he gloated over her wriggling bum and inflamed cunt. It looked very red and open, while the rich juices of her previous fuck trickled down her bottom.

"So you say master fucks better than I do, and that I am always in too great a hurry. Well, I will be slow enough now."

He took out his prick, and held it in his hand, while he opened the lips of her cunt.

It was the largest prick I ever saw, and had a tremendous head. I was curious to see how she could take it in. He pushed it against her cunt. She plunged about.

"Be quiet," he shouted, giving her a slap on the bottom. "Keep your arse quiet, I say, and mind your fucking."

He forced the head in, and, to my surprise, it passed easily in. The huge prick must have filled her belly. He grasped the cheeks of her bottom on each side, and held her up, as he plunged his great prick with wonderful force in and out of her smoking gap.

I had seen many a fuck, but never a fuck like this. I admired the wonderful size and strength of Robert's prick, and could not repress a longing for a taste of its prowess.

Tom too was greatly excited by the scene, and fucked me in his best style. But it was the idea of Robert's prick that filled my mind.

The next afternoon, drawn by an irresistible attraction, I went into the stable.

"Robert, I have come to look after my mare, I think she wants to be clipped," and I stepped up.

"Take care, Miss," he said, putting his hand on my shoulder, "she is very restive just now."

"Oh, I am not afraid," and I began to pat her.

He made some kind of noise that caused her, I think, to plunge and kick

"I told you so, Miss," he said, passing his hand down over my bosom, and drawing me towards him. "It is a mercy you were not killed." And he pressed me in his arms.

"Robert, let me go—where are you drawing me—you will make me fall. Oh! what do you mean—don't push your knees there—don't attempt to raise my dress. Robert, what are you about—I won't let you—take it away—you must not do it—Oh! oh!!—you are hurting me—Oh, my! what are you pushing in—yes, I do feel it—hold me in your arms—yes, I like that—you may fuck me, Robert, as hard as you like."

The monstrous prick was in my cunt. I felt it everywhere. He grasped my buttocks. He lifted me up. As he arose I clasped my arms round his neck, and crossed my legs over his back. He carried me around the stable, with his prick still embedded in my cunt. It seemed to penetrate to my very heart. Every nerve within me thrilled with rapture, as he shot into my vitals a stream of gushing sperm.

It was the first time I had ever received into my cunt the seed of man, and the feeling was intensely delicious.

"What have you done Robert? Perhaps you have ruined me for life."

"Not at all, Miss, look here," and he showed me a large syringe, "and there happens to be warm water in this bucket. Let me syringe your cunt at once, it will remove all danger."

I lay back with my thighs widely extended, while he poured such a flood of water into my cunt as must have washed out every trace.

Robert then wiped and kissed it, after which he knelt by my side, and presented before me his prick once more in splendid condition.

"What a great fellow you have, Robert," I said as I chafed it in my hand, and uncovered its rosy head. I kissed it, and with difficulty took part of it in my mouth.

"Oh, Miss May, you are very good, and you have the sweetest cunt I ever fucked, may I put it in again?"

"Not this time, Robert, I would rather pet this fine fellow, while you are tickling my cunt."

So keeping its glowing head in my mouth, with one hand I frigged the shaft, and with the other stirred his balls and touched his bottom, while he was equally busy about my seat of pleasure, deliciously frigging with his fingers each sensitive orifice.

And just as I felt my cunt flooded with love's effusion, he shot into my mouth such a torrent of seed that I could not swallow it fast enough, and it squirted out on each side of my mouth. It was pungent and pleasant to the taste.

Before I left him he swore on his oath never to speak of what had just happened, and he proved loyal and true.

I had now two esquires both able and willing to gratify me at any time, or in any way. And although I soon found out more of papa's secret amours, yet I myself exercised the greatest care and circumspection.

A few days after this adventure papa told me that as he

considered I must be very lonely so much by myself, he had asked a young lady named Kate L—— to come and stay with us for some time.

In due course she arrived. She was a nice, pleasing girl, with dark hair and eyes, and three years older than I was. I found her amiable and obliging, and ready to enter into my plans and share in my amusements.

Papa paid her particular attention, and I observed she did not seem at all averse.

They were often alone together, and I guessed something was going on, but she never told me anything.

Her bedroom was separated from mine by a bathroom, into which both our rooms opened.

One night, when we went upstairs, I sat for some time with her, and after bidding her good night, I passed through the bathroom, leaving the doors slightly opened. When I had undressed I put out my candle, and sat by the fire to warm my feet before going to bed.

I had not sat long when my curiosity was excited by hearing whispering in Kate's room.

I crept softly to the open door and listened.

"Oh, sir, why have you come into my bed?"

"Because I am so fond of you, my darling."

"If you were really fond of me you would not come to me in this way—don't—I pray you leave me—oh, my!—how can you be so nasty—take your hand off me—I don't like it —no, it is not nice—let my hands go—I won't hold it—I won't move it up and down—don't separate my thighs with your knee—what are you getting over me for? What are you pushing into me?"

"My prick, darling Kate. There, don't struggle, my pet, let it in, don't be frightened, I won't harm you in any way. Open your thighs, that's the sweet girl. Now I'll push it in as gently as possible. There, it is in, it is all the way up."

Then the bed began to creak, and the clothes to rustle.

"Put your arms around me, my love. Heave up your dainty little bottom. That's right. Do you know what doing this is called?"

"No sir."

"It is called fucking. Isn't fucking very pleasant?"

"Yes, it is now. Do I heave up right?"

"My darling, you heave as if you had been fucking all your life. Pinch my bottom. May I pinch yours?"

"Yes, as hard as you like."

"Now place your hand here. Hold my prick. Hold it tight. Oh! there it comes."

And rolling off her he lay panting at her side.

I felt greatly excited, and crept into the room, close up to the bed. I heard them kissing.

"Did I hurt you, my love?"

"You did a little at first, but when your prick was well in, and you commenced fucking, there was no feeling but pleasure. Would you like me to pet your prick now?"

"I would, darling, rub it up and down, this way, put your other hand on the balls, move your fingers further back, still further, there."

"Have you much feeling there?"

"Yes, there is great feeling behind the balls; don't you feel the root of the prick extending back to the little hole? That's a dear girl, the touch of your finger there is delicious. Push it in a little, my sweet pet. Kate, did you ever look at May's cunt?"

"Yes, I have seen it when she was in the bath; it looks well covered with hair."

"I am sure if you made free with her you would have great fun together, for, unless I am greatly mistaken, she has a very randy disposition. Promise to try to-morrow night, and tell me next day all that you have succeeded in finding out."

She promised to carry out his wishes.

"But now that you have worked up my prick we must have another fuck. Lie over me this time."

I heard her getting over him.

"Now it's in, heave away my love. You must do all the fucking yourself."

She panted as she worked her nimble bottom up and down over him.

"Do you like it this way, my love?"

"Yes, as a variety, but I like better to have you lying over me, and pushing in your prick."

He now prepared to leave, and I started for my own room, and was soon fast asleep.

I had several amorous dreams that night. I thought that

Robert was fucking me in the loft, when papa came behind, pulled him off, and thrust his own prick into my cunt, and fucked me most delightfully. In my dream I felt no surprise at papa's fucking me; on the contrary, the idea seemed to add greatly to my enjoyment.

The next evening Kate offered to sleep with me. I could not repress a smile as I consented.

When we were undressing Kate said: "I would like to see you quite naked, May. You know we girls need not be ashamed of one another, and I will set the example."

She threw off her shift and stood before me, then pointing to my cunt she remarked that I had a great deal of hair there.

I replied that her dark hair was prettier, for it set off the whiteness of her skin.

She put her hand on my cunt, and asked me to let her feel it, "and you may feel mine if you like."

She touched the clitoris, and passing her finger down the slit pushed it up the passage, and said:

"Dear May, you are very open, were you always as open as you are now?"

"No, I was not; but are not you very open too?"

She smiled as she said: "May, if you will give me your full confidence I will promise you mine."

"Agreed," said I.

"Did you ever see what a man has here?"

"I did, did you?"

"Yes, do you know what it is called?"

"I have heard it called a prick, is that it?"

"It is. Had you ever a prick in here?"

"I have Kate, haven't you?"

"Yes, dear. Now tell me how it happened, and I'll tell you about myself afterwards."

I related my adventure with Mr. T——, and how he was so fond of kissing and sucking my cunt.

"Would you like me to kiss it?"

"I would, dear Kate, and I'll kiss yours too."

"Well, lean back, lift your legs, open your thighs as widely as you can. There, do you like that?" Holding my buttocks with her hands she sucked my cunt with great ardour, rolling her tongue round and round, and thrusting it up the passage

After enjoying it for a while I said, "It is my turn now dear Kate, let me pet and kiss your sweet cunt, while you are giving me the account you promised."

I sat on a stool between her thighs, and with my mouth buried in her open cunt, listened to her narrative

---

CHAPTER III.
KATE'S NARRATIVE.

You know I am a native of the West Indies. I was born in Santa Cruz, where my father had a plantation, and lots of slaves.

The little boys and girls were naked until they were eight or nine years old: I remember being greatly struck with the fine little cocks of the boys, and wondered why they differed so from girls.

The son of our overseer was just my age, about ten. He was a smart intelligent boy, and we used to play together. His name was Joe.

One day I caught him piddling and looking at his cock. I laughed and told him he ought to cut it off, it was so ugly.

He said he would be sorry for he would much rather be a man than a woman, "and when I grow to be a man," he said, "this will grow big."

"How do you know?" I said, putting my hand on it.

"Because I have often seen men naked. Do you know what a man calls it?"

"No. What?"

"He calls it a prick."

"Oh?"

"And do you know what he does with it?"

"He piddles with it, I suppose, like yourself."

"Ah!" he said, looking very sly, "he does more than that with it."

"What?"

"He can put it into a woman between her legs, in that queer little slit you girls have."

"There's no room for it there," I said.

"Yes there is; I'll show you if you'll let me, may I?" he said, lifting my frock.

"You may, just for a minute."

He put his fingers into my cunt and felt about for the opening. At last he found it, and, to my surprise, pushed his forefinger up.

"Stop," I cried, "that hurts."

"I won't hurt you bye-and-bye," he said, with his sly look

"How, what do you mean?"

"I'll tell you, but mind, it's a great secret. You know Jim who has the cat and flogs the slaves when they misbehave. Well, when the women are sent, he flogs their backs; but when girls are sent he flogs their bottoms. I was near the place when a fine plump girl came from your papa with a note, which I saw afterwards. It had only these words: 'Give this girl twelve lashes.—E. L.'

"Jim brought her in and shut the door but I stole round to a window on the other side and peeped in. He had her kneel on a bench and tied her hands to the block. Then he threw up her petticoat, uncovering her shining black bum, and took out his cat.

"He said: 'Be quiet, Norry. If you let me have my will of you I won't hurt you, but if you won't I'll give it you.'

"He opened his pantaloons and out started, oh! such a big one, it would have frightened you as he pushed it against her bottom. She cried more than ever.

"He brought down the cat with a smart stinging blow on her bottom.

"She jumped and yelled.

"'Be quiet now or you'll get more.'

"She stopped, while he separated her legs as widely as he could. Then stooping, he looked up into her slit, which he kept open with his fingers. I could see that it was very red inside, had plenty of black woolly hair on it.

"Then he put in the head of his prick, and giving a great push, it went in every bit of it. Then he withdrew it out all wet and red looking, and putting his arms round her hips he went on pushing in and out with all his might.

"She did not mind but only poked out her bottom as if to get more of it.

"Then he stopped suddenly, and pressed in hard against her.

"After which he untied her, and giving her a kiss, sent her away."

"That's very odd Joe. It must have hurt her very much."

"Indeed it didn't. She liked it beyond anything. I know it by the way she stuck out her bottom. Will you just try and you'll feel how pleasant it is."

My amorous feelings were aroused, so I did not object to his having a trial.

I kneeled on the seat, as he told me, and jutted out my bottom.

He tried to get his cock into my slit, but failed. I put down my hand and kept the lips open, but whether from my immaturity or his inexperience, he could not succeed.

A few days afterwards he came running up to me in great glee, crying out: "I can do it now, Katie, I can do it now!"

"Stop your noise. What do you mean?"

"Stay, Katie, and I will tell you. You know father and I live in the cottage. He has, however, generally one or two of the slave girls with him in the evening. They like to come to him for they get plenty of rum, and are sure of a half holiday next day.

"He sends me to bed and then produces the rum, sugar and water. Last night he had three with him. He sent me off to bed as usual, but I hid behind the door.

"They soon became very merry over the drink and capered about in style. He threw up their petticoats, slapping their bottoms and tickled their cunts, while they pulled out his prick and handled his balls. Then he made them undress and chased them naked around the room. Whenever he caught one, he felt her cunt, and making her kneel would stick his prick into it from behind while the others tickled his balls and bottom. In the midst of the fun, one of them suddenly opened the door, and spying on me, seized me, and dragging me into the room, cried out: 'Oh, here's massa Joe playing bo-peep. What shall we do with him?'

" 'Let's strip him,' cried another, 'and we will make him fuck Fanny. She is the youngest and her cunt will fit his little prick best.'

"My father only laughed and said: 'All right, he'll be man enough for any of you some of these days.'

"So I was stripped, nothing loath, and placed over Fanny, who was lying on the floor. She had her legs wide apart and with her fingers kept the lips of her cunt open while one of the others, after kissing and sucking my little cock, pushed it in. Then they clapped my bottom, and sat around to watch the performance.

"Oh, Katie, you can't think how easy my prick slipped into her cunt. And I felt it growing bigger when it got in; she was so hot inside. She then hugged me in her arms and jerked up her bottom, while I worked and pushed as I had seen father do until the nice warm feeling came and I nearly fainted with pleasure.

"I was then glad to get away and creep off to bed, for I was tired and sleepy.

"Look at it, Katie, isn't it larger and stronger than before?"

He held it in his hand and drew back the skin until its head stood up round and red as a cherry.

"Put your hand on it, Katie. Feel how firm it is!"

I took it in my hand and rubbed it up and down.

"Yes, Joe, it is larger and stronger. You may put it in if you like."

He laid me back, lifted my dress and looked at and felt my cunt.

"Yours is much prettier and nicer than the black girl's, Katie. These soft round white lips are beautiful. Hold them open like a dear girl while I push it in."

I put my hands down and opening the lips with one while with the other I directed the head of his prick to the right spot and told him to push. He did so. It entered. He pushed harder. It got in more and more until it was all enclosed and I felt its head far back.

Oh, sweet sensation! Nothing can exceed the pleasure of feeling one's cunt for the first time filled up with a throbbing, heaving prick!

His eyes sparkled and his breath came hard and fast as I hugged him in my arms, and told him to push in his prick and fuck me very well.

Having now ascertained for ourselves the wondrous power we each possessed of conferring pleasure on the other, our play always turned on the practice and enjoyment of love.

We were never tired of examining and petting each other's privates.

And our senses being now fully aroused, we were always on the watch to enlarge our experience of the ways and means of enjoyment.

My father had several slaves almost white, and most of

155

them good-looking. These were all retained in the house and never sent into the fields.

One pretty little girl named Nina was assigned to me as my waiting-maid. She always attended me in my bath, and used to dry me when I came out. She was particularly attentive to my little slit, on which the hair was just beginning to grow. She used to perfume it, and comb it, and kiss it.

"You have a beautiful cunt, Missy, the sight of it would set any young fellow wild!"

"I suppose it is much the same as other girls', your own for instance. Show it to me, Nina."

She lifted her dress, and opening her thighs, gave me a full view of her cunt. It was a pretty little mouth, with a full rosebud clitoris, and the lips covered with brown silky hair. I put my hand on it, and pushing up my finger, said: "Did this ever set any young fellow wild?"

"Oh, Missy, you must not ask me such questions, or I will have to tell you lies."

"Nina, if you want me to be your friend you will tell me everything. But this will do for the present."

My father was in the habit of walking in the garden after sunset when it was nearly dark, to smoke his cigar, and I found out that he always had with him one or the other of the white slaves.

One night I missed Nina, and guessing where she was, I threw on my shawl and went out softly into the garden. I heard voices in a sheltered walk, and as it was almost dark, I was able to get within range of hearing without being seen.

"Now, Nina, be kind and you'll be my pet, and I will give you all sorts of pretty things—there, let me feel it, that's a sweet girl, open your legs more, lean against this tree, hold up your dress, give me your hand, place it here, close your fingers round it. That's the way. You have a dear little cunt, very fat and plump. But I wonder you have much hair on it. How old are you, Nina?"

"Just fifteen, sir."

"Now then, press out in front. Hold my prick, while I push it—there it's in—put your arms round me—press my bottom. How do you like the feel of my prick in your cunt?"

"It feels very nice, push it in more."

I heard them kissing and panting as they shoved together, and then they rested in each other's arms.

She soon left him, after promising to go out at that same hour that day every week.

I often followed him out now, and found he always had one of the slave girls with him.

I then learned all the terms and ways of enjoyment, for he was fond of variety, and loved to make them talk, and say all manner of words while he fucked them. And I was astonished to hear how freely they spoke of pricks, cunts, arses, frigging, fucking, pissing, etc.

Joe had been sent to school and my cunt, not having been entered for a long time, was in an aggravated state of longing and desire.

So, when Nina's turn came next, the thought flashed upon me, why not personate her for one occasion.

I was about her height and size, and my cunt was now pretty well furnished with hair. So when the hour came, I set her to a task which would occupy her for some time, and said I was in a hurry to have it done.

Then, going out in the dark I quietly strolled up the walk. Someone met me, put his arm round me, and pushed his knee in between my thighs.

"How is your sweet cunt tonight?"

I said nothing but only pressed against him as he lifted my dress and felt my cunt.

Moving his finger about, he said: "It's very hot and juicy tonight. I am sure it is longing for a fuck. Put your hand here, my love."

I felt his firm upstanding prick. I moved the loose skin up and down as Joe had taught me. I put my other hand below and felt the two soft balls in their hairy bag.

"Take it in your mouth, dear, for a moment."

I had gone too far to recede now, so I stooped and sucked its glowing head while I tickled him behind the balls.

"Oh, Nina, that's delicious! Now lie back on this moss bank, raise your legs, open your dress, that I may press your soft bubbies, while my prick is in your cunt."

He knelt between my uplifted thighs. He leaned over me. He opened the lips of my cunt. He introduced his prick. He moulded my breasts. He kissed me and darted his tongue into my mouth.

"Say you like it, Nina, my love!"

"Oh, yes dear sir!" I whispered heaving up my bottom. "I

feel your prick in my cunt—fucking—fucking—oh! so—deliciously!"

The rapturous feeling increased. He pushed and panted: I heaved and gasped: "Oh, yes, push, fuck, oh! oh! oh!"

He lay over me, his face on my shoulder and his prick buried in my cunt.

After a while he said: "I don't know how it is, Nina, but I never enjoyed fucking you so much before, your cunt closes on my prick with such a hot compression, and you nipped the head of my prick when I drove it home as you never did before, and which only a few women can do. Oh! there! I feel it now!"

(Here I interrupted Kate by asking: "What do you mean by nipping the head of his prick?"

"Well, my dear, I'll teach you. When you feel the entire prick driven in as far as it can go, draw up your bottom inside, as hard as you can. If you do it right you will squeeze the head of the prick as it rests on the mouth of your womb. Try it now while I have my finger in. Yes, that's the way."

"Well, go on, what did he say next?")

He asked me: "Is Miss Kate kind to you?"

"She is," I whispered in reply.

"Don't you attend her in the bath?"

"Yes."

"Does she let you see her cunt?"

"Yes, I dry it and sometimes kiss it."

"Is it a nice little cunt?"

"Very nice."

"Do you think she has any longing to have it fucked?"

"I am sure she has, it is always red and hot."

"I guessed as much. Indeed, I often think of it when I observe her swelling hips. How I would enjoy fucking her, if I could only do it without letting her know who it was."

"Perhaps I could manage it for you. Come to my bed tomorrow night and I'll prevail on her to take my place. I'll tell her I expect a young fellow who will take her for me, and give her the greatest pleasure but without doing her any harm. If you find the door of my room unlocked you will know I succeeded."

Next evening, papa did not go out at all and I saw he was regarding me with a peculiar look in his eyes. He was also more affectionate and made me sit on his knee when I was bidding him good-night and he pressed my bottom and thighs in the warmest way.

Nina readily agreed to my taking her place for the night when I told her I had been restless of late and thought a change of my bed would do me good.

About midnight someone entered the room and felt his way to where he heard me breathing. He quietly put off his clothes, and slipped into bed. He put his arm over me and felt my cunt. He opened the lips and rubbed about the clitoris and then tried to push his finger up.

I held his hand. "Oh, you hurt me!"

"Why, you are not my Nina at all."

"No, I am only Nina's friend."

"Well, whoever you are, you have a sweet cunt. Put your hand on this, it won't hurt you."

"But it will do me harm."

"No, trust me, my pet, I won't harm you."

He then got over me and began to push his prick against my cunt.

"Oh, no, I can't, I am afraid. Oh, pray don't, it is too big!"

I held him by the hips and pushed him back.

"I can't bear it—it will kill me!"

Every time he pushed the head of his prick at the en trance, I shrank from him.

He begged me. He prayed me just to let it in and he would be so very gentle.

He got it in a little way inside the entrance.

"Oh, push easily, or you'll kill me. Oh! Oh!"

"There, now—it is quite in. My precious I shall not hurt you any more."

He moved his prick very slowly in and out, in and out.

I began to heave and twist.

"Darling, this is exquisite! Your cunt is delightfully tight, and its soft pressure most delicious. Put your arms round me, my love! I only once before had such a fuck as this."

I pressed him in my arms, thrust up my bottom to meet every thrust of his prick. I raised my thighs and crossed my legs on his back.

He ran his prick with delightful friction in and out of my throbbing, heaving, panting cunt. I felt a soft hand on my bottom and soft fingers playing about my cunt. I knew they were Nina's, I did not mind. I was intoxicated with pleasure. I squeezed in my bottom to nip his prick.

"Oh! That's grand, who taught you that sweet trick—do it again. Oh! That's splendid!"

Nina got into the bed and pressed against his bottom.

"Oh, Nina you are just in time. Let me get on you that I may spend in your cunt."

He drew out his prick, saying to me: "You know I promised not to harm you; but Nina does not mind the risk for she knows she will be well taken care of. Let us get outside the clothes and take off everything, the night is so warm."

He then got between her uplifted thighs, and resting on her breast, told me to put it in.

I felt her cunt, it was very hot and flowing. I took his prick and rubbed its throbbing head between the soft lips, placed it at the entrance. He pushed, it passed in. I went behind him and holding him around the hips rubbed my cunt against his bottom while he fucked.

He discharged immediately and soon afterwards he bid us good-night and went away.

Nina begged me to excuse her. She said she heard all that passed and got so excited that she could not help coming in to us.

I asked: "Did papa know who your friend was?"

She said she was not certain but thought he did.

There was something peculiar about papa's manner the next morning. He put his arms around me several times, called me his sweet girl, his darling pet. He told me he was making arrangements to send me to England, to have my education completed there. He told me that he had taken my passage in a sugar-brig which was to start in a few days, and which was commanded by a friend of his, a Captain Lemberg, who would take good care of me.

I said I would like it very much but would be sorry to leave him and put my arms round his neck kissing him.

He enfolded me in his; he lifted me off the ground, carrying me to a sofa and laid me down. He sat by me and slipping his hand under my dress put it on my naked bottom. "My darling," he said, "let me pet you, I feel so fond of you and I won't have you long."

"Dearest papa, you may do anything you please with me, I love to give you pleasure."

He kissed me warmly, turned me on my back, lifted my dress, opened my thighs, and looked at my cunt.

"You are beautifully made here. Tell me, my darling, was it you in Nina's bed last night?"

"It was I, dearest papa; was I very wicked?"

"No, my darling, you gave me the sweetest pleasure I ever had in my life. Did you enjoy what I did to you then?"

"I did indeed, it was most delightful."

"Might I do it to you again?"

"You may, dear papa, if you like."

He drew me to the end of the sofa, made me raise my legs and open them as widely as possible. Then kneeling on the floor, he kissed my cunt. He praised its shape and colour. He opened the lips, put in his tongue and licked the inside round and round. He introduced his prick, pushing it slowly up, and fucked me most delightfully.

I tried all I could to increase and intensify his pleasure. I asked if he was enjoying it much.

"Do you like it, papa?"

"Yes, my sweet pet, your cunt is perfection itself. I envy the man who gets you for a wife."

I now ventured on a request I had long in mind.

"Dear papa, I have one thing to ask you for."

"What is it my pet? I would do anything in the world to gratify you."

"Will you give Nina her freedom and send her to England with me?"

"Surely, my pet, I will do more; if she marries with your consent and approbation I will allow you to present her with £50 dowry, and besides, you may order whatever dress she may require for the voyage."

Need I describe the response I made to these kind words, how I clung to him, how I tightened the pleasure girths within, what a glowing reception I gave to his prick as it darted into my quivering cunt, or how he grunted his satisfaction: "Oh, Katie! Oh! Katie, my pet!"

Nina was overjoyed when she heard that she was to have her freedom. She thanked me on her knees and promised to be the most faithful of servants.

Now, dearest May, I have told you more than ever I told

anyone else, because I find in you a kindred soul and I want someone to sympathize with me. Don't judge me too harshly; I was little more than a child and alone, my father has been a widower ever since I could remember. Do you love me less?

"No, dearest Kate, I love you a hundred times more for your confidence and affection; but go on and tell me about the voyage and how you first met papa."

"I will dearest; but not to-night. I am tired and sleepy. Kiss me, my love, good night."

Chapter IV.
Kate's Narrative Continued; The Voyage; Captain Lemberg and His Niece Hilda

On the next occasion that May and her friend Kate were snugly stretched in bed, their arms fondly circling one another and their hands tenderly plucking the hair of each other's cunt, they soon grew so excited that she, throwing off everything and May reversing her position, lay over her friend and gamahuched her most lovingly, Kate's tongue returning those fiery kisses of love with such interest that in a few minutes both were dissolved in a balmy emission.

As soon as they were recovered a little and more composed, May said softly: "Now, dear Katie, proceed with your most interesting and exciting narrative."

Well, when the time came, papa brought me word to board the brig, and after taking a most affectionate leave he left me in charge of Captain Lemberg and his niece, Hilda. I was delighted to have her as a companion for she was a merry, spritely girl, and had made the voyage before.

I had a little cabin adjoining hers and opening on the salon.

Nina was accommodated in the forepart of the ship and was with a soldier's wife, a Mrs. S and her sister Jenny. The vessel sailed early the next morning and soon began to pitch and roll. The motion made us all sick. Nina was not able to leave her berth and Hilda was nearly as bad. As for me I never felt so bad in my life.

About noon the Captain came into my cabin. I was lying down, only half dressed and so sick that I did not care what was done to me.

He said he was so sorry to find me so bad; but that if I would allow him to prescribe for me he knew what would be sure to give relief.

I said I would take anything he gave for I could not be worse than I was.

He went out and soon returned with a tumbler of hot brandy and water. When I tasted it I said: "I cannot take this, it is too strong."

"All the better, my dear, it will do you more good. Come, trust an old sailor."

He put his arm round me and supported me while I gulped it down. Then he laid me back. It relieved the sickness but threw me into a stupor.

Before he left he arranged my dress and was very particular in setting it over my breast. Seeing I did not move he passed his hand down over my stomach and pressed the mound at the bottom of my belly. Then he lightly kissed my forehead and went away.

After a short time he returned and finding me tossing about, but still in a state of stupor he softly rubbed my stomach over my chemise, bringing his hand lower and lower, until he reached my cunt. Finding I did not mind him, he passed his hands up under my chemise and boldly grasped my cunt.

"Oh, Captain," I muttered, but could say no more.

He pushed his hand between my thighs so as to feel the lips. He separated my thighs more and felt them round about. Indeed I don't know what he did, I was so stupefied, but I think he kissed it.

In the evening the sea calmed down and I felt much better.

He brought me a cup of coffee, which roused me up. He supported me with his arm while I was drinking and then stooped to kiss me. I could not refuse him my lips, he was so kind.

In a few days I recovered from the effects of my sea-sickness, and I began to feel at home in the vessel.

Hilda brought me about and showed me everything.

At the opposite side of the salon the Captain and the mate, Mr. Carle, occupied cabins corresponding to ours.

Mr. Carle was a young man, good-looking and very agreeable. He was most attentive to Hilda and did not mind me much. But the Captain was unremitting in his attentions to me. He got into the way of kissing me every night and used to squeeze my bottom when I passed near him.

With Hilda he was still more free, but then she was his niece.

In arranging my cabin I found there was a sliding panel between Hilda's cabin and mine which, when open, gave a full view either way.

The Captain generally kept the first night-watch and remained on deck until after twelve; then he would come down, take grog, and turn in.

One night I was awakened by talking in Hilda's cabin and I heard her say: "Now behave yourself, I won't have you coming this way into my cabin at night. Ah, stop, I will call out, if you don't let me alone."

"Hildy, my pet, let me, just a moment."

"No, you mustn't put your hand there—you mustn't raise my shift—you mustn't open my thighs. Oh, Uncle, do—take it away. You are a terrible man, why don't you go and fuck Kate? What would Carle say if he knew you did this to me?"

I got up, opened the panel and peeped in. Her lamp was burning. I could see that he had drawn her to the edge of her berth, over which her naked bottom projected. Her legs were raised up and resting on his arms while his large prick was darting in and out of her open cunt. I could see that she was beginning to enjoy it for she wriggled her bum and threw her arms around his neck.

"Press it, dear Uncle! You make me like it in spite of my self."

At every thrust he banged against her rump, crying. "There, there, you have it all."

Before he left I heard him talking of me and telling her to show me some books and pictures.

The next day, coming suddenly out of my cabin I caught her sitting in Mr. Carle's lap. He had his arm round her and was kissing her. They started and blushed when they saw me and he got up and went on deck.

She then told me that they were engaged to be married at the end of the voyage. "And do you know, Kate, though I am fond of Carle I dread it."

"Why?" I asked.

"Oh, don't you know what a man does to a woman when they are in bed together?"

"No," I said, looking very innocent. "What?"

"Oh, you must know that he has something that he puts

into her stomach."

"What is it like, Hilda? Tell me about it."

"It's a thing called a prick, eight or nine inches long, with a purple head. It hangs between his legs and when it stiffens he can push it into our slits, which are called cunts, you know. Then after working it in and out, something comes out, and it makes the child."

"How queer! Did you ever see it, Hilda?"

"I have often seen pictures of it. Uncle has curious books with pictures, that tell all about it. Would you like to see it? I was looking over his books and I came upon a secret drawer which was open, and there I found them; come, I'll show them to you."

We went into his cabin and on opening the drawer saw a number of books full of coloured pictures of the most lascivious evolutions of love.

There were naked men and naked women with their cunts and pricks and bottoms displayed in every kind of attitude and position. They were frigging, sucking and fucking in all varied positions.

There were some large French prints also. One depicted a beautiful girl with her bare shoulders and legs, seated on the lap of her lover. Between her voluptuous thighs her cunt is seen delightfully gorged with his standing prick. Her arms are round his neck and her face is turned up, beaming with the satisfaction she experiences in her well-filled cunt.

Another showed a fat nun with her frock up and her breasts bare, stretched on a couch before a large mirror; she had been working a dildoe, that is, an artificial prick into her voluptuous cunt. She has obtained an emission and is now lying back in delicious languor, while two randy monks, peeping round the curtain, and beholding the luscious scene reflected in the glass, have pulled out their pricks and contend who shall be the first into her lustful orifice.

Then there was a scene in a café in Paris: a number of naked men and women dancing together. As they circle round, their pricks and cunts are presented in most exciting points of view; one is pressing the soft buttocks of his partner, while she holds with loving grasp his standing prick. Another squeezes the breasts of his beloved, while she supports his pendant balls. Another couple falls, but they so manage that he falls between her extended thighs and his eager prick soon finds lodgement in her expectant cunt. Some are lying their partners, nothing loath, upon the surrounding couches and relieving their excitement by plunging into their melting cunts. While others again regale their senses of taste and smell between the voluptuous thighs of their delighted fair ones.

These pictures excited me greatly. I had never seen anything like them before. "Oh, Hilda," I muttered as I pressed together my thighs, while she pointed out each lascivious detail.

"But we must not remain here," she said. "Let us take some of these books into your cabin and there we can observe them at our leisure."

So, taking three, we shut the drawer and made off.

When we had comfortably settled ourselves on a little sofa at the side of my cabin, we opened the first. It contained a thrilling description of a doctor's exploits with a buxom young widow. How he gained her confidence and then excited her amorous feelings, until he succeeded in raising her snowy smock and in feasting his eyes on the ripe beauties of her voluptuous form. The next depicts her standing thus at his side with her splendid cunt protruding its full rounded lips from the midst of a thick covering of crisp curling hair, while the crimson line between gives promise of a warm reception to his prick

He has put her hand on his standing prick, which she looks at with shy pleasure as she draws the skin down from its glowing red head

In the next plate she is seen lying across his lap, her beautifully rounded bottom with its milk-white globes is turned up to meet his amorous gaze. He pats the cheeks and titillates the furrow between, while his prick is luxuriating in the soft folds of her melting cunt.

In another plate she is represented as astride of him, her bottom rubbing against his belly as he leans back. By the sweet suction of her mouth she has restored his prick to vigorous life, and, as it now stands up between her widely separated thighs, she presses it warmly against the lips of her longing cunt.

"How would you like to be in her place, Kate? And to feel a fine lusty prick pressing against your cunt and then pushing up into it filling you with rapture and delight?"

"I am sure it would be very pleasant if it were the prick of one I loved "

166

"No doubt that would vastly increase the pleasure; but don't you feel when your cunt gets excited that any prick, if it were in the right condition, would give you pleasure? How does your cunt feel now? Would you mind my putting my hand on it, Kate?"

"Not in the least, Hilda, if you want to."

"Lean back, dear, open your thighs. Might I see it?"

"I have no objection."

I now became aware that the sliding panel was slightly open and though I saw something like an eye peering through the slit, I pretended to take no notice. I replied: "You may, Hilda, provided you let me see yours afterwards."

She quickly raised my petticoats, uncovering all my belly and thighs right up before the panel, which was now opened a little further. She played with my hairy turf and praised its colour. Then, separating my legs as far as possible she drew the lips apart. "You have a sweet little cunt, Kate, with a wonderful clitoris, and a deep red recess. Oh, how hot it is inside! And how it sucks and presses my finger. If I only had a prick I would like to fuck you myself." She stooped and kissed the lips and sucked the clitoris. I then got up and made her display her secret charms before the panel, which made her blush for she well knew what was there.

She had a very pretty cunt, daintily fringed with light red hair and the inside hot and juicy.

That night the Captain changed watches with Mr. Carle and before he went to our cabins made us take some of his grog. Hilda took it very freely and made me take more than I wished; in fact, when I stood up I felt quite giddy.

The Captain took me in his arms and made me sit on his knee. While I was warding off his kisses he slipped his hand under my dress and pushed it up between my thighs.

"Oh, Captain! Stop. Take your hand away—no, I won't allow it!"

"What is he doing?" Hilda asked, laughing.

"No matter, I won't allow it—stop! Oh, stop, how can you be so impudent?"

"Don't be angry, Kate, my pet. I won't harm you. Sure every pretty girl likes to have her cunt tickled. Doesn't she, Hilda?"

"Well, I don't, and I won't let you. Oh, Hilda, don't let him raise my dress—don't let him—you make me ashamed —how can you be so wicked?"

I was now stretched on my back and he over me holding my arms and stifling me with kisses.

"Hilda! What are you doing? don't let him push it in! Oh! Oh! Oh!"

Hilda with her sly cunning had trapped me. It was she that opened the lips of my cunt, pushed in the head of his prick and then held it by the roots.

At each thrust he cried: "Sweet Katie—sweet pet—you have it now—in your delicious cunt—fuck—fuck—fuck! Hold my balls Hilda! Slap my arse, slap hard!"

At every smack she gave his bottom I felt his prick rush up with increased vigour into my cunt. I began to wriggle and heave.

"Ah, little one, you like it now—ah—oh, it comes—there —there it is."

He then put himself in order and hurried on deck to take his share of the night duty.

When I stood up I could hardly walk, so Hilda supported me into my cabin and helped me to undress.

When she had settled me in my berth she kissed me and wished me good night.

I stopped her and said: "It was a shame, Hilda, to allow me to be so treated."

"Don't mind, dear," she replied, laughing. "You are nothing the worse. And if I am not much mistaken you will enjoy it better before you leave the ship. Good night."

Though I was tired yet I was too excited to be sleepy.

After a short time I heard someone open the door of Hilda's cabin.

"Oh, Carle, what do you want here at this time of the night?"

"I want you, my pet, I can't live without you."

"Sure you have me all day."

"But I want you all night, too."

"But that you can't have yet, you know."

"Why not, love, don't you trust me?"

"Wait until we are married, Carle. You will have enough of me then. Go away now, there's a dear fellow. There, you've kissed me enough already to serve for a month. Well, I will sit on your knee just for a moment, if you promise to go away at once. Ah, where is your hand stealing?"

"Let me, my pet, I am curious to know if you are as nice

here as I expected."

"And if I am not, what then?"

"Well, let me try anyway—there—open."

"Will you swear on your soul that you will marry me at the end of this voyage?"

"I will, indeed, dearest, on my soul. Thanks Hilda. Now I love you more than ever because you have confidence in me. You are very nice indeed, my sweet pet, you have a darling little pussey. Oh, how soft and warm it is. Now put your hand here and you will find something that is just made for it. Move it up and down, my love, it is all your own. Feel how strong and hot it is; it's longing to make acquaintance with its friend here. Won't you let them kiss, just to touch those loving lips?"

"Ah, Carle, it's not kind of you; you know I am so fond of you! You won't hurt me?"

"Open your legs more—there—it's in—in your sweet cunt. Darling Hilda, don't you like to feel my prick there, fucking, fucking?"

"Yes, but push gently, there's a dear."

"My love—oh, my love!—How my prick loves to fuck your sweet cunt."

Then they went on hugging and kissing for ever so long.

After a while I heard her asking questions about his prick and balls. "Now it is beginning to get large again. There, see how it has stiffened up. Would you like me to put it into my mouth and suck it?"

"Yes, my love, that would give me great pleasure. Thanks, darling Hilda, your mouth is almost equal to your cunt. That's delicious."

"But who can tell what queer places this has been in. How many girls have you had, Carle?"

"Ah, Hilda, don't be getting jealous. I have fucked, as you know, a good many girls. And if you are a wise little wife you won't object to my fucking a few more besides yourself, even after we are married. Now, let us make an agreement, love, which I am certain will tend to our mutual happiness. Give me perfect liberty and I will promise never to do anything without your knowledge and consent. I will give you the same liberty to have anyone you please and as often as you please, on the same conditions. I am satisfied we will love each other better and enjoy each other more than ever

169

when we are not tied up exclusively to each other. Do you agree?"

"Well, Carle, I don't desire any liberty myself but if it will make you happier and cause you to love me more, I agree. But, remember, the condition must be carried out."

("Just a moment, Kate! Were they married afterwards, and did they follow that agreement?"

"They were, and the last time I met them, I thought I never saw a happier or more loving couple."

"Another word: what do you think of the arrangement yourself, Kate? I ask you because Mr. T has proposed the same thing to myself, that is, if I marry him."

"Well, dear, it is hard to give an opinion. Most women like to have a man all to themselves and as a rule they are satisfied with one; but in cases where either party has led a free life before marriage, I can quite understand that such an arrangement would be expedient and wise. But you may have an opportunity of judging for yourself as your papa intends inviting them here as soon as Carle returns from his present voyage."

"Oh, that will be delightful. I am longing to see Hilda and we may have Mr. T also, for he says he can't wait any longer for me and he has written to papa. But go on, dear Kate, and tell me what happened next.")

Just this: The following day Carle told the Captain of his engagement with his niece and that he had promised to marry her as soon as they arrived in port.

The Captain replied: "All right, old fellow, I congratulate you. She is a thorough good girl and will make a jolly wife. But you may have her at once so far as I am concerned, if you sign the marriage contract in my presence, which you know has legal force in Danish law."

Carle jumped at the idea. So the contract was drawn up and signed by Hilda and himself, the Captain and I adding our names as witnesses.

"Now," said the Captain, "I pronounce you man and wife together, etc. Have at her as soon as you like, my boy! And as we have witnessed the wedding it would be only fair that we should witness the bedding too."

Carle found her in his arms and placed her on his knee. The Captain caught hold of me and moving his leg under me, said: "Kate, you will have to be my niece now." And in spite of my struggles he forced his hand up between my legs.

Carle was not slow in following his example, and soon amidst many "Ah, Carle," "Stop Charlie" our cunts were taken in full possession of by exploring hands while two standing pricks boldly upreared their rosy tips.

Finding that they were bent on enjoying us openly, we saw no use in further resistance and so let them have their way.

The Captain smiled when he saw how skillfully and lovingly Hilda caressed Carle's noble tool, and under cover of a kiss placed my fingers on his own. "Now, Carle, lay her on the locker and don't spare her maiden-trap. Kate will guide the bird into the nest and I will look on, and see fair play and no favour."

Carle laid her back and tenderly lifting her dress uncovered her belly and thighs. Then raising her legs, he spread her thighs widely apart and paused to admire her cunt, fringed with golden hair, and cosily placed himself between her luxuriant thighs. He then leaned over her so as to place his prick upon its opened lips.

"Kate, now pop it in and hold it firm."

I stooped forward and taking hold of Carle's bounding tool pushed its head into her soft recess. In doing so my bare bottom became exposed to the Captain's view.

He caught me round the hips and cried: "Oh, lovely arse!" He kissed it and I felt his warm pliant tongue playing in and about my cunt and penetrating my bottom-hole itself. Then quickly rising up he thrust his rampant prick into my cunt and fucked away all the while leaning over my back, watching Carle and crying out at every thrust: "That's the way, old fellow! Send it home—rattle your bullocks against her arse—fuck—fuck—fuck—ah, oh!" And we all fell together, our cunts overflowing with the discharge from their excited pricks.

After lying over her for a few moments Carle began to heave his bottom again and gave her the benefit of a second fuck, without taking out his prick.

This pleased the Captain greatly. He stooped over his niece and kissing her asked how she liked being fucked.

She smiled, and stretching out her hand took hold of his prick, now soft and hanging down.

Carle laughed to see her frigging her uncle's prick and went on slowly driving his own in and out of her cunt.

The Captain's prick began to stand; he pushed it towards her face. She drew it to her lips and calling me, raised my clothes and placed Carle's hand on my cunt, then looking up she said: "Now we are quits."

He kissed her and said: "Darling Hilda, you are the best and sweetest of wives, you will never regret it."

Then bending down he asked me to lean back and open my thighs. He kissed my cunt and sucked the clitoris all the while with a slow and measured stroke, fucking Hilda's cunt.

"What are you doing to Kate, Carle?"

"I am sucking her sweet cunt while I am fucking yours. And what are you doing to the Captain?"

"I am sucking his prick and squeezing yours in my cunt."

The Captain now heaved his great heavy bum and worked his prick in and out of her mouth, just as Carle with increasing vigour drove his prick in and out of her cunt. She heaved up and down, and in the height of her excitement, grasped one of the cheeks of my bottom and at every thrust of Carle's prick gave me such a squeeze that I could hardly suppress a shout.

But I felt nearly as excited as herself, for the action of Carle's lips and tongue in my cunt was almost as exciting as that of his prick in hers, while the view of his fine bottom rising and falling between her wide-spread thighs, and the Captain's tool darting in and out of her mouth, caused me fully to share in the general form of excitement.

The Captain feeling the tide of pleasure rising to the flood, cried: "Fuck her, Carle—fuck her cunt."

Carle replied: "Suck him, Hilda—suck his prick."

Whilst I, I pressed my cunt against Carle's mouth and spent on his tongue, called out the names—prick—cunt—arse—frigging—sucking—fucking—oh!

Carle went on deck and the Captain soon after tumbled into his berth. Hilda and I retired to our cabins and were soon fast asleep.

I need not tell you that after all reserve was laid aside amongst us we certainly enjoyed ourselves amazingly.

Carle and the Captain seemed to delight in fucking us turn and turn about, but everything was done openly and by general consent.

The books and pictures were freely used and we tried to act the scenes depicted or described.

The Captain would lay Hilda on her back across the table. Then, placing me over her so that her face was between my thighs while my feet rested on the floor, he would produce his prick, and Hilda looking up, would pop it into her cunt and hold it while he fucked.

Carle would be at the other side of the table between Hilda's uplifted thighs, while I, stooping forward, would take his prick and stick it into her open cunt and then handle his bottom and balls. The Captain leaning over my back would watch the operation with great interest, and, waiting until Carle's prick was all absorbed within the hairy lips, would cry:

"Now, old fellow, let us make a fair start! Draw out first, and when I say one, push."

"ONE."—The two bottoms heaved, driving the two pricks deep into the recesses of our cunts.

"TWO."—Another energetic shove, making our breasts and bellies rub together.

"THREE."—A vehement push; the Captain's belly smacked against my bottom, and Carle's balls banged against Hilda's rump.

"FOUR."—The two excited pricks rushed with delicious force into our throbbing cunts, making us bound to meet them.

"FIVE."—We felt the pricks rammed home, they seemed to reach our very hearts.

"SIX."—A flood of boiling seed burst into our cunts and filled our reservoirs so that they overflowed and the hot sperm poured out, saturating pricks, ballocks, and cunts in love's sweet juice.

The next time that Hilda and I were alone she pointed to some whipping scenes among the pictures and suggested that we should make a trial of the boasted efficacy of the birch rod in producing emotion.

"But where shall we get a rod on board ship?" I asked.

She at once replied: "Oh, I know where there is a broom without a handle. I can easily abstract some of the twigs and tie up a rod with enough for our purpose."

So, that evening, when I was in my nightdress, Hilda came into my cabin and showed me a rod which she had prepared and neatly tied with ribbon.

I was a little frightened at the sight of it and said:

"Won't it hurt?"

"Oh, it may a little at first, but when one begins to get the feel, the pain will be turned into pleasure. However, begin with me, I am not afraid"

She then placed herself on the sofa with her naked bottom up, and making me tuck up my shift, she put her arm round my hip and told me to whip away.

I touched up her beautiful white posteriors while she played with my cunt.

"You may hit harder than that, Kate," she said, wriggling her bottom about.

I began to enter into the sport and struck her so smartly that the cheeks of her bottom assumed a rosy hue like two blooming apples.

"Oh," she cried, as she rolled over, "my cunt is on fire—put your finger into it, Kate. How I would enjoy being fucked now. How I wish Carle was here."

"Well, you have your wish," he said, as he stepped in quite naked and holding in his hand his fine red-headed prick in stiff erection.

He seized her round the waist and making her stoop forward he plunged his prick into her cunt from behind.

"Stay a moment, Carle," she said. "Kate is to get her whipping now, and lest you should cover it with your hands let me tie them here."

And without asking my leave she secured my wrists and tied them firmly to the legs of the sofa, and then to keep my legs apart, she tied my ankles, too. I did not quite like my position but as I was helpless I only said:

"Remember, you must stop when I tell you."

Then she leaned forward and Carle introduced his prick into her cunt from behind.

They both laughed while she played away at my poor innocent bum. At first I tried to bear it as patiently as I could; but Carle became more energetic in his strokes, and she imported more force to her blows. At last I said: "I say—Hilda —stop! Hilda, you wretch, what do you mean? You cruel girl let me up, you are torturing me!"

My whole bottom felt in a flame. I made frantic efforts to release my hands and I began to sob. Just then she fell forward, and Carle pressing against her bottom discharged into her cunt. Then, coming to me, she untied my hands and laying her cheek against mine, said: "Forgive me, dearest

174

Kate, I was so excited. I am just burning!"

"Oh, Hilda, you cruel girl, how could you? Oh, I am so hot; I am just burning!"

"Where are you so hot, darling Kate?"

And I felt a hand slip up between my thighs and press the lips of my cunt. Looking up I saw the Captain's good-humoured cheery face.

"Never mind, Kate, we will punish her for this. Let me give you what relief I can."

Then, gently separating my thighs he pushed in his prick while Hilda kissed away my tears. The soft head of his prick had a most soothing effect on the terribly excited folds of my cunt and as it gradually passed up I forgot the pain of the whipping in the intensely amorous excitement I now experienced. I never felt anything more delicious than the sweet friction of the Captain's cock in my fevered cunt; it made every nerve thrill again with pleasure.

"Does not that repay you?" Hilda whispered.

"Oh, yes," I replied. "Push it in; drive it home, fuck me—fuck me. Oh, fuck—fuck—fuck!"

The Captain now declared that Hilda ought to be well whipped for her cruel treatment of my poor bottom.

"Very well," said Carle, "but as I am the real offender I will bear it in her place."

So putting the rod into my hand he leaned over the berth and stuck out his great fleshy rump, while Hilda sat below him, holding his prick and sucking it in her mouth.

"Now, Kate," said the Captain, "lay it on strongly; don't spare his impudent backside, hit him, hit him hard! Don't mind, he used to be flogged every day at school!"

I whipped away and soon his bottom began to glow, his balls were tightened up and his prick swelled and stiffened. He heaved gently so as to work it in and out of her mouth and then with a tremendous "Oh!" he spurted his seed down her throat.

Now, sweet May, that must do for the present. Good night, my love, good night.

———————

Before I resume Kate's narrative I must tell something that happened to myself the following night.

Kate was later than usual in coming and when she did I was in bed, my lamp out and the room quite dark. When she got into bed she put her hand on my cunt, and asked if I had ever any longing for a prick now. I told her I had but that I was waiting for my lover to come and then I should have plenty of fucking.

"But would not any other prick do you as well as his," she asked, all the while frigging my cunt until she had it in a glow.

"Well, Kate, you have so excited my cunt with your finger that I could enjoy being fucked by most any prick."

"Well dear, your finger has done the same for me. Let us try to relieve each other and as the night is hot let us get outside the clothes. Come, lie over me."

And placing herself on the edge of the bed with her feet on the floor, she put me astride over her, my breast and belly resting on hers, and my bottom turned out. Then she threw her arms around me and thrusting her tongue in my mouth held me firm. I felt something touch my bottom and then a soft round stiff thing poked against my cunt. I spluttered out: "Let me up, Kate, I am sure there is someone behind us."

"Nonsense," said Kate, "it is only your own overheated imaginative mind."

"I tell you it is no imagination. Oh!—it is pushing in—let me up—there is someone fucking me. Oh, Kate, I feel his prick, my cunt is filled with it, do let me up."

But she held me tighter than ever.

"Don't be foolish, keep your bottom quiet. It is only my finger."

"No, it is a prick, I feel its head—in—ever so far. Oh!"

"What is it doing?"

"It is fucking, fucking, fucking, fucking. Oh, there the feeling comes, how delicious!" And I lay motionless on her bosom. Then the prick was suddenly drawn out and must have been thrust into her for I felt a belly with hair on it rubbing against my bottom as the prick was worked in and out.

Then a pair of strong arms clasped us both together and after holding us for a moment, quickly withdrew.

After we had returned to our usual places in the bed I asked: "Who was it, Kate?"

"Oh, never mind, let me go on with my story."

"Both the Captain and the mate had good voices and they sometimes sang for us when taking their grog in the evening.

"Our custom was to sit reclining on the broad stern locker which was well covered with cushions. Carle was generally between Hilda and me, and with a hand on each of our cunts. I would be occupied petting his prick and balls while she would be similarly engaged with the Captain. The latter while sipping his grog would strike up one of his favourite ditties in a bold rollicking tone, and Carle would quickly follow suit. After which there would be a general fuck such as I have already described.

"I only remember two of their songs, which I will repeat for you as specimens if you like."

"Do please, I would like to hear them."

THE CAPTAIN'S SONG.

I care not what squeamish lovers may say,
    The maiden that best suits my mind
Is the sweet girl that will meet me half way;
    And while she is free, be as kind.
With her rich beauties I never am cloyed,
    Fresh pleasures I find at her side;
I don't love her less because she's enjoyed
    By many another beside.

Shall I try to describe all her merit,
    I feel that I'd never have done;
She is brimful of sweetness and spirit,
    And sparkles with freedom and fun.
It is bliss then to hold her and win her,
    She never proves peevish or coy;
But the farther and deeper I'm in her,
    The fuller she fills me with joy.

She opens her thighs without fear or dread,
  She points to her sweet little crack,
Its lips are so red, and all overspread
  With hair of the glossiest black.
Reclined on her breast, and clasped in her arms,
  With her my soft moments I spend;
And revel the more in her melting charms,
  Because they are shared with a friend.

THE MATE'S SONG.

My Jamie is a lover gay,
  He is so very funny.
When last we met to sport and play,
  He took me by the cunny.
Then drawing out his sturdy prick,
  Right in my hand he placed it,
And said 'twould be a jolly trick,
  If in my mouth I'd taste it.

I kissed its bright and rosy head,
  And then began to suck it;
He felt about my cunt, and said,
  He wanted now to fuck it.
  Down on the bed he laid me,
With bursting balls, and prick's round head,
  Love's sweetest debt he paid me.

Let maidens of a tim'rous mind
  Refuse what most they're wanting;
Since we for fucking were designed,
  We surely should be granting.
So when your lover feels your cunt,
  Do not be coy, nor grieve him;
But spread your thighs and heave your front,
  For fucking is like heaven.

When Kate had repeated these songs she asked me what I thought of them.

I told her they were excellent, especially the mate's, and that I certainly should learn that one and sing it to Mr. Trevor. Kate then continued her narrative:

I ought to tell you that during our voyage my maid Nina had not been idle. She attended me every morning to assist in giving me a sponge-bath and in dressing me. She amused me by the recital of her adventures with the sailors who coaxed her to come to them at night in their hammocks. She said fucking in that position was quite new.

She had an adventure which I must repeat to you. Our passengers were a sailor, Jim Murphy, sent home on sick-leave, his wife and her sister Jenny, a buxom damsel about twenty.

Now, Mrs. Murphy kept a sharp look-out on Jenny, with whom the boatswain soon fell in love, and he tried to find opportunities of being alone with her to press his suit, or in plain language, to get a fuck out of her.

Mrs. Murphy had at times to be in her husband's cabin to give him medicine or attend to his wants, so she told Nina in her absence never to leave Jenny alone with the boatswain.

Nina faithfully promised and kept her word in the following manner.

One evening Mrs. Murphy was sent for to attend to her husband and the moment she was out of sight the boatswain came and sat down by the side of Jenny and Nina and asked Jenny to sew a button on his shirt.

"Yes," said Jenny.

"Then come to my cabin and I will give it to you."

Nina said: "Yes, Jenny, we will both go."

So all three went into the boatswain's little cabin and Nina said: "Now if you want to show Jenny your prick Mr. Boatswain, now's your chance, and I will unbutton your breeches for you." And suiting the action to the word she did so, and released his noble pego from prison. His swelling head stood proudly erect, and Nina, taking hold of it, said: "Look, Miss Jenny, here's a noble plaything for you to put in your cunt."

Jenny blushed scarlet all over neck and face, and said: "Oh, for shame, Nina, to talk about such names!"

BOATSWAIN.—"Well said, Nina! You know a thing or two and pretty Jenny here will soon know how pleasant it is to make love. Come sit on my knee, darling, and give me a kiss before your mother comes back. You know, I want to make you my wife if you will marry me as soon as we get ashore. And then I have a nice little house of my own we can live in. Give me a kiss and sit on my knee, there's a darling "

Jenny did both and the boatswain made her grasp his prick

with one of her hands while one of his own quickly slipped under her dress and touched her knee. Jenny called out, "Don't, don't," but the hand goes further up until the bower of bliss is reached and one finger gently intrudes and tickles her slit.

"Say yes, darling Jenny, and I swear to marry you and to give you a silk dress and a home of your own. For I am very sure your mother is cross to you."

JENNY.—"Yes, that is true, she is cross, but I'm afraid."

NINA.—"Now Jenny don't be a fool! Do you expect to get a better husband than the boatswain who earns more than a pound a week? You do all he asks and I will be a witness for fair play! You will find it most delicious to have his sugar-stick stirring you up—you will like it so much that you will ask for it afterwards."

"But will you be certain to marry me, Mr. Boatswain?"

"Yes, by the Holy Virgin, I will, as soon as ever we get on shore and can find a priest to marry us."

"I should like a house of my own and to live away from mother, for she is very cross at all times."

"Then that is all settled, darling Jenny! I consider you my wife; and now I will teach you a wife's duty. Lay down on my bed here, dear Jenny, I suppose you know a wife and husband occupy one bed?"

JENNY.—"Yes."

BOATSWAIN.—"Now, Nina, keep watch at the door. There now, my prick is getting into Jenny's cunt. Oh, it's heavenly! Why, Jenny, what is the meaning of this? Where's your maidenhead?"

"Oh, the priest took that when I had my first communion. Mother knows all about that."

"Well, I'm going to have a good fuck now."

And Nina said it was half-an-hour before he left off and she saw Mrs. Murphy coming. I went into the boatswain's cabin and Mrs. Murphy followed me and saw him fucking her daughter.

"Oh, you villain, you dirty blackguard!" she exclaimed: "you have ruined my daughter, my precious Jenny! Stop your fucking this minute," trying to pull him off and turning to me: "As to you, you promised to keep a close watch over Jenny, you wretch!" And she gave Jenny a look and Nina a blow on the shoulder with her fist that stretched her on the floor.

Nina got up and said: "And so I did keep close to Jenny and I have watched over her, and I it was who saw Mr. Boatswain's prick slip in and out of her cunt, and I have been watching her while he did it! What could be closer watching than that, Mrs. Murphy?"

"But he has promised to marry me," called out Jenny.

"Yes," said the boatswain, "I swear I will, but she must let me have a fuck every day until we are ashore."

Mrs. Murphy was obliged to give her consent as she saw the mischief was done.

All our love-matters went on in much the same manner, until at last our brig reached London docks, when we wished Jenny and the boatswain good-bye, and with Nina and our luggage, Captain Lemberg took us to the hotel, where he usually put up when he returned from his voyages.

Captain Lemberg was very kind and chose a bedroom for myself and Nina next to his own, and both opened into a parlour intended for our mutual use.

Captain Lemberg decided I should remain a week or two at the hotel with him, to rest after the voyage and to see some of the sights of London, before I went to the school. In fact he told me he did not think I need go to school until he was obliged to return to the brig, which would be a couple of months, and I told him I would prefer to obey my father's wishes. So we decided I was to go to school in a week.

My father had given me a letter to hand to Madame Stewart, the school-mistress, who lived at Hampton Court.

Captain Lemberg took us to the theatres, which pleased me extremely, also to the Tower and Monument and British Museum.

The time passed very rapidly away in seeing the wonders of London by day and the theatres in the evening, and then we had nice suppers at our hotel and Nina and I retired to our bed, soon to be followed by Captain Lemberg to continue those loving fucking matches like those on the ship.

At last the week ended and Captain Lemberg took me in a coach to Madame Stewart together with Nina, who was to continue to wait on me as lady's-maid.

We had a little fucking in the coach and at last arrived at the school which was a large house surrounded by ornamental grounds and gardens, enclosed by high walls. The grounds sloped down to the Thames, on the banks of which, of course, there was no wall.

Madame Stewart received the Captain and myself and Nina in a large drawing-room, and I handed her my father's letter and told her Nina was my servant.

She told Nina to retire for the present to the housekeeper's room.

Madame was a fine-looking woman of about fifty, with dark hair and eyes and a fine bust.

After reading the letter she kissed me and said she was acquainted with my father many years before and would try to make me happy, provided I obeyed the rules of her establishment.

Captain Lemberg then paid her £100 for one year's fees in advance and asked for a receipt.

Madame asked him to step into the next room with her as she kept her writing materials there, and she wished to ask him a few questions in private.

So pouring me out a glass of wine and giving me some cake and a book of pictures, they withdrew into the next room and shut the door.

You may be sure my eye was at the keyhole in a moment and I saw that the Captain had pulled out his prick! And I heard him say:

"Madame, I am entitled to the usual commission for bringing you a new pupil and I will take it in dog-fashion."

"Hush!" said Madame, "or the young lady will hear you."

"Nonsense—now get down on all fours so as not to derange your dress."

Madame did so and the Captain tossing up her clothes exposed her bottom, and standing behind her, leant over her back and fucked her in that position.

When this was over they each took a chair and I overheard the following conversation:

MADAME S.—"Is this young lady a virgin?"

CAPT. L.—"Yes, as much as you are!"

MADAME S.—"Shall I read you the letter her father has sent me?"

CAPT. L.—"I shall be delighted to hear it read."

Madame then read the letter aloud, and I heard every word that follows:

My Dear Madame Stewart:

These will be handed to you by my daughter Kate, a fine girl just over twelve years of age. Captain Lemberg has kindly undertaken to see her safely to your house, and I have authorized him to pay you for the first year's expense, one hundred guineas.

My daughter's education has been neglected in such matters as penmanship, grammar, drawing, and music. Be pleased to spare no pains in instructing her in these.

In some other things she is in advance of her years. On account of living all her life on a slave plantation she has always seen boys, girls and women in a state of nakedness, so the difference in sex is familiar to her. She has seen men and women in the act of coition.

You will please pay special regard to her religious duties, and also try to inculcate that modest demeanour which is such a characteristic to your own movements that I shall never forget being struck with on occasion of my last visit to your school some fifteen years ago when I had the felicity of watching you slowly strip naked at noon before a large mirror in your dining-room previous to your honouring my pego with a visit to your fine quim.

Alas! Madam, these remembrances quite overpower me and make me regret the distance that separates us!

I have sent a very fair mulatto-girl named Nina, to wait on my daughter.

From your obedient servant,
Sebastian de Lorme.

P.S.—Nina is not a virgin although she is very tight in her cunny. She may be useful at your conversations. Neither Kate nor Nina have ever been birched."

CAPT. L.—"What a very interesting letter. Do you use the birch still, Madame?"

MADAME.—"Certainly, when my young ladies deserve it."

Capt. Lemberg then insisted on having another fuck, for reading my father's letter of his interview with Madame Stewart had given him a cockstand.

So they had another bout and the Captain said he must leave. So I hastened from the keyhole and was apparently absorbed in my book when Madame and Captain entered the room.

The Captain kissed me as he bade me good-bye and thrust his tongue into my mouth as he did so, bidding me obey Madame in everything and all would be well.

He promised to take me for a day's holiday before the brig sailed if Madame would kindly consent.

I promised to endeavour to please Madame, and with another kiss he departed.

Madame Stewart then had a long talk with me and urged me to be candid and truthful in my answers to her questions. She asked: "Have you ever seen the slave men quite naked?"

"Yes."

"And the slave women?"

"Yes."

"And is it true that neither of them ever have any hair on their private parts?"

"Do you mean their cocks and cunts, Madame?"

"Yes, my dear."

"Then it is not true, because I have seen short curly hair on those places, and in the case of the men, quite as much as was on my dear father's prick."

"Do you mean to say you have seen your father's prick?"

"Yes, Madame, and felt it too!"

So I told her all my history, at which she was delighted and wanted to look at my cunny. I complied and she complimented me on my rich growth of hair.

She told me I must never let a man's prick enter my cunny without her consent being first obtained as she was desirous of shielding me from harm whilst I was under her roof; but she promised I should have all the coition that was good for me at proper times if I was diligent in my lessons.

You may be sure, dearest May, I was pleased with this intelligence and gave the required promise, thinking what a wise and kind schoolmistress she was.

I told her my father had fucked Nina and sent her to be my waiting-maid, and as we were very fond of each other I hoped she would allow us to be together as much as possible. She agreed to this saying she quite understood from my father's letter that it was his wish Nina should be with me. She made me repeat the tale I had told her about my taking Nina's place in the garden with my father and also the scene with him just before the brig sailed.

Nina was then called into the room and I told her that Madame Stewart was a very kindly lady and was willing we should occupy the same room like we did at home.

Poor Nina was profuse in her thanks and asked permission to kiss Madame's feet as a token of her gratitude.

Madame then told us to follow her upstairs, and she took us down a long passage with bedrooms opening from both sides of it. Here she pointed out a room and told us it was ours, but shared with another girl, the daughter of a wealthy baronet, Sir Thomas Moreton.

The room had three narrow beds in it, as Madame said her rule was for each pupil to have a bed of her own.

Madame then kissed me and told me to read the rules, a copy of which was fastened on the wall. As nearly as I can recollect they ran as follows:

Rule I—Every pupil, before retiring to rest, must strip naked and wash her person in every part.

Rule II—No pupil may examine her secret part before the mirror.

Rule III—No pupil must occupy a bed that is not her own.

N.B.—The penalty for breaking either of these rules is one dozen stripes with the birch.

When Nina heard me read these rules she said: "But how will Madame know if we break them?"

I replied: "Perhaps the other girl will tell tales on us! Or, perhaps she will be a nice girl and we can do as we like."

"Hush!" said Nina.

And Madame entered our room with Miss Moreton, saying, "Let me introduce you young ladies, as you will occupy this room together. Miss Moreton has been in this establishment for two years, so she knows all the girls and all the customs. You will soon get acquainted."

Madame withdrew and Miss Moreton asked my age and who my father was and we were soon chatting away glibly.

She said she was sixteen and should leave the school next holidays. Her name was Alice. She asked me if I had ever had a lover. I told her yes—Captain Lemberg—and that my father had sent me in his ship from home to England.

"Oh!" said Alice, "then you had a fine time together, I know! Please tell me all about it."

185

I said I would someday, but now I wanted to know all about the girls at school as I was never at school before.

Alice was surprised at this but I informed her my mother died when I was young and my father would not part with me, but preferred teaching me himself.

Alice told me Madame was very strict with the new girls until she had the chance to whip them a few times, after which she was very indulgent.

She told me that Saturday evening was punishment time and she had found out that gentlemen were admitted to Madame's room to peep at the girls punished. I enquired how she knew that. She said I had no doubt noticed that the grounds reached the water's edge.

Well, said Alice, one Saturday Madame sent me into the garden to get some fruit the gardener had forgotten and I saw two boats stop at the boat-house. I hid behind some bushes and saw four gentlemen, muffled up in cloaks, walk up the path which leads to the side entrance of the house. They were admitted by Mrs. White, the housekeeper. My curiosity was excited, so I quickly brought Madame the fruit and ran into her private room, and crept under the sofa to listen, thinking I would be certain to find out something. Nor was I wrong in my conjecture, for in a few minutes Mrs. White ushers in the four gentlemen and two of them sit down on the very sofa I was under. They talked to each other about the superior manner in which Madame's establishment was conducted. Two of them said they had daughters at present in the school and hoped they would have broken some of the rules that week.

This remark astonished me but my surprise was greater when by the voice of the next speaker I recognized my own father, Sir Thomas Moreton! He had visited me that very morning, gave me a supply of pocket money, wished me good-bye and said he was going back home at once; and here he was in the same house!

The other speaker was the rector of the parish church, the Hon. and Rev. Algernon Stanley. I knew his voice, for in the course of the conversation he was addressed as Stanley by my father.

Evidently the party of four were acquaintances, for they all chatted away on good terms.

In a few moments I heard my father's voice:

"Well, gentlemen, I will bet you five pounds that when you see the punishment this evening you will allow my daughter's bottom to be the plumpest and most exciting of any you shall see tonight!"

RECTOR.—"But suppose your daughter is not birched tonight?"

SIR MORETON.—"Then we will let the bet stand over till some other Saturday when she is flogged and we all are here."

Here, dear Kate, was a revelation to me! My father and three other gentlemen evidently were here for the purpose of witnessing the punishments about to be inflicted on the schoolgirls' bottoms! And my father must have seen my bottom on some previous occasion, or how could he make this bet! I knew I was to be punished that evening for my name was on the blacklist.

How should I escape from under the sofa and reach the schoolroom? For my ambition was fired by my father's words of admiration about my plump bottom and I wanted him to win that bet!

Fortunately for my intentions, Madame came into the room and invited the gentlemen to adjourn upstairs.

Directly they were gone I crept from my hiding place and ran up to the schoolroom by the back staircase and seated myself at the piano and commenced practicing my exercises.

In a short time the German governess, Fraulein Hoffman, came to me and said:

"My dear you must prepare for punishment."

"Yes, Fraulein," I answered.

And, according to the custom, I retired to my bedroom, took off my form, skirts and corset and returned to the schoolroom in chemise, drawers and stockings, which was the regulation dress for punishment.

Three other girls were to be punished; one rebelled from Fraulein's order and had to be dragged to her room and undressed.

At last we heard a bell ring and each of us, the culprits, was escorted by a governess to the room especially used and fitted up for punishment. It was lighted from the roof and had ladders, Berkeley horses and other appliances, such as ropes from the ceiling, rings in the floor and ceiling to which to fasten refractory culprits.

On this occasion we were made to slowly take off our

drawers and then kneel on a kind of table with our heads low down and our posteriors sticking well out, with our hands and ankles tied securely.

Next, our offences were read out to us by Madame as follows:

"Margaret Stanley, your offence is as usual peeing in bed. I give you notice that I intend telling the worthy rector, your uncle, of this most disgusting habit of yours.

"Fimeline Chesterfield, your offence is greediness in eating up the cake you brought from home, and not sharing it with your schoolfellows

"Constance Le Ray, you were discovered viewing your naked person in the glass; such vanity must be checked by the rod."

And then Madame read my name.

"Alice Moreton, your offence is one against decency. It is that of having received a letter from a lover whom you obstinately refuse to name or give any information as to how you have carried on this clandestine correspondence.

"I will read it aloud to you, Miss Alice Moreton, and I hope your cheeks will blush with shame as much as the cheeks of your bottom will blush under the rod, presently. This is the horrid letter:

My Dear Alice:

How I do long for another kiss on the lips of your pussey! The last I had was delicious! I dream of you every night and sometimes fancy I am in one of those high pews at church with your naked bottom sitting in my face, so I can kiss and suck your pussey! At other times in my dreams you catch hold of me by the cock and sing: "I will not let thee go, unless you fuck me!"

You cannot wonder at these dreams, sweetheart, for they are only repetitions of the facts of the day!

Give my love to Madame and asked her to notice the beauty of your cunny!

From your devoted love,
Henry.

Madame having finished the letter told the governesses to commence flogging us, and to strike as she called out, One, Two, Three

They were stationed close to our heads so they had to

strike over our backs to reach our bottoms, which were
turned towards the end of the room at which Madame was
seated on a dais, raised up six steps above the level of the
floor.

I remembered the conversation of the gentlemen and the
bet of my dear father, and I had no doubt they were watching us from some secret peep-hole, or were perhaps under the
dais. So at every blow of the rod I writhed and twisted my
posteriors as much as possible, in order to display all its
beauties.

Margaret received fifty stripes, Emmeline sixty, Constance
eighty, and I, the greatest offender, received one hundred,
which caused me to faint away.

What do you think of that, Kate dear?

I told her I thought it was a great shame and asked if the
gentlemen ever came again.

Alice said no doubt they did although she had never had
an opportunity of proving it; still, on Saturdays occasionally
she had slipped into the garden and found boats moored to
the boat-house. "However, my dear Katie, I have told you all
I know, perhaps someday we will make more discoveries."

Kate said she warmly thanked Alice for telling her all the
circumstances, and they kissed and went to bed.

Chapter VI.
A Letter from Susey.

About this time I received a letter from Susey, who, when
the vacation commenced, went to her uncle in Scotland, and
I may as well give her adventures in her own words:

My Darling May:
You remember the morning you took leave of me, I
had to walk a mile to meet the coach. John Cox, my sister
Jane's intended husband, came to start me off, and he carried
my box on his shoulder as we walked across the fields and
down to the crossroads where the coach takes up passengers.
John told me he and Jane were soon to be married, and he
said her belly was so big that it looked beautiful.

I asked him what made it so big and he laughed as he said:

189

"Why, Susey, because I have made a baby inside of it to be sure, you little goose!"

John also said that he was now obliged to fuck Jane behind, because her belly sticking out quite prevented his approaching the front.

He told me that he had a special message from Jane to me which was to be sure to do my pee just before getting on the coach, as I should have to ride for many hours and it was very painful to be obliged to hold your water.

"So," says John, "you had better squat down at once, and I can see your little cunt at the same time."

So I got close to some bushes and had a good pee and John had a good look at my cunny, and afterwards kissed and sucked it. Just then we heard the guard's horn announcing the near approach of the coach. So I had only time to give John's prick a farewell kiss, and then we hurried to the little ale-house at the crossroads.

The coach was full inside so I had to take an outside seat, and as there was no ladder I climbed up as well as I could. But I felt John's hand on my thigh as he stood beneath me.

When the coach started I looked at my fellow passengers and saw there were two gentlemen—one evidently a clergyman and the other, from remarks made, was his son, apparently about my own age. He asked me how far I was going and I replied, to Scotland.

"Have you never been there before?"

"No, sir," I replied.

"They have some very curious customs in Scotland," he said.

"What are they?" was my enquiry.

"The wearing of the kilt, for instance," said he.

"I do not know what a kilt is," was my reply.

"I will show you a picture of a Scotsman dressed in his kilt," said he, taking a book from his coat-pocket, and turning over the leaves, he showed me the picture of a tall man with naked knees and a short petticoat which he explained was the kilt.

I laughed at the odd figure in the picture and asked: "Do the Scotch girls and women dress like that too? If so, they must be cold."

"I wish they did," said he, "don't you, father?"

"Well, my son, it would have a very delightful effect, no doubt," said the clergyman.

I interposed: "But the poor man must feel very cold here."

"Not at all," said the clergyman. "When I was at college as a young man, I wore that dress once at a fancy ball and found it very comfortable."

"Did you waltz in your kilt?" I asked.

"Yes, certainly, and why not?"

"Because I should think the whirling motion of dancing would cause your kilt to fly up and expose your . . ." and I stopped suddenly—laughing.

"Bottom, you were going to say, my dear! And where would be the harm in that? Ladies like to get a glimpse at a man's bottom sometimes," said he.

"I'm sure they don't," I replied.

"Oh," said the son, "you think the ladies would rather look at him before than behind, eh? Well, what do you say at this picture," and he moved aside the kilt, which was a separate piece of paper, and showed me the Scotsman's prick in full erection.

"That's more in your way, my dear," said he. Then speaking to the clergyman, he said: "Father, this young lady, evidently, from her blushes, thinks a man's prick is more beautiful than his bottom."

"I am very glad to hear it," said he, "for it proves that her education has not been neglected and that she has learnt from her catechism: 'What is the chief end of man?'"

"My dear father," said the young man, "we have the back part of the coach to ourselves and the guard is sitting with the coachman, so we are quite private here. Would it not be a good opportunity for letting this young lady look at your reverend prick?"

"Most certainly, my son," replied the clergyman, unbuttoning his trousers. "I am always ready to please the ladies."

So he pulled out his noble tool, fondly stroking it. "There, Miss, there is something for a man to be proud of, and I am proud to have such a father."

"I hope you may have just such another someday," I said.

"Thank you, my dear," said he, "I will show you what I have at present."

And he exhibited his own prick. I told him it was as big as he had any reason to expect, and he quite agreed with me

191

and then regretted the fact that our being outside the coach would prevent his father and himself from looking at anything I would like to show them. "But," continued he, "the coach will stop to change horses in a few minutes' time, and then the passengers generally get down and go inside the inn for half-an-hour for refreshments. But my father, the rector, is well known to the landlord and we will ask for a private room and take our refreshments there; and then, Miss Susan, you will have the wished-for opportunity."

By the time he had finished speaking we arrived at the Royal George, and the parson and his son helped me down from the coach, and I soon found myself in an upstairs parlour with them. They told me their journey terminated there, as they had to drive in a gig to their home, five miles distant, and they both begged me to lose no time.

I replied: "I am in your hands, gentlemen! Only don't harm me."

They promised they would not, and the father then raised my clothes, called his son's attention to my white thighs and the pouting lips of my cunt.

Both father and son kissed and sucked it for a few minutes and then the father insisted on his son having a fuck before he had one.

By the time each had finished, the horn blew the warning to get ready. So hastily swallowing a glass of wine, I arranged my clothes and bade them good-bye.

They accompanied me to the coach and this time I was able to get inside, there being one place vacant, and the parson kindly paying the difference in fare.

With mutual farewells the coach started again and I looked at my fellow passengers and found one who appeared young, the other two being grey-haired gentlemen.

They all accosted me very politely and hoped we should have a pleasant journey together.

The young man enquired how far I was going and when I replied to Edinburgh, he expressed his pleasure that we should be going to the same city.

"What a fortunate circumstance," said he, "that you were not travelling by this coach last week."

"How so?"

"Because the notorious Dick Turpin and his gang stopped the coach just a little way from here and robbed the passengers, and used the ladies very cruelly."

"Oh! how you frighten me! Do tell me all about it," said I.

The elderly gentleman opposite now spoke and said:

"I can give you the correct account, for I was one of the passengers and one of the victims, I may say."

"Oh, do tell me if there is any danger of Dick Turpin coming again today?" I asked.

"Not the slightest," said the old gentleman, "and that is the reason why I am travelling again so soon. Besides, I am armed with my horse-pistols."

"Oh," said I, "don't show them to me, I am so terribly frightened! But tell me about the villains."

The old gentleman continued: "It was just about three in the afternoon when, as we were bowling along, as we are now, I heard several horsemen ride up on each side of the coach and call to the coachman to stop or he should be shot. And two shots were fired at him, and one wounded him, the other broke the lamp.

"Of course the coach was stopped and the robbers then called: 'Stand out and deliver your money and valuables, or you are all dead men.'

"There must have been ten or twelve men—some on foot, and some on horseback.

"I should mention that the inside of the coach was occupied by some girls going to York to school. There were four besides their mistress and outside there were four more girls—that makes nine ladies, and there were six men passengers besides the coachman and guard.

"I should say that two of the misses were my grandchildren, aged about thirteen and fourteen.

"Well, the villains first looked inside the coach and made the madame give up her gold watch and rings, then they made us men come down and stand in the road while they searched our pockets, one man standing with the muzzle of a pistol pressed close to my forehead while he searched my pockets.

"When this was done, they abused us for giving them so much trouble for so little money and declared they would be revenged on the women for it.

"I begged them to spare my poor grandchildren.

" 'Point them out,' said one of the villains.

"I did so, thinking that he was going to listen to my re-

193

quests, but no; to my surprise he tied their hands behind them and then lifted up their clothes and threw them over their heads, exposing their bodies from the waist downwards!

"I rushed forward to replace their clothing when two of the villains caught hold of me and tied my hands behind my back, and then to my indignation, they actually cut open my breeches in front and pulled out my prick."

"Horrible!" I exclaimed.

"Monstrous," said the young man.

"Yes," continued the old man, "and that is not all. There is something more horrible to tell."

"Oh, do tell," said I.

"Pray," said the young man, "continue."

"Well, the villains made me kneel down and kiss the slits of my two granddaughters and made me suck them and push in my tongue! Then they uncovered the poor girls' faces, and tying their clothes tight under their arms, ordered them to suck my cock! In vain they and I protested. A loaded pistol fired off close to our ears was the warning of what our fate should be if we disobeyed. So first one and then the other dear girl went through the task. And the villains made me say the sucking was pleasant!"

"And what did you say?"

"Of course I told the truth, that the sucking gave me great pleasure."

"And what became of the other men who were passengers?"

"Oh, they were made to suck the slits of the schoolgirls and to submit to have their pricks sucked in turn."

"And how did the school-madame fare?"

"Oh, the villains grossly insulted her by examining her cunt, and telling her she was too old to allow them to give her any pleasure of that kind, so they cut a bunch of twigs from the bushes and forced her on all fours, bared her backside and gave her a good flogging."

"Do you mean to state that all these outrages took place on the high-turnpike road?"

"Well, yes, that is to say, close to it, for there was a piece of turf or grass-land rather wide at the side of the road at this place. In fact, there were a few trees and bushes growing there."

"Did no person pass in travelling along the road, while this took place, for it must have taken some time?"

"Yes, it took an hour or more, but a farmer with his wife riding behind on a pillion, and one wagon loaded with hay accompanied by the wagoner, were all that passed by during the time. Part of the hay was unloaded to serve for beds on which to extend the unfortunate lady-passengers and the farmer was compelled to fuck his wife in public."

"Did Dick Turpin take part in these outrages?"

"No, he told his men to fuck any way they took a fancy to, but he kept watch most of the time and gave the necessary directions to his men so that several of them kept watch in turn, while the others committed these outrages on their victims."

"Do you mean to say that the ten schoolgirls were all raped and their maidenheads taken?"

"Certainly; if they had any to lose! They were all fucked before my eyes."

"How did it all end?"

"Oh, after a while Captain Dick said: 'That's enough for this time, boys. Mount and away!' And so they rode off leaving all the victims tied and bound until some passer-by should come and relieve them. Of course we called for help directly after our tormentors had left us and in half-an-hour some foot passengers and also the returning mail-coach came by and released our bonds and we all made the best of our ways to our destinations "

The young man now spoke. "It is all quite true, Miss, I assure you; I was one of the passengers by the down-mail on that occasion and I saw the condition of the ten schoolgirls as described by our friend here. They were all tied to trees with their arms behind them, and their clothing raised and tied close to their shoulders so as to expose their bellies and all below.

"I could not help being delighted with the sight, although of course I pitied the poor things, and I delayed helping to release them in order to have a good view of their naked charms. I was much amused at the remarks of a worthy tradesman and his wife who were also looking at those schoolgirls. The wife spoke sharply: 'Well, Mr. Jones, I am ashamed of you to stand staring like a stuck pig at those naked shameless young hussies. Why don't they put their dresses down?'

" 'Well, my dear,' said her husband, 'they have their hands tied behind their backs and can't help themselves, and as to my looking at them, my excuse is I never saw such a sight before! Why, there are ten naked bellies for me to look at and four have hardly any hair on their slits and the others all have black hair on them, but one, and she. . .'

"Here his wife angrily interposed: 'You have made good use of your eyes for these few minutes, Mr. Jones; I must say I am astonished at you, a married man and the father of six girls and four boys, so to demean yourself! Why don't you shut your eyes until this disgraceful exhibition is over?'

" 'No, Mrs. Jones, I am not going to close my eyes! I may be called as a witness against the villains if ever they are caught, and if I shut my eyes how am I to describe to the jury the cruel state in which the girls are left?'

" 'Well,' said his wife, 'had you not better try and catch those villains?'

" 'No, my dear, my duty does not lie in that direction.'

" 'Nor your inclination either,' retorted his wife, 'for evidently you prefer the safer course of feasting your eyes on these poor girls' nakedness.'

" 'Well, my dear, you know I am always delighted to look at yours but you so seldom allow me to do so.'

" 'I should think not, indeed,' said Mrs. Jones, 'and that reminds me that last Sunday I saw you take two of our daughters on your knee and I think you had your hands under their clothes!'

" 'Nonsense! Mrs. Jones, only a little play and romping, for my girls are very fond of their old father; besides it is a father's duty to see if his girls' underclothes are clean and in the fashion.'

" 'Now, Mr. Jones, do be quiet. What right has a man to be troubling himself about his girls' clothing?'

" 'Why what I buy and pay for with my own money I have the right to examine, and you know I should never have married you if I had not examined you first!'

" 'For shame, Mr. Jones, to speak about that here in the open air where anyone might overhear you!'

" 'Now Mary Ann, dear, will you untie these poor girls' clothes from their necks and help me undo their hands?'

"So I then offered my assistance to several of the girls and helped to put their clothing down over their bellies, taking care to touch much of their naked bodies in doing so, and getting my hand on each of their bellies in the performance of this duty.

"I ought to mention that the place where these outrages took place was a kind of valley between two hills, and where a house was not in sight for many miles. It was up a lane through this valley that the highway-men came on horseback to do their unlawful work, and when they had completed it they went away down the valley again."

At this moment as the young man finished his account the coach gave a lurch forward, probably from the coachman suddenly whipping up the horses; however, I found myself flung against the elderly man sitting opposite me and he caught me firmly in his arms and kissed me, saying: "God bless me, Miss, don't be frightened, come to my arms, I'll take care of you."

I replied I could not help it and then felt a hand passing up my thighs from behind, and another hand patting my bottom.

I cried out: "Oh, this conduct is most shameful gentlemen, do leave a poor girl alone!"

"Why, what's the matter, my dear?" said the young man.

"Nobody is touching you," growled the old gentleman.

"Well, my dear, I am kissing you," said the one on whom I had been thrown.

"I know that," I replied, "but more than that has been done to me."

"Well," said he, "I am a magistrate and my name is Squire Johnson, and if you will sit by my side and make your complaint you shall have justice done to you."

The other elderly-looking gentleman said: "Well, Squire Johnson you have known me for years as the parson of the parish and my name is the Rev. Mr. Scarlett and I expect you to take my oath against any other person's."

The young gentleman now spoke: "Oh, I am a medical student going home from college. My name is Charley Stuart and I am sure to fall in love with every pretty girl I see, especially such an angel as this!" giving me a most loving look.

"Now, then," said Squire Johnson, "if you, Miss, will give us your name we will proceed."

I replied: "My name is Susan Gardiner and I charge Parson

Scarlett and Charley Stuart with touching my naked body.'

Squire Johnson wrote this down in his pocket-book and then said: "Miss Susan, you say you charge these gentlemen with an indecent assault! Please state the particulars."

I did so, saying the Parson put his hand on my bottom, "when the coach by that sudden jerk threw me into your arms and you kissed me. The other gentleman, called Charley Stuart, put one of his hands between my thighs, very high up, at the same time."

SQUIRE JOHNSON.—"Now Parson, what is your reply to those charges?"

PARSON.—"Oh, I saw the young lady's petticoats disarranged and I tried to replace them."

SQUIRE J.—"And you, Charley Stuart?"

CHARLEY.—"Oh, I plead guilty and promise not to do it again until the next time."

SQUIRE J.—"Gentlemen, from your replies I am quite satisfied that you are both guilty of the offence charged against you; and my sentence is that you each pay Miss Susan immediately the sum of half-a-crown, that you each beg her pardon and that you each offer to show her your pricks. Come, Parson, you first, out of respect of your cloth, as you are in holy orders."

PARSON.—"Never did I hear a more impartial and righteous sentence."

So he paid me the half-crown at once and pulled out his tool; it was short and thick with an enormous red head.

Charley said: "See Miss Susan, I offer you this half-crown for the sweet kisses you gave me. Here, balanced on the head of my prick and it is cheap enough."

And Squire J.—"Now, Miss Susan, I offer you this half-crown, and as it is now four o'clock, before the coach will stop, I propose that you should give us some entertainment —and answer all our questions truthfully."

PARSON.—"Also obey us in all our wishes."

CHARLEY.—"And Miss Susan, if you do, you shall be paid a guinea from me."

SQUIRE.—"And another from me."

PARSON.—"And I will give another, that will make three golden guineas! Think, what a lot of money!"

Dear May, do not blame me for acceding to their wishes. I knew I was completely in their power, and then the presents of the guineas! It seemed riches indeed to me, who had never possessed more than a few shillings at one time in my life.

So I dried my tears and taking up the three half-crowns, said: "Do not harm me, good gentlemen! I will agree to your proposals and trust to your honour, as I am only a girl entirely at your mercy, but I should vastly like three guineas."

"A very sensible good girl," said the Parson.

"You are an angel," said Charley.

PARSON.—"I will ask Miss Susan if she has any hair on her little slit?"

"Yes," I replied.

SQUIRE.—"What colour?"

"Light red"

"Did you ever allow a man to look at your cunt?" said Charley.

"Yes."

PARSON.—"And suck it, I'll be bound?"

CHARLEY.—"And kiss it?"

"Yes."

SQUIRE.—"Then Miss Susan shall be laid across the laps of two of us, and the other shall kiss and suck her pretty cunny."

"Agreed!" they all cried.

And this was done in succession, until all three had had their turn. To do this my petticoats and smock were raised so as to expose to view my thighs and belly. Then each gentleman knelt on the floor of the coach and kissed and sucked my cunny.

The Parson asked: "How much time, Squire, do we have before the coach stops?"

"Three hours."

The Parson then said: "That will be ample time for Miss Susan to strip herself naked, and to let us enjoy looking at her charms in the nude state."

"Yes," said the Squire, "plenty of time."

I replied that I should take cold.

"No, I'll take care of that," said Charley. "I will keep you warm. I will give you brandy from this bottle."

"But I shall be seen by passers-by," again I objected.

But the Parson and Squire agreed to keep the curtain of the coach-windows drawn down, sufficient to prevent all chance of anyone seeing me.

"Now," said Charley, "I will be your lady's-maid and disrobe you."

He then took off my bonnet and shawl, then my frock stays and petticoats. I begged hard to be allowed to retain my smock, but all in vain as the Parson said it would interfere with the full view of my naked body; besides, he said: "Eve was naked in the Garden of Eden, so there's Scripture for you, Miss Susan."

I was praised for the whiteness and firmness of my skin, and my shape was much admired.

Two of them sat on one seat of the coach and one on the other, with their knees as close to one another as possible, and on this broad lap I was laid and rolled over and over, their hands roving over my back, shoulders and bosom, belly and bottom, in succession, one pointing out to the other some attraction that he specially admired.

My mouth and both hands were next occupied with three pricks at once, and I was obliged to change from one to the other, until each had his prick sucked.

Next I was seated between two of them on the edge of the seat. Then they raised my legs higher than my head, and told me to jut my belly well forward. This had the effect of exposing my bottom-hole as well as my cunny. Then one gentleman would fuck me in this position and then the others would change places, until all three had fucked me. But I will say, they all withdrew their pricks before spending and spouted their sperm over my belly, as it was solemnly promised by them all that there should be no risk of getting me with a child.

By the time they managed to get a couple of fucks each, the time came for me to resume my clothing, which I was thankful to do. And I was only decently dressed when the guard's horn warned us the coach was about to stop.

I was glad to learn we had to stop one hour for dinner, but was amused at Charley telling the chambermaid I was his wife, and so accompanying me up to the bedroom where he actually produced the pot from under the bed and made me sit down and do my pee, while he, lying at full length on the floor with his head close to my belly, watched the waterfall, as he called it.

Then he went down the stairs with me to the dinner-table, where we all did justice to the repast and had some good wine.

My companions were all very attentive to my wants and paid my score between them.

We then resumed our places in the coach as before, the coachman telling us we should have another four hours without stopping at all.

I noticed the Parson and Squire soon felt the efforts of their wine and good feeding, for they were soon sound asleep and snoring.

Charley said he was glad of that as now he could have me all to himself. So we first had a mutual prick-and-cunt-sucking match, each trying to hold back the juice of love as long as possible.

Next, sitting in Charley's lap with his tool ensconced in my cunny, I gently rode up and down, till he was compelled to withdraw and spend all over my belly.

We tired ourselves out with our varied loving encounters and at last we both fell asleep and were only aroused by the guard's horn announcing our arrival at our destination in Edinburgh.

My uncle was waiting for me at the inn and after thanking my travelling companions for their polite attentions, I took my uncle's arm and walked with him to his home.

My uncle kept talking all the way and enquired the name of my late companions.

I answered truthfully and he was pleased to think I had been in such good respectable society: "For," said he, "now-a-days there are so many villains about that a young girl might be ruined before she knew her danger."

I mentally resolved to act the part of an innocent girl in dear uncle's presence and also I determined to put in practice the instructions of Charley Stuart, who, being a medical student, told me many things about a woman's private parts that I did not know before. One thing he told me was to get a lump of alum and push it up in my cunny and keep it there all night. It would act as an astringent and make it as tight as a virgin's cunny. And he also advised me to use a solution of alum in water with a female syringe as often during the day as was convenient.

Dear May, I advise you to do the same. When you send a messenger to buy the alum you can say it is for a sore throat or to use in dyeing—as it is used for both those purposes.

Only, dear May, let me give you a caution—don't let the piece of alum be very large, for I will tell you what a fright I had.

One night I put a lump as large as a hen's egg up my cunny and in the morning I could not get it out! It had caused such a contraction of the inside folds of my cunny that I could barely insert the tip of my finger so you may imagine my dilemma. At last I thought: "Why of course, hot water will dissolve it." So I sat over the bidet for nearly an hour and bathed my poor cunny with warm water and it gradually dissolved some of the alum, and I was none the worse for my fright.

Well, to resume, Uncle and I came at last to his house which was a bookseller's shop with rooms for residence over the shop and a milliner's shop on one side, and a dressmaker's shop on the other, while opposite was an inn called "The Royal Standard," and next door to that was a board-school for young ladies.

I mention these details because Uncle called my attention to them, saying they were all his best customers.

On arriving at Uncle's house he took me upstairs and introduced me to the housekeeper, who was going to leave to get married the following week, and I was to take her place in Uncle's household.

She took me to a comfortable bedroom, and kissing me, praised my good looks and enquired if I would like a bath after my long journey.

I replied it was the one thing I was longing for. So she opened a door leading from my bedroom and showed me the bath, saying she would be back in half-an-hour to help me dress and get ready for dinner.

Oh, May, how I enjoyed that cold bath! I splashed and dashed the water all over my naked body and took the opportunity of removing the alum Charley had considerately slipped into my cunny in the coach, for, said he, who knows how soon you may have to pass for a virgin?

I had just finished my washing and stepped out of the bath and was seated on a stool drying myself when the door opened and in came the housekeeper, Jemima, and rushing up to me, exclaimed: "Oh, Miss Susan, please stand before this pier-glass for a moment!"

I did so and found it was as tall as myself and reflected

my figure as large as life.

Jemima now began to rub me with a towel, all the time praising my skin, my back, my belly, and my thighs, in such a loud voice that I began to fancy she intended someone in the next room to hear. However, I kept my thoughts to myself and only said: "Make haste, Jemima, and help me dress for I want my supper so badly."

At last she was obliged to leave off her rubbings and she brought me a clean smock and petticoat which she helped to put on. Then I sat on a low stool and drew on clean white stockings; but Jemima would help put on a new pair of garters, which fastened with a silver clasp. I was so pleased with them that I jumped up and stood before the mirror to admire my garters, and of course had to raise my smock rather high to do so.

"Those garters are a present from your uncle," said Jemima, "you will not forget to thank him presently."

"Of course I shall thank him," I said.

Jemima now put on me a very low-necked blue frock.

"And this also is your uncle's present," said she.

"Oh, what a dear, kind uncle he is! How much I love him already," I replied.

"Well," said Jemima, "now go down to supper and tell him so."

On entering the room downstairs I found supper on the table and Uncle in his dressing-gown and slippers sitting by a bright fire.

Uncle got up and came to meet me, saying: "Welcome, Susey, I am glad you have come! How blooming you look! You must want your supper after such a long ride."

I threw my arms around his neck and kissing him, said: "Thank you, dear Uncle, for all your great kindness and especially for this lovely silk dress and the pretty garters you gave me."

"Does the dress fit you, my dear?" he asked, placing his hands on my bosom and squeezing it gently.

"Yes, Uncle dear," I said.

We then had supper, and Uncle insisted on my drinking four glasses of the champagne, which I found warmed up my blood as doubtless Uncle intended it should do.

After supper he said: "Susey, if you love me, show me your garters."

"Oh, Uncle!" I replied blushingly, "would that be decent and proper?"

"You are an ungrateful girl to refuse the first trifling request I make," he said.

"Not ungrateful, Uncle," I replied; "see here, please examine my pretty garters," and I stretched out both my legs as I continued sitting in my chair.

Uncle was on his knees between my legs in a moment, and put his hands first on one garter and then on the other, unclasping them and kissing my thighs just above the stockings.

Then he said: "Dear Susey, do you know that your mother was my favourite sister? And that as children we used to sleep together, and were fond of taking off each other's nightdress and of examining the difference in our naked bodies, and making water in the same pot. And now, dear Susey, I want to tell you that your dear mother on her death-bed confided you to my care, and I have paid for your education and maintenance all your life; and now I hope you will love me and be a comfort to me in my declining years."

"Yes, dear Uncle," I said, "you may depend on my doing everything in my power to give you pleasure."

"That's a good girl," said Uncle. "But now you can do something this minute to please me, and that is to show me your cunny!"

I told him he could look at it if he wished. So as I was seated in an easy-chair he lifted one of my legs over an arm of the chair and telling me to hold my clothing and chemise out of the way, he exposed my cunny and bottom-hole to his delighted view, and covered both with kisses, sucking and putting his tongue as far as possible into both places. The end of this, of course, was that I gave down my liquor of love over his tongue and he greedily sucked up every drop, declaring it was most delicious.

After this he pulled out his prick and pretended to me that he had fucked my mother, therefore he had a right to do the same to me!

I laughed at this reasoning and feigning ignorance of his meaning asked him to explain everything.

He then laid me on the sofa before the fire and undressed me and also himself, all the time praising the whiteness of my skin, and then, dearest May, he fucked me, and fancied he

204

was the first that had penetrated my virgin slit, as he fondly called it.

Now I must close this letter, hoping you have had as much pleasure as I have in the way of fucking.

By the way, dear May, why don't you get your father to fuck you? Uncle says you would find it delicious, for he knows your father well and says he remembers that his cock is both long and very thick!

I remain, darling May, your loving friend,

SUSEY.

P.S.—Be sure and keep this letter a secret and don't let your father see it for the world! Write soon and tell me everything.

———

I put this precious letter in my pocket and then remembered that Kate had never told me how she first became acquainted with my father. So I went into the dining-room in search of her and found her and papa sitting on the sofa, with their private parts exposed and each was fondling and touching the other's genitals.

Papa caught sight of me and called out: "Come in May, I want you most particularly."

I went up to him.

He continued: "I want to see if the hair on your cunny is as fine and silky as this on Kate's cunt. Now be a good obedient girl and I will give you a silk dress and you shall choose the colour yourself."

How this promise dazzled me! I had had only one silk dress many years before and now the promise of choosing one myself conjured up visions of beauty to my mind's eye.

I replied quickly: "Yes, dear papa, I will do all you require," and I raised up my clothing as I stood in front of him.

"That is not convenient," he said. "You had better slip off your clothes except the chemise. Kate will help you."

So in a few moments my dress and petticoats were on the ground and I was en chemise as I did not wear drawers in those days. In taking my dress over my head my pocket was emptied on the carpet and the letter caught my father's eye.

"Oh, a love letter," he cried, "fine goings on, Miss May! I must read this letter from your favoured lover!" and he picked it up and commenced to read it.

"It is not a love letter," I said, "but one from my school-friend Susey who is in Scotland with her uncle."

"All the same I shall read it aloud," said my father.

And he did so. And Kate whispered to me: "Don't be afraid of anything, May dearest, I will take your part."

My father was delighted with Susey's letter and as his breeches were unbuttoned as he sat on the sofa I could see his pego rise to a fine erection as he came to some of her descriptive passages.

At last he came to the end where she advised me to get my father to fuck me, and then he cried out: "Sensible girl this Susey! I wish she were here now. I must invite her and her uncle, my old friend, on a visit this summer, and we will have glorious times! But at present I am concerned to examine closely my daughter's cunny! And if she consents, willingly will I fuck her for I cannot use force to my own daughter, I love her too well for that! Only if she cheerfully consents to let me have my will, she shall have five guineas in addition to the silk dress and I will take her to the theatre one night each week!"

I exclaimed: "You dear kind papa! How much I love you! Yes, do whatever you like with me and teach me how to give you pleasure. I hope, dear Kate will not be jealous of poor little me?"

"No, no, dearest May," said Kate. "I shall never be jealous of you or any other girl your papa wished to fuck; in fact I should like to see him fuck all the girls in the parish, if he wanted to!"

Papa said: "Generous-hearted Kate, you shall never have cause to regret such unselfish conduct. It was the perfect nobleness and disinterestedness of your character which attracted me to you, and the more I see of your mental superiority the more I bless the hour we first became acquainted with each other! Now May, I am ready to fuck you!"

"And I, dear papa, am ready to be fucked," I replied smiling.

Kate insisted on papa stripping himself perfectly naked and also on removing my smock. She then told papa to lie flat on his back with his prick standing erect; she then made me lie on top of him and she slapped my bottom in time to papa's heaves and thrusts until the crisis came and my womb was deluged with paternal sperm.

I was swimming in delight and could not help calling out: "Thank you a thousand times, dear papa, for this delicious treat!"

"And thank you, my darling child, for giving me such exquisite pleasure," replied papa.

In the next bout our positions were altered and Kate took part in the pastime, placing herself in such a position that papa could see her cunny while he fucked mine.

We changed positions many times until papa said he must rest from his labours of love, and after partaking of refreshments we all three went to papa's bedroom and fell asleep on his bed, one on each side of him.

In the morning I asked papa to tell me how he became acquainted with Kate, and he replied as follows:

"Last Christmas I went up to London for a holiday and at my club I met with several old friends, who had daughters at school with Madame Stewart at Hampton Court. Sir Thomas Moreton, my neighbour, was one of the party, and while drinking our wine, we talked about our experiences in fucking, and afterwards the conversation turned to the subject of schoolmistresses whipping their scholars' bottoms. I argued that it was not done nowadays but might have been done years ago.

"Sir Thomas laid me a £50 bet that I was wrong and offered to take me to Mme. Stewart's to prove it.

"I accepted his wager and on the following Saturday evening accompanied him to Mme. Stewart's to put his wager to the test.

"We were conducted to a room fitted up with all kinds of punishment apparatus and at one end was a raised dais or platform, under which we seated ourselves, and the door being closed we found the front of the platform was pierced with peepholes in all directions so we had a perfect view of the room, which was brilliantly lighted up with wax candles whilst our recess was dark.

"Presently six girls were brought in by the governess and Madame Stewart ascended the dais over our heads and gave orders for the number of stripes and read the list of offences

"The fair culprits were placed with their bottoms towards the dais so we had a full view of their struggles and wrigglings as the rod fell on their thighs and bottoms and we had many a peep at the tender cunny which peeped from between their legs.

"My Kate was one that was punished on that occasion and I was especially attracted by the quivering of the lips of her cunny as the rod fell on her lovely bottom. At last I was sure I could see the dear girl give down the peaily drops in pleasurable emission. Such sensitiveness charmed me, and when the punishment was over I made an offer to Madame Stewart to take Kate home with me as a fucking-piece, offering her a bribe.

"Madame demurred at first then said the matter should be left to Kate's decision.

"She was called into the room and I told her how I was smitten with the sight of her naked charms and wanted her to come and live with me a few months every year.

"She first looked at my standing prick and then enquired if it would be any advantage to Madame Stewart and that if it would, she would come with me.

"I told her I offered Madame £50.

" 'Then,' said Kate, 'I will go with you and trust in your honour as to your treatment of me.'

"Such disinterested conduct is most uncommon in this money-loving age and I love and honour Kate for it."

I told my father I was sure he would be generous to both Kate and myself.

He told me he was anxious I should be married to a gentleman of his acquaintance, an elderly rich widower.

I enquired how he knew anything about me and what was his name? To which my father replied his name was Mr. Sinclair and it was his cock I had become acquainted with, that he was over eighty years old, so I should be a rich widow probably in a few years. That the old gent was able to do a fair amount of fucking, but if I wanted more I could easily get a young man for a pound a week to do it for me.

I consented to my father's propositions and we invited Mr. T (the resident tutor at the school mentioned at the beginning of my tale), to come to the wedding. We also invited Susey and her uncle.

They all came and I was marired one fine May morning out of compliment to my name. After the ceremony the clergyman asked permission to have the first kiss on my cunny, which I granted him in the vestry.

We went for our wedding tour to the Isle of Wight for a

month during which time my husband was satisfied he had got me with a child. He then gave me permission to have as much outside fucking as I wanted

I told him I should wait until we got home as I was longing for a taste of Mr. T's noble tool and also for my dear father's prick.

My husband was pleased with my determination and engaged Mr. T as librarian, and in that capacity he remained until the lamented decease of Mr. Sinclair at the age of ninety, who left me with one daughter nine years old, and all his money.

As soon after his death as was decent I married Mr. S—— whom I found to be one of the best husbands.

Susey often pays us a visit and brings young girls with her to please Mr. T who has a penchant for the unfledged cunny, and often has a game of blindman's buff with the naked children, and a romp with my little Agnes when she is naked. The little darling is now twelve years old and very proud of being able to make "her new papa's cocky get big," as she says, by rubbing her little cunny against its head.

Mr. T anticipates the pleasure of taking her maidenhead when she is fourteen. I tell him that it is too early and that he ought to wait until she is fifteen, but he is so impatient that I fear he will have his own way.

So good reader, both lady and gentleman, farewell!

> And may you never want a fuck,
> Nor yet a prick or cunt to suck.

FINIS.

When Mrs Conwell was in this country, she showed me a copy she had made of a large picture of a Turkish soldier on horseback She had made the horse's testicles very conspicuous, and then shamming ignorance, pointed at them, saying, "That is the rider's foot on the other side." "Yes," said I, with a low bow, "very like a foot!" This made her giggle.

CONUNDRUM.

My first expresses, or joy, or woe,
Each passion that touches the soul;
My second's as far as you can throw;
And my whole—you may suck my whole.

My first tells every passion of man's,
Each feeling that moves his soul;
My second supports the pots and pans;
And my whole—you may suck my whole.

O—range.

NURSERY RHYMES.

There was a young man of Calcutta
   Who thought he would do a smart trick;
So anointed his arsehole with butter,
   And in it inserted his prick.
     It was not for greed after gold;
     It was not for thirst after pelf;
     'Twas simply because he'd been told,
     To bloody well bugger himself.

There was a young lass of Dalkeith,
Who frigged a young man with her teeth;

She complained that he stunk;
Not so much from the spunk;
But his arsehole was just underneath.

There was a young Jew of Torbay,
Who buggered his father one day;
    Said he, "I'd much rather,
    Thus bugger my father,
Because there is nothing to pay."

There was a gay parson of Norton,
Whose prick, although thick, was a short 'un;
    To make up for this loss,
    He had balls like a horse,
And never spent less than a quartern.

There was a young man of the Tweed,
Who sucked his wife's arse thro' a reed;
    When she had diarrhoea,
    He'd let none come near,
For fear they should poach on his feed.

There was an old man of Balbriggan,
Who cunt juice was frequently swigging;
    But even to this,
    He preferred tom-cat's piss,
Which he kept a pox'd nigger to frig in.

A cabman who drove in Biarritz,
Once frightened a fare into fits;
    When reprov'd for a fart,
    He said, "God bless my heart,
When I break wind I usually shits."

A young woman got married at Chester,
Her mother she kissed and she blessed her.
    Says she, "You're in luck,
    He's a stunning good fuck,
For I've had himself myself down in Leicester."

There was a young parson of Goring,
Who made a small hole in the flooring;

He lined it all round,
Then laid on the ground,
And declared it was cheaper than whoring.

FABLES AND MAXIMS.

Translated from the Indian of Shitpot, the great Brahmin Confucius.

THE TWO WOLVES.

"What a nasty smell there is in this den," said one wolf to another; "have you shit yourself?" "No," said the other. "Then," said the first wolf, "I must have done so myself." So he had. The moral of this fable is that though ever ready to spy into the defects of others, we are apt to overlook our own imperfections.

THE DOG AND THE COCK.

"What a large fellow you are!" said the Cock to the Dog. "I can fuck half-a-dozen hens, while you are getting half way in." "Very likely," said the Dog, "but when I am in I stay there fancy; look at my prick compared to yours. I don't call yours fucking at all, it's over before it's well begun." This fable teaches that I like a long prick best.

THE MONKEY AND THE DILDOE.

A pet monkey who had watched his mistress fill her dildoe with cream, waited a chance when she had ceased using it, being called away for a few minutes. "Now," said he, "I will have my fill of cream," so he sucked away, but unfortunately the lady had contracted syphilis, and the monkey died in convulsions. The moral of this fable is, that you should never suck dildoes.

"You want a good stiff prick up your arse," said the Fox, when he found he could not catch the Gander. "I've got one; I always wear it there," said the Gander, chuckling. "Sold again! Yah! Bloody Fool!" The Fox slunk off abashed. This shows that the same repartee does not suit everyone.

THE OTHER WAY

Henry lived six gay years in Rome,
 His mistress was a kind Machese.
Her daughter bright in childish bloom,
 Charmed him with pretty loving ways.

Mama encouraged him to take
 The budding virgin's maidenhead,
But this displeased the virtuous rake,
 The girl was soon about to wed.

Mama replied, "Why should you hesitate?
 True it is disapproved by some,
But if you are so very delicate,
 Can't you just fuck her in the bum?"

THE REVERIE.

What dull and senseless lumps we'd be,
If never of felicity
We tasted; and what bliss is there
To equal that of fucking rare?
An age of grief, an age of pain,
I would endure and ne'er complain;
To purchase but an hour's charms,
While wriggling in a maiden's arms!
And hugging her to heavenly rest,
My hand reposing on her breast!
Her arse my own, her thighs my screen,
My penis standing in between!
My bollox hanging down below,
And banging 'gainst her arse of snow;
Or else grasped firmly in her hand,
To make my yard more stiffly stand.
How soon the blood glows in the veins,
And nature all its power now strains;
The belly heaves, the penis burns,
The maiden all its heat returns,
Till passion holds triumphant sway,
And both the lovers die away.

A MAIDEN'S WISH.

When wishes first enter a maiden's breast,
She longs by her lover to be carest;
She longs with her lover to do the trick,
And in secret she longs for a taste of his prick!
Her cunt it is itching from morning till night,
The prick of her lover can yield her delight;
She longs to be fucked, and for that does deplore,
For what can a young maiden wish for more?

If fever or sickness her spirits doth shock,
Why, we know what she wants, 'tis a stiff-standing cock!

Give her a prick, it will soon make her well,
Though perhaps in the long run, her belly may swell!
She'd like very well to be laid on the grass.
To have two ample bollox sent bang 'gainst her arse;
She longs to be fucked, and for that does deplore,
For what can a young maiden wish for more?

It's a pity any quim hungry should go,
All maids wish them filled, as you very well know,
And if the young men would be ready and free,
They'd up with their clouts in a trice, d'ye see!
She wants to be ask'd, but to ask is afraid,
And fearful she is that she'll die an old maid;
She wishes for prick, and for that does deplore,
For what can a young maiden wish for more?

———————————

THE JOYS OF COMING TOGETHER.

———————

Tell me where are there such blisses
    As the sexes can impart?
When lips join in heavenly kisses,
    When they both convulsive start!
        Throbbing, heaving,
        Never grieving;
        Thrusting, bursting,
        Sighing, dying!
All nature now is in a glow,
Now they're coming, oh! oh!! oh!!!
Mutual keeping to one tether,
Sweet it is to come together!
Decrepid age is only teasing,
    Shrivelled-up pricks, who can abide?
Vigorous youth, oh, that is pleasing,
    It is worth the world beside!
        Craving, wanting,
        Sobbing, panting,
        Throbbing, heaving,
        Never grieving,

Thrusting, bursting,
Sighing, dying!
All nature now is in a glow,
Now they're coming, oh! oh!! oh!!!
Mutual keeping to one tether,
Sweet it is to come together.

NURSERY RHYMES.

A parson who lived near Cremorne
Looked down on all women with scorn;
 E'en a boy's white fat bum,
 Could not make him come;
But an old man's piles gave him the horn.

A cheerful old party of Lucknow,
Remarked, "I should like a fuck now!"
 So he had one and spent,
 And said, "I'm content!
By no means am I so cunt-struck now."

There was a young man of Peru,
Who lived upon clap juice and spew;
 When these palled to his taste,
 He tried some turd paste,
And said that was very good too.

There is a new Baron of Wokingham;
The girls say he don't care for poking 'em,
 Preferring "Minette,"
 Which is pleasant, but yet,
There is one disadvantage, his choking 'em.

There was an Archbishop of Rheims,
Who played with himself in his dreams;
 On his nightshirt in front,
 He painted a cunt,
Which made his spend gush forth in streams.

There was a young man of Newminster Court,
Bugger d a pig, but his prick was too short;
    Said the hog, "It's not nice;
    But pray take my advice;
Make tracks, or by the police you'll be caught."

There was a young man of Cashmere,
Who purchased a fine Bayadere!
    He fucked all her toes,
    Her mouth, eyes, and her nose,
And eventually poxed her left ear.

There was a young party of Bicester,
Who wanted to bugger his sister;
    But not liking dirt,
    He bought him a squirt,
And cleaned out her arse with a clyster.

There was a young man of King's Cross,
Who amused himself frigging a horse,
    Then licking the spend
    Which still dripped from the end,
Said, "It tastes just like anchovy sauce."

A president called Gambetta,
Once used an imperfect French Letter;
    This was not the worst,
    With disease he got cursed,
And he took a long time to get better.

———————

AMEN.

Oh! cunt is a kingdom, and prick is its lord;
A whore is a slave, and her mistress a bawd;
Her quim is her freehold, which brings in her rent;
Where you pay when you enter, and leave when you've spent.

ADULTERY'S THE GO!

(A Song before the time of the New Divorce Court.)

When we were boys the world was good,
    But that is long ago;
Now all the wisest folks are lewd,
    For Adultery's the go.
        The go, the go, the go,
        Adultery's the go!

Quite tired of leading virtuous lives,
    Though spotless as the snow,
Among the chaste and pious wives,
    Adultery's the go.
        The go, the go, the go, &c.

Long life then to the House of Lords,
    They know a thing or two;
You see from all their grand awards,
    That Adultery's the go.
        The go, the go, the go, &c.

And Lady Barlow, Mrs. Hare,
    Case, Clarke, and Bolders;
Teed, Ashton, James, and all declare
    Adultery's the go.
        The go, the go, the go, &c.

Some husbands still are jealous,
  And guard the furbelow,
But spite such prudish fellows,
  Adultery's the go.
    The go, the go, the go, &c.

Horn'd cuckolds were mad raging bulls,
  A century ago;
Now, they're tame oxen, silly fools,
  For Adultery's the go.
    The go, the go, the go, &c.

Then, hey for Doctors' Commons,
  With horned beasts arow;
For man's delight, and woman's,
  Adultery's the go.

HER VERY SOUL.

On Sundays, in a church like this,
I joy to face the blushing Miss,
Eye within eye, agog for bliss,
Through touching not, I only kiss,
  Her very soul! Her very soul!

She falls at once into my plan,
I guess she prays, behind her fan,
"Oh, for a man! A real man!
To satiate, as he only can,
  Her very soul! Her very soul!

Heavens! what a glance! see her suck,
And lick her lips, on fire for cock.
I see her frisky bottom buck,
While with the prick of lust I fuck,
  Her very soul! Her very soul!

FIRST RONDEAU.

Ten years ago, on Christmas day,
Fair Helen stole my heart away,
I went to church—but not to pray,
    Ten years ago.

To pray? Yes—pray to Helen's eyes;
Ah! would that we had been more wise;
To-day, she would not recognize
Him, whom she kissed in ecstasies,
    Ten years ago.

SECOND RONDEAU.

Again we've met, and now I find,
Her still more luscious to my mind;
She was not to such pranks inclined,
    Ten years ago.

Though now a second time she's wed,
Hers is a most lascivious bed;
Though thirty years she now has sped,
She fucks still better than she did,
    Ten years ago.

There was a young man of Berlin,
Whom disease had despoiled of his skin;
 But he said with much pride,
 "Though deprived of my hide,
I can still enjoy a put in."

There was a young woman of Cheadle,
Who once gave the clap to a beadle.
 Said she, "Does it itch?"
 "It does, you damned bitch,
And burns like hell-fire when I peedle."

There was an old Chinaman drunk,
Who went for a sail in his junk,
 He was dreaming of Venus,
 And tickling his penis,
Till he floated away in the spunk.

There was a young man of Rangoon,
Who farted and filled a balloon.
 The balloon went so high,
 That it stuck in the sky,
And stank out the Man in the Moon.

There was a young man at the Cape,
On a maiden committed a rape.
 Said she, "You damned shit,
 You can't fuck a bit,
And you're knocking my quim out of shape."

There was a young parson of Harwich,
Tried to grind his betrothed in a carriage.
 She said "No, you young goose,
 Just try self-abuse,
And the other we'll try after marriage."

UP THE CHIMNEY.

When Captain Jones of Halifax,
   Was put in winter quarters,
His landlady, a widow, had
   The prettiest of daughters.

The Captain sued her lovingly,
   The girl was gay and ready
To join her lot with his and be
   The noble Captain's lady.

Their wedding was deferred; but soon,
   Impatient for the pleasure,
He found his way into her room,
   And swiv'd her at his leisure.

The chambermaid, who set to rights
   The different pots and pans,
Warn'd mistress there was ne'er a drop
   In that of this young man's.

The mother asked him tenderly,
   "As you're to wed my daughter,
Pray tell me why—my dear young man,
   Why—why—you make no water?"

"Ah, Madam!" cried he, "cannot you
   The real reason guess?
The fact is that I go to bed,
   So full of tenderness.

I get eager for the bliss,
   I feel so stiff and hot,
That really I'm obliged to piss
   Right up the Chimney Pot."

NURSERY RHYMES.

There was a young lady of Harrow,
Who complained that her Cunt was too narrow,
    For times without number
    She would use a cucumber,
But could not accomplish a marrow.

There was a young lady of Glasgow,
And fondly her lover did ask, "Oh,
    Pray allow me a fuck,"
    But she said, "No, my duck,
But you may, if you please, up my arse go."

There was a young man had the art
Of making a capital tart,
    With a handful of shit,
    Some snot and a spit,
And he'd flavor the whole with a fart.

There was an old man of Connaught.
Whose prick was remarkably short,
    When he got into bed
    The old woman said,
"This isn't a prick, it's a wart."

There was a gay Countess of Bray,
And you may think it odd when I say,
    That in spite of high station,
    Rank and education,
She always spelt Cunt with a K.

There was a young girl from Vistula,
To whom a friend said, "Jef has kissed you, la!"
    Said she, "Yes, by God!
    But my arse he can't sod,
Because I am troubled with Fistula."

There was an old parson of Lundy,
Fell asleep in his vestry on Sunday;
    He awoke with a scream,
    "What, another wet dream,
This comes of not frigging since Monday."

There was a strong man of Drumrig,
Who one day did seven times frig;
    He buggered three Sailors,
    Four Jews and two Tailors,
And ended by fucking a pig.

There was an Old Man of the Mountain,
Who frigged himself into a fountain,
    Fifteen times had he spent,
    Still he wasn't content,
He simply got tired of the counting.

There was a young man of Nantucket,
Who went down a well in a bucket;
    The last words he spoke,
    Before the rope broke,
Were, "Arsehole, you bugger, and suck it."

A native of Havre de Grace
Once tired of Cunt, said "I'll try arse."
    He unfolded his plan
    To another young man,
Who said, "Most decidedly, my arse!"

THE TRIAL OF CAPTAIN POWELL

For Ravishing Margaret Edson, a child under the Age of 12 Years, at York Assizes, March 31st, 1775.

Mary Edson stated: I am the child's mother. On the Friday before New Year's Day, I perceived my daughter was ill, I asked her what she had done to herself (as she had trouble in making water), if she had fallen and hurt herself; she said no. On Sunday, the 1st January, when I stripped her I saw her shift very much daubed with what had come from her, which gave me a great shock.

Q.—What colour was it?

A.—A yellow colour mixed with red. When I saw her in that condition, I said if you do not tell me what you have done with yourself I will take the skin off your backside. As she would not tell me I got a birch rod, and twining her over my lap gave her bum a sharp tickling, when she said that Captain Powell sent for her brother and her, and he gave her brother a halfpenny to buy some sweets. After the boy went out the Captain barred the door, and then he put his finger up her body and hurt her very much. I was much surprised, and sent for Mrs. Nurser, a neighbour, who advised me to send for Dr. Lee, who lives at Knaresborough. In the afternoon too we asked her what Captain Powell did to her, and she then said Captain Powell unbuttoned his breeches and took out his cock and put it into her. I asked her if she felt anything come from him. She said she thought he made water in her. She said he sat in his chair and took her before him, and she shewed the motion he made in the chair, then he took her upstairs and did the same again.

Q.—From the appearance of the colour on the shift did you think it had the same appearance as that which comes from a man on those occasions?

A.—To the best of my judgment I thought it was.

Mr. John Lee, a surgeon, said that Mr. Edson, the father of the child, making application to him to examine his daughter, he attended at his house, when he inspected the child, and found her private parts much inflamed and swelled, which convinced him she had received some injury; there was likewise a discharge from the parts, which made him afraid it was venereal. He attended and administered to her about six weeks.

Q.—Did it appear to you there had been any violence used by a man's penis?

A.—I cannot say I formed any judgment as to the cause.

Q.—Suppose a man had introduced his private parts, would it have occasioned this?

A.—Yes it would.

Q.—Would a finger being put there occasion the excoriation?

A.—Yes it might. If a man had entered the vagina of the child and entered into her body, I should have thought it would have had a different appearance. It would have brought away blood, but I observed none.

Margaret Edson (the child).

COURT.—What age are you?

A.—Ten-and-a-half.

Q.—Do you tell lies?

A.—No.

Q.—Will you tell me the truth?

A.—Yes.

Q.—Do you know Captain Powell? Look round and see if he is here.

A.—There is Captain Powell, pointing to the prisoner.

Q.—Now tell us what Captain Powell did to you.

A.—I and my brother was at Mrs. Raper's playing with her little boy; we did not stay long. My brother and I were going home, and Captain Powell said, "Come hither, Peg, come hither." My brother went with me to Captain Powell, and he gave my brother a halfpenny to go and buy sweets. My brother went, and then Captain Powell bolted the door.

Q.—What did he do after that?

A.—He put one hand round my waist and turned up my clothes.

Q.—Where was he?

A.—He was sitting in a chair.

Q.—How was you standing?

A—On the floor before him, between his legs.

Q   What did he do?

A.—He unbuttoned his breeches and took his cock out.

Q.—How did you know it was his cock?

A.—I saw it; I saw him take it out.

Q.—What did he do after that?

A.—He put his cock in my arsehole.

Q.—Tell us that again?

A.—He unbuttoned his breeches, took out his cock, and put it in my arsehole.

The jury did not wish to hear any more, and he was indicted at the next assizes for a common assault, and found guilty.

THE PATIENCE OF JOB.

A farmer and his wife, who had been to church one Sunday morning, were walking home through a country lane, when John said, "Excuse me, my dear, for a minute or two, I want to get over the hedge to do something for myself." After rather a long interval his loving wife, who had walked on a little, returned to look for him, and could hear her good man on the other side of the hedge, blasting, swearing, and damning at an awful rate. She managed to get over to him, and then seeing him stooping down as if troubled by a very hard motion, exclaimed, "John! John! how can you swear so, don't you remember what the parson said about the patience of Job?"

"Blast that damned Job," exclaimed the furious John, "he never had his balls caught in a rabbit trap! Why don't you make haste to help me?"

The poor fellow stooping down to ease himself, had really been caught, and his wife had to release him and help him home.

ORIGIN OF COPULATION.

Success to dame Nature, for 'twas by her plan,
That woman first thought of enjoyment from man;
She knew that of pleasure they'd never be sick,
And so out of kindness, invented a prick!
    A stiff-standing, glorious prick!
    Voluptuous, rubicund prick!
Oh, surely, of fortune it came in the nick,
Good-natured dame Nature to give us a prick!

Without it how lost would a poor maiden be,
It tickles her quim, makes her water run free;
Most women a handle would have to their front,
So they've only to thrust a long prick in their cunt!
    Their hairy, voluptuous cunt!
    Their sweet little, queer little cunt!
What damsel no handle would have to their front?
And prick e'er has been a great friend unto cunt!

When nature to woman gave two mouths, she will'd,
Of course, that they both should be equally filled,
And if women will look after one mouth, you know
That prick will look after the mouth that's below!
    Stiff-standing, glorious prick!
    Voluptuous, rubicund prick!
Oh, surely, of fortune it came in the nick,
Good-natured dame Nature to give us a prick!

When sorrow torments lovely woman. oh dear,
A mighty good fucking will banish despair;
If her belly but aches, why we all know the trick,
There's nothing can ease it so well as a prick!
    A nice luscious prick!
    A stiff-standing prick!
For any young maiden it can do the trick.
Oh, joys there are plenty, but nothing like prick!

TAKING A MAIDENHEAD.

Air—"Gee, ho Dobbin."

Oh, Maidenhead-taking's a very great bore,
It makes cunt and prick so confoundedly sore;
But fucking the third time's like heaven above,
For your prick then glides in as you draw on a glove!
    Gee up, Roger,
     Wag up, Roger,
Roger's a thing that all women admire!

Oh, give me a damsel of blooming fifteen,
With two luscious thighs and a mouse-trap between,
With the fringe on the edge, and two red lips I say,
In her cunt I'd be diving by night and by day!
                  Gee up, &c.

That woman would be a disgrace to our land,
Who would not take a prick, when it stiffy does stand;
And when it droops low as if it were in dread,
She must tickle the balls, till it lifts up its head!
                  Gee up, &c.

Cunt is a treasure which monarchs admire,
Cunt is a thing that my theme doth inspire;
Cunt is a mighty temptation to sin,
But cunt is a hole that I'd ever be in!
                  Gee up, &c.

Prick is its friend, its first cousin, I ween,
Tho' prick I confess is a rare go-between;
Prick to a woman much joy can impart,
And prick is a thing that she loves in her heart!
                  Gee up, &c.

Then here's to the female who yields to a man,
And here's to the man who'll fuck when he can,
For fucking creates all our joy on earth,
And from fucking you know, we all date our birth.
    Gee up, Roger,
     Wag up, Roger,
Roger's a thing that all women admire.

EPITAPH.

Here lies the amorous Fanny Hicks,
The scabbard of ten thousand pricks,
And if you wish to do her honour,
Pull out your cock, and piss upon her.

THE TRIUMPH OF SCIENCE OVER PHYSIC.

Home they brought the warrior, fed
  To repletion more than just;
And the servants, chuckling, said,
  "He must shit or he will bust."

Then they gave him castor oil,
  Pills and drugs of many a sort;
Yet despite their loving toil,
  He would not be taken short.

Stole a maiden to the spot,
  And emetics, laughing, dared;
Yet in vain she held the pot,
  For he only belched and glared.

Came a nurse of ninety years,
  An enema huge she bore;
Shoved it up amidst their jeers,
  And he shat for evermore.

SONG.

If anxious Venus, beauty's queen!
  Your empire should endure,
Borrow Cecilia's face and mien,
  Our homage to ensure.

Though perfect all the charms may seem,
    Tht famed Apelles drew.
Not half so sweet are they, I deem,
    As fair Cecilia's Cu.

The feelings of my faithful heart,
    My mouth shall still express,
Upon that Cu—, delicious part,
    In rapture's wild caress.

Oh! ye, who ne'er disquiet felt,
    Nor aught but virtue knew.
Whence is it? But your eye ne'er dwelt
    Upon Cecilia's Cu.

Cecilia, think not, from my brain,
    The souvenir can remove,
Of thy sweet Cu, 'twill there remain,
    Imprinted fast by Love!

But if my thread of life should break,
    Expire thy lover true.
May I flight 'mid kisses take,
    Imprinted on thy Cu!

A philosophical dandy thus vented his musings upon
Copulation: "The idea is old; the attitude queer; and the
motion fully ridiculous; but all tends to the acme of felicity."

GONE TO CA-CA.

Tom brought home some friends,
    And not finding his dear,
But only young Harry,
    Who look'd rather queer.

(Papa) Hush, Harry! What nonsense!
          Run, call your Mama!
(Boy)   Mama and de Captain
          Are gone to Ca-Ca.
(Papa) Hush, Harry! What nonsense!
          Just hear the child talk!
(Boy)   Captain pull down his breeches,
          Ma pull up her frock!

MISSY'S THOUGHTS.

(At a Boys' School.)

I'll tell my mammy when I go home,
The boys won't let my twat alone;
They pull my frock, and beg to see.
What can they want to do with me?

My sister Mary's twice as wild,
For she's fourteen, and I'm a child;
And if they tried to plague her so,
I think what bouncing Moll would do.

But why do the boys all tease me so,
And ask if I have a mouse to show?
They say there's a mouse in Bruce's clothes,
And when he was cuddling me, it rose!

When yesterday, I climbed for pears,
The boys all came to get their shares;
They giggled, and pointed into my slit,
I didn't know they were laughing at it.

232

The usher pretends to be my friend,
But ' don't know where his love will end;
For while he keeps his sober talk,
I catch his fingers under my frock.

They often make me lie down to show
The very inside of my belly below,
I do as they please, because they pay
A shilling among them for the play.

They're not content, though I open wide,
They grope for something or other inside;
You'd think them fools, to see how they kiss,
The smarting hole, by which I piss!

And then they show me all their shames,
And teach me all the nasty names;
I'll tell my mammy when I go home;
The boys won't leave my Cunt alone!

————————————

INTO THE BARGAIN.

Two lads were out on Hertford Heath
    And being flush of money,
Offered two shillings to a wench,
    To let them view her cunny.

They viewed it with extreme delight,
    Stark naked and provoking;
They paid their shillings for the sight,
    The touching and the stroking.

"Now," said the cunning little slut,
    "Just add a sixpence each;
And you shall see my very scut!
    I'll let you see my breech."

"What fun!" exclaim the simple boys,
    So they the shilling paid;
Then pulling up her smock behind,
    Her bottom she displayed.

And so they peeped, and felt their fill;
    Then cried the giggling lass,
"Your bargain shall be better still;
    Say 'Please,' and kiss my arse!"

AMENITIES OF LEICESTER SQUARE.

Girl to Ponce:—Go along, you bloody Mary Ann, and tighten your arse-hole with alum.

English Whore to French Woman:—Yah, you foreign bitches can only get a man by promising them a bottom-fuck!

French Woman:—Yes, I do let the English gentlemen have my arse-hole but my cunt I do keep for my husband.

THE OLD DILDOE.

Tune—"The Mistletoe Bough."

The beds were all made in the bawdy house fine,
And the whores were rejoicing in gin and wine;
And the old bawd herself, dressed out so gay,
Was making them drunk on Xmas day
And there was "Peg Watkins" the brothel's delight,
Got lewd on a cove, as was there that night.
And said she to herself: "If I don't have a go,
I'll content myself with the old Dildoe."

Chorus—Oh! the old Dildoe, oh, the old whore's Dildoe.

"Oh! I am weary of lashing," Peg now did cry,
Come upstairs with me Joey, and let's have a shie."
But Joey determined to stick to the gin,
And wouldn't leave his liquor to have put in.
And Peg cursed him and told him to go to hell;
But drunk as a fart, from the chair he fell.
So away she ran with her blood in a glow,
Determined to try the old Dildoe.

Chorus: Oh! the old Dildoe, oh! the old whore's Dildoe.

To the old bawd's bedroom at once she went,
To seize upon the implement.
She looked in the cupboard, she looked in the pot,
She searched high and low but found it not.
She rushed to the couch, she searched the bed,
Underneath the pillow she spied its head.
She seized it and cried: "Full well I know,
Far better than Joe's the old Dildoe."

Chorus—Oh! the old Dildoe, oh, the old whore's Dildoe.

She flew with the treasure into her room
(Its size was the handle of a broom).
Oh! what ecstatic moments she passed there,
As she threw up her legs on the back of a chair.
Through each vein in her body the fire lurked,

Surely and quickly the engine worked;
Face her, back her, stop her no! no!
Faster and faster flew the old Dildoe.

Chorus: Oh! the old Dildoe, oh! the old whore's Dildoe.

Minutes soon passed and the hours flew by,
When there suddenly came a fearful cry,
Which was followed at once by a fearful scream,
Which awoke the whores from their drunken dream.
They all jumped up in a hell of a fright,
In an empty gin-bottle they stuck a light;
And the old whore herself away did go
To look after the safety of the old Dildoe.

Chorus: Oh! the old Dildoe, oh! the old whore's Dildoe.

But the old whore very soon did return
With a look of agony and deep concern;
For her heart was filled with dire remorse,
As she told the whores of her fearful loss;
She questioned them all and implored them to tell,
Where the treasure had gone that she loved so well;
When one of them said: "I think I know,
Peg Watkins is using your old Dildoe."

Chorus: Oh! the old Dildoe, oh! the old whore's Dildoe.

Away they all flew to Peggy's room.
But, ho! 'twas filled with smoke and fume,
And a terrible stench came forth from the bed,
Where poor Peggy lay all burnt and dead.
Sad, sad, was her fate, when, instead of a fuck,
With the old Dildoe she had tried her luck;
And when at the short digs she so hard did go,
It caught fire with the friction—the old Dildoe.

Chorus: Oh! the old Dildoe, oh! the old whore's Dildoe.

———————

It has without doubt been Truscott's ambition
To get the new Temple Bar in position.
He thought of it by day, dreamt of it by night
And one morning woke in a terrible fright.
"I dreamt, my dear love, that this thing came to pass,
That the public had shoved Temple Bar up my arse;
That they greeted me loudly with hisses and calls
And the dragon grew lively and bit off my balls."

NURSERY RHYMES.

There was a young bride of Antigua,
Whose husband had said: "Dear me, how big you are!"
 Said the girl: "What damn'd rot,
 Why, you've often felt my twot,
My legs and my arse and my figua!"

There once was a young man of Bulgaria,
Who once went to piss down an area,
 Said Mary to cook:
 "Oh, do come and look,
Did you ever see anything hairier?"

There was a young lady of Harwich,
Who said on the morn of her marriage:
 "I shall sew my chemise,
 Right down to my knees,
For I'm damned if I fuck in the carriage!"

Rev. J. Spurgeon will Address the Young Women's Christian Association on the subject of:
CIRCUMCISION.
With practical examples of the advantage of removing the hood or foreskin from the penis.

Admission to women only. No collection.

THE LOVER'S KISS.

"Give me, my love, that billing kiss,
    I taught you one delicious night,
When, turning epicures in delight,
    We tried inventions of bliss.

Come gently steal my lips along,
    And let your lips in murmurs move;
Ah, no—again—that kiss was wrong,
    How can you be so dull, my love?"

"Cease, cease," the blushing girl replied,
    And in her milky arms she caught me;
"How can you thus your pupil chide?
    You know 'twas in the dark you taught me!"

An old and favoured servant of two maiden ladies had been frequently reprimanded by them for his free behaviour with the female servants. Caught one day in *flagrante delicto*, he was summoned to their presence, and while the girl was sacked, he was told that if he did not do better and turn over a new leaf, much as they valued him—his next escapade would be the last. He promised amendment and matters went on very well for a time. One evening, he was not to be found when wanted, and on a search being made, was discovered in the beer-cellar, buggering the page boy.

"How now," he was asked, "is this your amendment? You promised to turn over a new leaf." "So I have" said he, "only I have begun at *the bottom of the page!*"

History does not give the conclusion of the matter.

The Rev. Kettle of Battersea met on the Rhine-boat a lady who had not seen him for years. "How do you do, Mr. Kettle, I heard you were married. Any family?"

"Yes, Madame, six."

"Six, dear me! how many are boys and how many girls?"

"The number is divided, Madame, there are six little Kettles, three with spouts, three without."

A' THAT AND A' THAT.

Put butter in my Donald's brose,
    For weel does Donald fa that;
I love my Donald's tartan hose,
    His naked prick, and a' that.

    For a' that and a' that,
    And twice as mickle as a' that:
    The lassie get a skelpit gnat,
    But wan the day for a' that.

For Donald swore a solemn oath,
    By his first hairy gravat,
That he would fight the battle there,
    And fuck the lass and a' that.

    Chorus: For a' that and a' that, etc.

His hairy cock, both side and wide,
    Hung like a beggar's wallet;
His prick stood like a rolling-pin,
    She nicker'd when she saw that.

    Chorus: For a' that and a' that, etc.

And then she turned up her cunt,
    And she bade Donald claw that;
The devil's dizzen Donald drew,
    And Donald gave her a' that.

    Chorus: For a' that and a' that, etc.

LINES FOR VALENTINES.

What a fate this poor girl in her lovers befalls,
A prickless old man, and a youth without balls.

Boast not that you have won a rich wife,
Length of tool, not of purse, makes the comfort of life.

Your prick is so useless for love's pleasant game,
  Your nose long and hooky and fuck of such muck,
Go, stick then your nose in the cunt of your dame,
  And you'll have at one go both a blow and a fuck.

To his bed he went sleepy and drunk, oh, very!
  He wanted to piss, felt about for the jerry,
Took up by mischance a big mousetrap instead,
  Which snapped off, alas! his old gentleman's head!